Also by Sarah Bennett

The Butterfly Cove series

Sunrise at Butterfly Cove
Wedding Bells at Butterfly Cove
Christmas at Butterfly Cove

The Lavender Bay series

Spring at Lavender Bay
Summer at Lavender Bay
Snowflakes at Lavender Bay

Sunrise at Butterfly Cove

Sarah Bennett

ONE PLACE. MANY STORIES

HQ
An imprint of HarperCollins*Publishers* Ltd
1 London Bridge Street
London SE1 9GF

This paperback edition 2018

1
First published in Great Britain by
HQ, an imprint of HarperCollins*Publishers* Ltd 2017

Sarah Bennett asserts the moral right to be
identified as the author of this work.
A catalogue record for this book is
available from the British Library.

ISBN: 978-0-00-829251-5

MIX
Paper from
responsible sources
FSC™ C007454

This book is produced from independently certified FSC™ paper
to ensure responsible forest management.

For more information visit: www.harpercollins.co.uk/green

Printed and bound in Great Britain by
CPI Group, Croydon CRO 4YY

This one is for my mum

PROLOGUE

October 2014

'And the winner of the 2014 Martindale Prize for Best New Artist is…'

Daniel Fitzwilliams lounged back in his chair and took another sip from the never-emptying glass of champagne. His bow tie hung loose around his neck, and the first two buttons of his wing-collar shirt had been unfastened since just after the main course had been served. The room temperature hovered somewhere around the fifth circle of hell and he wondered how much longer he would have to endure the fake smiles and shoulder pats from strangers passing his table.

The MC made a big performance of rustling the large silver envelope in his hand. 'Get on with it, mate,' Daniel muttered. His agent, Nigel, gave him a smile and gulped at the contents of his own glass. His nomination had been a huge surprise and no-one expected him to win, Daniel least of all.

'Well, well.' The MC adjusted his glasses and peered at the card he'd finally wrestled free. 'I am delighted to announce that the winner of the Martindale Prize is Fitz, for his series "Interactions".'

A roar of noise from the rest of his tablemates covered the choking sounds of Nigel inhaling half a glass of champagne. Daniel's own glass slipped from his limp fingers and rolled harmlessly under the table. 'Bugger me.'

'Go on, mate. Get up there!' His best friend, Aaron, rounded the table and tugged Daniel to his feet. 'I told you, I bloody told you, but you wouldn't believe me.'

Daniel wove his way through the other tables towards the stage, accepting handshakes and kisses from all sides. Will Spector, the bookies' favourite and the art crowd's latest darling, raised a glass in toast and Daniel nodded to acknowledge his gracious gesture. Flashbulbs popped from all sides as he mounted the stairs to shake hands with the MC. He raised the sinuous glass trophy and blinked out at the clapping, cheering crowd of his peers.

The great and the good were out in force. The Martindale attracted a lot of press coverage and the red-carpet winners and losers would be paraded across the inside pages for people to gawk at over their morning cereal. His mum had always loved to see the celebrities in their posh frocks. He just wished she'd survived long enough to see her boy come good. Daniel swallowed around the lump in his throat. *Fuck cancer.* Dad had at least made it to Daniel's first exhibition, before his heart failed and he'd followed his beloved Nancy to the grave.

Daniel adjusted the microphone in front of him and waited for the cheers to subside. The biggest night of his life, and he'd never felt lonelier.

***

Mia Sutherland resisted the urge to check her watch and tried to focus on the flickering television screen. The latest episode of *The Watcher* would normally have no trouble in holding her attention—it was her and Jamie's new favourite show. She glanced at the empty space on the sofa beside her. Even with the filthy weather outside, he should have been home before now. Winter had hit earlier than usual and she'd found herself turning the lights on mid-afternoon to try and dispel the gloom caused by the raging storm outside.

The ad break flashed upon the screen and she popped into the kitchen to give the pot of stew a quick stir. She'd given up waiting, and eaten her portion at eight-thirty, but there was plenty left for Jamie. He always said she cooked for an army rather than just the two of them.

A rattle of sleet struck the kitchen window and Mia peered through the Venetian blind covering it; he'd be glad of a hot meal after being stuck in the traffic for so long. A quick tap of the wooden spoon against the side of the pot, and then she slipped the cast-iron lid back on. The pot was part of the *Le Creuset* set

Jamie's parents had given them as a wedding gift and the matching pans hung from a wooden rack above the centre of the kitchen worktop. She slid the pot back into the oven and adjusted the temperature down a notch.

Ding-dong.

At last! Mia hurried down the hall to the front door and tugged it open with a laugh. 'Did you forget your keys—' A shiver of fear ran down her back at the sight of the stern-looking policemen standing on the step. Rain dripped from the brims of their caps and darkened the shoulders of their waterproof jackets.

'Mrs Sutherland?'

No, no, no, no. Mia looked away from the sympathetic expressions and into the darkness beyond them for the familiar flash of Jamie's headlights turning onto their small driveway.

'Perhaps we could come in, Mrs Sutherland?' The younger of the pair spoke this time.

Go away. Go away. She'd seen this scene played out enough on the television to know what was coming next. 'Please, come in.' Her voice sounded strange, high-pitched and brittle to her ears. She stepped back to let the two men enter. 'Would you like a cup of tea?'

The younger officer took off his cap and shrugged out of his jacket. 'Why don't you point me in the direction of the kettle and you and Sergeant Stone can make yourselves comfortable in the front room?'

Mia stared at the Sergeant's grim-set features. *What a horrible job he has, poor man.* 'Yes, of course. Come on through.'

She stared at the skin forming on the surface of her now-cold tea. She hadn't dared to lift the cup for fear they would see how badly she was shaking. 'Is there someone you'd like us to call?' PC Taylor asked, startling her. The way he phrased the question made her wonder how many times he'd asked before she'd heard him. *I'd like you to call my husband.*

Mia bit her lip against the pointless words, and ran through a quick inventory in her head. Her parents would be useless; it was too far past cocktail hour for her mother to be coherent and her dad didn't do emotions well at the best of times.

Her middle sister, Kiki, had enough on her hands with the new baby and Matty determined to live up to every horror story ever told about the terrible twos. Had it only been last week she and Jamie had babysat Matty because the baby had been sick? An image of Jamie holding their sleeping nephew in his lap rose unbidden and she shook her head sharply to dispel it. She couldn't think about things like that. Not right then.

The youngest of her siblings, Nee, was neck-deep in her final year at art school in London. Too young and too far away to be shouldering the burden of her eldest sister's grief. The only person she wanted to talk to was Jamie and that would never happen again. Bile burned in her throat and a whooping sob escaped before she could swallow it back.

'S-sorry.' She screwed her eyes tight and stuffed everything down as far as she could. There would be time enough for tears. Opening her stinging eyes, she looked at Sergeant Stone. 'Do Bill and Pat know?'

'Your in-laws? They're next on our list. I'm so very sorry, pet. Would you like us to take you over there?'

Unable to speak past the knot in her throat, Mia nodded.

Chapter One

February 2016

Daniel rested his head on the dirty train window and stared unseeing at the landscape as it flashed past. He didn't know where he was going. Away. That was the word that rattled around his head. Anywhere, nowhere. Just away from London. Away from the booze, birds and fakery of his so-called celebrity lifestyle. Twenty-nine felt too young to be a has-been.

He'd hit town with a portfolio, a bundle of glowing recommendations and an ill-placed confidence in his own ability to keep his feet on the ground. Within eighteen months, he was *the next big thing* in photography and everyone who was anyone clamoured for an original Fitz image on their wall. Well-received exhibitions had led to private commissions and more money than he knew what to do with. And if it hadn't been for Aaron's investment advice, his bank account would be as drained as his artistic talent.

The parties had been fun at first, and he couldn't put his finger on when the booze had stopped being a buzz and started being a crutch. Girls had come and gone. Pretty, cynical women who liked being seen on his arm in the gossip columns, and didn't seem to mind being in his bed.

Giselle had been one such girl and without any active consent on his part, she'd installed herself as a permanent fixture. The bitter smell of the French cigarettes she lived on in lieu of a decent meal filled his memory, forcing Daniel to swallow convulsively against the bile in his throat. That smell signified everything he hated about his life, about himself. Curls of rank smoke had hung like fog over the sprawled bodies, spilled bottles and overflowing ashtrays littering his flat when he'd woven a path through them that morning.

The cold glass of the train window eased the worst of his thumping hangover, although no amount of water seemed able to ease the parched feeling in his throat. The carriage had filled, emptied and filled again, the ebb and flow of humanity reaching their individual destinations.

Daniel envied their purpose. He swigged again from the large bottle of water he'd paid a small fortune for at Paddington Station as he'd perused the departures board. The taxi driver he'd flagged down near his flat had told him Paddington would take him west, a part of England that he knew very little about, which suited him perfectly.

His first instinct had been to head for King's Cross, but that would have taken him north. Too many memories, too tempting to visit old haunts his mam and dad had taken him to. It would be sacrilege to their memory to tread on the pebbled beaches of his youth, knowing how far he'd fallen from being the man his father had dreamed he would become.

He'd settled upon Exeter as a first destination. Bristol and Swindon seemed too industrial, too much like the urban sprawl he wanted to escape. And now he was on a local branch line train to Orcombe Sands. Sands meant the sea. The moment he'd seen the name, he knew it was where he needed to be. Air he could breathe, the wind on his face, nothing on the horizon but whitecaps and seagulls.

The train slowed and drew to a stop as it had done numerous times previously. Daniel didn't stir; the cold window felt too good against his clammy forehead. He was half aware of a small woman rustling an enormous collection of department store carrier bags as she carted her shopping haul past his seat, heading towards the exit. She took a couple of steps past him before she paused and spoke.

'This is the end of the line, you know?' Her voice carried a warm undertone of concern and Daniel roused. The thump in his head increased, making him frown as he regarded the speaker. She was an older lady, around the age his mam would've been had she still been alive.

Her grey hair was styled in a short, modern crop and she was dressed in that effortlessly casual, yet stylish look some women had. A soft camel jumper over dark indigo jeans with funky bright red trainers on her feet. A padded pea jacket and a large handbag worn cross body, keeping her hands free to manage her shopping bags. She smiled brightly at Daniel and tilted her head towards the carriage doors, which were standing stubbornly open.

'This is Orcombe Sands. Pensioner jail. Do not pass go, do not collect two hundred pounds.' She laughed at her own joke and Daniel finally realised what she was telling him. He had to get off the train; this was his destination. She was still watching him expectantly so he cleared his throat.

'Oh, thanks. Sorry, I was miles away.' He rose as he spoke, unfurling his full height as the small woman stepped back to give him room to stand and tug his large duffel bag from the rack above his seat. Seemingly content that Daniel was on the move, the woman gave him a cheery farewell and disappeared off the train.

Adjusting the bag on his shoulder as he looked around, Daniel perused the layout of the station for the first time. The panoramic sweep of his surroundings didn't take long. The tiny waiting room needed a lick of paint, but the platform was clean of the rubbish and detritus that had littered the central London station he'd started his journey at several hours previously. A hand-painted, slightly lopsided *Exit* sign pointed his way and Daniel moved in the only direction available to him, hoping to find some signs of life and a taxi rank.

He stopped short in what he supposed was the main street and looked at the handful of houses and a pub, which was closed up tight on the other side of the road. He looked to his right and regarded a small area of hardstanding with a handful of cars strewn haphazardly around.

The February wind tugged hard at his coat and he flipped the collar up, hunching slightly to keep his ears warm.

Daniel started to regret his spur-of-the-moment decision to leave town. He'd been feeling stale for a while, completely lacking in inspiration. Every image he framed in his mind's eye seemed either trite or derivative. All he'd ever wanted to do was take photographs. From the moment his parents had given him his first disposable camera to capture his holiday snaps, Daniel had wanted to capture the world he saw through his viewfinder.

An engine grumbled to life and the noise turned Daniel's thoughts outwards again as a dirty estate car crawled out of the car park and stopped in front of him. The passenger side window lowered and the woman from the train leant across from the driver's side to speak to him.

'You all right there? Is someone coming to pick you up?' Daniel shuffled his feet slightly under the blatantly interested gaze of the older woman.

His face warmed as he realised he would have to confess his predicament to the woman. He had no idea where he was or what his next move should be. He could tell from the way she was regarding him that she would not leave until she knew he was going to be all right.

'My trip was a bit spur-of-the-moment. Do you happen to know if there is a B&B nearby?' he said, trying to keep his voice light, as though heading off into the middle of nowhere on a freezing winter's day was a completely rational, normal thing to do.

The older woman widened her eyes slightly. 'Not much call for that this time of year. Just about everywhere that offers accommodation is seasonal and won't be open until Easter time.'

Daniel started to feel like an even bigger fool as the older woman continued to ponder his problem, her index finger tapping against her lip. The finger paused as a sly smile curled one corner of her lip and Daniel wondered if he should be afraid of whatever thought had occurred to cause that expression.

He took a backwards step as the woman suddenly released her seat belt and climbed out of the car in a determined manner. He was not intimidated by someone a foot shorter than him. *He wasn't.*

'What's your name?' she asked as she flipped open the boot of the car and started transferring her shopping bags onto the back seat.

'Fitz...' He paused. That name belonged in London, along with everything else he wanted to leave behind. 'Daniel. Daniel Fitzwilliams.'

'Pleased to meet you. I'm Madeline, although my friends call me Mads, and I have a feeling we will be great friends. Stick your bag in the boot, there's a good lad. I know the perfect place. Run by a friend of mine. I'm sure you'll be very happy there.'

Daniel did as bid, his eyes widening in shock as—*unbelievable!*—Madeline propelled him in the right direction with a slap on the arse and a loud laugh.

'Bounce a coin on those cheeks, Daniel! I do so like a man who takes care of himself.' With another laugh, Madeline disappeared into the front seat of the car and the engine gave a slightly startled whine as she turned the key.

Gritting his teeth, he placed his bag in the boot before moving around to the front of the car and eyeing the grubby interior of the estate, which appeared to be mainly held together with mud and rust. He folded his frame into the seat, which had been hiked forward almost as far as it could. With his knees up around his ears, Daniel fumbled under the front of the seat until he found the adjuster and carefully edged the seat back until he felt less like a sardine.

'Belt up, there's a good boy,' Madeline trilled as she patted his knee and threw the old car into first. They lurched away from the kerb. Deciding that a death grip was the only way to survive, Daniel quickly snapped his seat belt closed, scrabbled for the aptly named *oh shit!* handle above the window and tried to decide whether the journey would be worse with his eyes open or closed.

Madeline barrelled the car blithely around the narrow country lanes, barely glancing at the road as far as Daniel could tell as she sang along to the latest pop tunes pouring from the car radio. He tried not to whimper at the thought of where he was going to end up. What the hell was this place going to be like if it was run by a friend of Madeline's? If there was a woman in a rocking chair at the window, he'd be in deep shit.

The car abruptly swung off to the left and continued along what appeared to be a footpath rather than any kind of road. A huge building loomed to the left and Daniel caught his breath. Rather than the Bates Motel, it was more of a Grand Lady in her declining years. In its heyday, it must have been a magnificent structure. The peeling paint, filthy windows and rotting porch did their best to hide the beauty, together with the overgrown gardens.

His palms itched and for the first time in for ever, Daniel felt excited. He wanted his camera. Head twisting and turning, he tried to take everything in. A group of outbuildings and a large barn lay to the right of where Madeline pulled to a stop on the gravel driveway.

Giving a jaunty toot on the car's horn, she wound down her window to wave and call across the yard to what appeared to be a midget yeti in the most moth-eaten dressing gown Daniel had ever seen. *Not good, not good, oh so not good...*

Chapter Two

It had seemed like such a good idea at the time. Mia lay on her back staring up at the large water stain on her bedroom ceiling. She squinted a little to try and work out if it looked bigger than the day before. There were many cautionary tales about money pits and impulse buys and buying sight unseen and Mia had disregarded every single one of them.

She'd thrown a large portion of her widow's settlement into what she thought would be the perfect new start at Butterfly House. Her lip twisted at the romantic name attached to the monstrosity she now owned. Whoever had owned the place had a wild imagination to attach such a pretty name to the ugly old pile.

She couldn't regret the purchase though, even if the reality had failed to live up to the romance of the name. Over a year of inertia, surrounded by everything they had made together, their friends, their special places, had finally come to a head when she realised that she couldn't remember a day when she hadn't cried. She felt terrible, looked worse, and in her heart knew that Jamie would've hated it if he'd had any idea.

Not going there, not today... Mia gave herself a mental shake and contemplated leaving the cosy nest she had made in the middle of the double bed that dominated the small but airy room she had set aside for herself. Well, she hoped it would be airy in the summer, but just now on a dank, cold February morning it was not that appealing.

Taking a deep breath, she slid her leg from beneath her flannel sheets and quickly drew it back as her toes touched the freezing cold floor. Where the hell were her slippers? Mia rolled to the side and peered over the edge of the mattress in the vain hope the slipper fairy had come through for once and left them helpfully by the bed. Nope, just cold boards still needing to be filled, sanded and waxed.

'Bollocks,' Mia huffed, wincing as her breath misted in the cold air.

With a mental count to three, she threw back the covers and dashed from the bed, swearing and hopping from foot to foot as she made her way across the cold floor and into the bathroom and the relative warmth of the bathmat. She grabbed her dressing gown from the hook behind the door and burrowed into it, turning her face instinctively into the collar to seek out an elusive hint of Jamie's scent.

The man-sized garment swamped her; the sleeves were rolled back at the cuffs several times and still her hands only just peeked out. It dragged a little on the floor unless Mia hiked it up slightly with the belt from her old dressing gown. The fluffy pink belt clashed with the dark green tartan pattern but it did the job and there was no-one around to care about her bedroom attire.

She scrubbed her face until it glowed before cleaning her teeth vigorously in the hopes of generating a little extra body warmth. She spat and rinsed and then made the mistake of looking in the mirrored doors of the little cabinet above the sink. The problem with short hair, she mused, was that it just *never* looked good in the morning.

Wetting her hands, she made a vague effort to try and flatten the dark crop into some semblance of order but quickly lost interest. She had another dirty day ahead cleaning out the grate of the fireplace in what would one day become the dining room, so there was no point in more than basic ablutions as she would be filthy in no time.

With no more reason to linger on the little island of material any longer, Mia hurried from the bathroom and down the sweeping staircase that dominated the hallway of the house. She hopped and skipped her way down, well-versed in which of the boards were half rotten and ready to try and capture her foot in their splintery jaws.

Reaching the bottom, she dove on her cosy boots, shoved her freezing feet into their fleecy warmth, and sighed in relief. She scuffed her way into the kitchen, moving by rote as she made a cup of builder's strength tea and gathered the bucket, brush and other cleaning implements she would need to tackle the fireplace. The worst of the old soot and rubbish had been removed from the grate the day before, but the whole thing was still stained from years of neglect.

Carrying her tea into the dining room, she paused to catch her breath as the view from the French windows caught her, as it did every time. This, *this* is what made her carry on when she wanted to throw in the towel and give up on the whole idea of running her own guest house. The view spread out before her: across the sad-looking collection of cracked paving in front of the window, through the weed-filled garden and beyond. Windswept dunes rolled down towards the sea. Churned to a murky green by the winter winds, it swelled and undulated like a living beast.

Dark clouds glowered above and the horizon was blurred by mist and rain out to sea. It looked dangerous and utterly captivating. Mia had seen pictures of it taken in the summer looking like a benign, soft blanket of blue edged with white lacy waves. She was determined that in a few months she would be sitting out on the patio in the sunshine with a cold glass of wine in her hand as she watched pleasure boats sailing across that blanket.

Finishing her tea, she ran through a mental list of things she had already achieved as she slowly put the house to rights. The daily exercise had become a motivational lifeline and thinking of the positives helped to offset the mountain of tasks outstanding. 'One thing at a time, one step forward.' Muttering the mantra, she turned back to the kitchen to fetch the first of many buckets of hot soapy water.

A couple of hours later, Mia sat back on her ankles and wiped her face on the increasingly dirty sleeve of her dressing gown; it would have to go in the washing machine that night, taking her another wash away from Jamie's scent. It was a foolish thought; it had long ago stopped smelling of anything other than her fabric softener and, she gave a rueful sniff, her sweat.

The fireplace looked amazing; the enamel panels set into the red brick surround had come to life under her determined ministrations and were now a gentle shade of cream with a riot of colourful butterflies dancing over the deep green vines running up the centre of them. She had scrubbed the bricks with several different brushes so they varied in shade from dark, almost black, to nearly new red brick.

The house had history, had been lived in by many others, and each person who had passed through the front door had left their mark. Mia was determined to retain the lived-in, homely feel lurking beneath the layers of grime.

She climbed to her feet, rotating her hips a little to release some of the stiffness in them from prolonged kneeling at the hearth, and then lifted the bucket of cold, dirty water. Trying not to spill the filthy contents, she lugged it through the house and out into the yard. A large drain sat next to the barn and she'd taken to emptying the contents into it, rather than spoil the old butler's sink in the kitchen. One last trip and then it was time for a shower.

The toot of a car horn and a brisk call of 'Ooh hoo, Mia darling!' startled her, sending cold water sloshing onto her boots, which whilst soft and warm were not waterproof.

'Well, shit,' she said with feeling. Setting the bucket down, she folded her arms across her chest. She loved Madeline, she really did, but it had been a long day and Mia wasn't in the mood for a gossip. She shrugged off the unkind thought.

Both Madeline and her kind-hearted husband, Richard, were a welcome blessing in her life. They had taken her under their wing from the moment they had called around to welcome Mia to the village and found her a sobbing mess on the front porch. *In the front porch* was more accurate as her foot had gone straight through the rotten wood and been stuck fast until they rescued her.

With a mixture of kindness, humour and tough love when the situation required it, the older couple were helping to turn the ramshackle house into the guest house she dreamed of. Mia turned her attention back to Madeline as her words filtered through. 'I've brought you a present, darling. Your first of what I am sure will be many guests.' Madeline disappeared back inside the car although her voice carried clearly across the cold air. 'Out you get, Daniel, there's a good boy. Mia will see you right.'

The passenger door swung open and Mia prayed to every god that she had ever heard of for a sinkhole to open and swallow her whole as a broad-shouldered, dark-haired, bearded man uncurled from the car, eyeing her with some trepidation.

Madeline appeared out of the driver's side, opened the boot and wrestled out a duffel bag nearly as large as she was. She dropped the bag on the ground, swiftly closed the boot, and before Mia could utter a word, the gears of the car crunched, forcing the stranger to jump clear to avoid being sideswiped as Madeline spun the car around and disappeared back up the drive with a toot and a wave.

'Well, shit,' Mia said again as the situation clearly warranted it, before she picked up the bucket and slopped over to the drain to empty what remained of the water.

'Umm, Madeline said you run a B&B.' The man's voice rumbled pleasantly in his chest and Mia decided she needed to make the best of the situation, if she could only work out what the hell that was.

'I am hoping to open the house to guests later this year; it's just taking a little bit longer than I anticipated to put things straight,' she said, with what she hoped was a confident smile as she skirted around the man. She was ripe and in dire need of a shower.

'Daniel, is it? Would you like to come in for a cup of tea while I try and find out if somewhere else in the area is open and taking in guests?' Mia tried to sound more confident than she felt about letting a stranger into her house. It was something she was going to have to get used to and surely Madeline wouldn't leave her alone with a crazy man?

She continued briskly towards the kitchen door. He would follow or not but she needed to get her feet out of her wet boots before they started to rot or hypothermia set in.

Chapter Three

Daniel watched the woman, *Mia*, disappear through the back door, bucket swinging in hand and a large swathe of her dressing gown dragging along the ground behind her. He suppressed a shudder, wondering whether the inside of the house would be as grubby as its owner. He wandered over to fetch his duffel bag and, as he bent over, he noticed a wizened stone face peering out from the depths of the evergreen shrubbery that shielded the back of the house.

Reaching into the pocket of his jacket, he retrieved the digital camera that was always somewhere about his person and stepped closer to take a shot of the green man, for surely that was what the little statue was with its hair and beard carved to resemble ivy. The dark, almost waxy sheen of the leaves of the shrubbery framed the moss-covered stone and he knelt, heedless of the cold, damp gravel of the driveway to take a series of pictures.

The sun found a small break in the cloud and its weak but welcome warmth bathed the back of his head. A glint to the right caught his eye and he turned to study another half-hidden fancy: a bronze fairy this time, standing on tiptoe with her hands held out as though drawing down the sunlight.

Daniel scrambled closer, swearing to himself as the gravel dug into his knees through his jeans. Sitting back on his heels, he brushed a few stray stones from the two damp circles over his knees. He glanced towards the still-open door of the house, intrigued by the woman. She clearly had a sense of humour and imagination if these little secret figures were anything to go by.

He rolled his head on his shoulders then pushed up to his full height and collected his bag, slipping the camera back into his pocket. He was stiff and tired from the long train journey and he could certainly do with the cup of tea he'd been offered. He'd drunk plenty of tea from dirty mugs in his art school days after all. Trying not to look too closely at the cobweb-strewn windows and the patches of weeds poking up through the driveway, he headed for the back door.

Mia glanced over her shoulder from where she stood at the large white sink, scrubbing her hands with a brush. Catching a closer look, he realised she was a lot younger than he'd first assumed. Probably close to his own age. 'Take your shoes off, please.' She nodded to where her wet boots were drying on a piece of newspaper on the floor next to the radiator on the spotless stone floor. 'And shut the door behind you. The boiler's new but this house takes for ever to heat up.'

Daniel paused to survey the kitchen, relieved to find it immaculately clean. A wooden table dominated the centre of the large square room and a huge cooking range surrounded by granite worktops filled most of the back wall. The appliances looked modern and were a soft duck-egg blue, providing a nice contrast to the stone surfaces and wooden cupboards. He toed off his shoes and placed them carefully on the newspaper as requested.

'Have a seat. I'll just grab my cup from next door and get the phone book and see if we can find you somewhere with a bed.' His reluctant hostess spoke again and Daniel moved towards the table just as she took a step forward and they nearly collided. He reached out a hand to brace her, but she shied away. Wrapping her arms around her body tightly, she took an exaggerated route around the kitchen to keep well away from him. He dropped his hand swiftly, feeling big and awkward in comparison to her delicate height.

'I'm sorry, I didn't mean to startle you.' Mia turned in the doorway and offered a weak smile at his apology before disappearing.

Heat rose on his cheeks as he sank into a chair; he was clearly not wanted here. How the hell had he got himself in such a mess? Getting away from London had seemed like such a good idea, but clearly he was not a spur-of-the-moment kind of guy. He was the man with the plan, the designated driver, always booked a table, always thought ahead.

He was not impulsive usually, but he'd woken that morning with a stinking hangover. The scent of cigarette smoke and stale perfume on the pillow next to him had turned his stomach. A wash of guilt over his bad behaviour the day before added to his misery.

His dreams of being an artist, a serious photographer, had taken him from his home to the bright lights of the capital like so many before him. London was where it all happened: where the connections were, the dealers who would frame his quirky black and white pictures and sell them to people with lots of money. His simple but arresting shots had captured attention and sooner than he could have ever dreamed of, he was flavour of the month with his pictures appearing in magazines and on the walls of the hip young things who set the trends others followed.

Before he knew it, Daniel was attending parties and premieres and his picture started appearing in the magazines in the gossip sections more often than images of his work did. Then there was Giselle. Always perfectly dressed and styled, she knew the perfect places to go and be seen with lots of other perfect people.

She was also a perfect bitch, although he hadn't realised it until they'd somehow ended up living together. He still wasn't sure how the hell that had happened, but Giselle had decided that she was going to be Daniel's girlfriend and had attached herself to him like a limpet. He'd been too lazy, too enamoured with his own celebrity, and frankly, too stoned to do something about it until it was too late. The cold contempt in her voice had chased him halfway down the street as he scurried away with his hastily packed bag.

Shaking off his melancholy thoughts, Daniel roused at the sound of Mia shuffling back into the room. 'This is Orcombe's idea of Google.' She dropped the local phone directory on the table before skirting past, back over to the kettle.

Daniel pulled the book towards him and started flipping through until he came to the section for hotels, inns and guest houses. He smiled slightly at using the old-fashioned book. So used to instant access to the world through his phone, it felt strange to be manually searching for information again.

Several of the entries carried small ads detailing seasonal opening so he ignored those. His eyes skimmed down the list but nothing sounded appealing. Even the simple decision to choose which number to try first seemed too much of a trial. Desperate for a distraction, he leaned back in his chair and studied the room around him.

Mia bustled around from the butler's sink to the large retro-style fridge to fetch a pint of milk, which she plopped on the table before turning to rummage in one of the lower cupboards. Her bottom wiggled a little as she reached deeper into the cupboard.

A man might notice such a thing, even under the swathes of material she was layered in, if he was so inclined. Not that he was so inclined, of course. This pale, scruffy little creature was nothing compared to the sleek London girls he hung with.

Mia found what she was looking for apparently, given her little hoot of triumph as she backed out of the cupboard. She brandished a decorative cake tin in hand before dropping it on the table next to the milk. A quick rattle in the cupboard above the kettle and a side plate appeared, swiftly followed by two mugs of strong tea and a bag of sugar with a teaspoon poking out of the top.

Circling the battered oak table, she pulled out a chair for herself, as far away from him as possible he noted. She added a splash of milk to her tea and nudged the cake tin closer to him, then sat back on her chair with one foot tucked underneath her.

Raising the mug to her face, she blew across the surface of her tea before raising her eyes to meet his across the table. Deep brown, with thick sooty lashes framing them and large, almost purple bruising underneath. Her face was pale, *too pale*. It made her eyes seem huge above her button nose and dry lips that looked as though she chewed on them too often. As if to confirm his assumption, Mia drew her lower lip between her teeth and nibbled on it. She squinted her eyes at Daniel as though trying to come to a decision.

Daniel ducked his head away from her scrutiny and raised his own mug of tea to his mouth, venturing a sip before quickly pulling the cup away with a rueful expression. 'No milk,' he muttered before adding some and taking another drink.

'Are you hungry? There are scones in the tin. No cream, I'm afraid, but there's butter and jam if you want it.' Mia nodded with her head towards the cake tin. He put down his mug and pried open the lid of the tin, giving the contents an exploratory sniff. The sweet, buttery scent of the scones teased his nose and his stomach gave an appreciative rumble.

He reached into the tin then pulled back to quickly head to the sink and wash his hands. Returning to his seat, he lifted out his prize from the baking tin. He sliced the scone in half and slathered on a generous layer of butter.

The first bite had his eyes rolling back into his head and he was afraid a little moan of bliss may have escaped him as the sweet taste of home baking filled his mouth. He couldn't remember the last time he'd had something that hadn't been mass-produced from a supermarket chain. Not since his mam had passed away probably. He cut his eyes to Mia and was surprised to see her pleased smile.

'Baked by my own fair hand, those are,' she said before taking a deep drink from her mug. 'I'd better let Richard know that he's got competition for my culinary attentions.'

'Mnphfod?' Daniel mumbled around another huge mouthful of scone.

'Madeline's husband. He trades labour and heavy lifting around the place in exchange for treats.

It's quite the bartering system we have going. I'm holding out on a Dundee cake until he regrouts the tiles in one of the guest bathrooms.' She paused and some of the merriment fell from her eyes. 'I think he does it to try and make me feel less guilty for all the hard work that he and Madeline have put in here. I would be lost without them, well, even more lost...' Mia trailed off and blushed as she stuck her nose back in her cup.

'So you'd pay me in cake if I offered to lend a hand around here?' The words were out before Daniel realised what he was saying and he mentally kicked himself as Mia stiffened visibly in her chair, her fingers whitening as she gripped her tea.

'You can't stay. I've no room for you,' she stammered and Daniel crooked an eyebrow and raised his eyes to the ceiling. *How many bedrooms would a place this size have? Five, six maybe.* 'No room fit for habitation. I don't know you; you can't be here. It's a ridiculous notion.'

Mia slammed her mug down on the table and pulled the cordless phone out of its holder on the wall and shoved it across to him. 'Get dialling. I'm going for a shower and to get dressed and then I'll drop you off wherever.'

She whirled away and shot out of the kitchen into the hallway. Daniel leaned sideways in his chair and caught sight of her disappearing through another doorway with the stairs framed in the background. The door slammed and he heard the snick of a key as she locked it behind her before climbing the stairs, her passage marked by creaks and groans from the half-rotten staircase.

Daniel blew out a breath and scrubbed his hand thoughtfully across his chin as he tried to decide on what to do for the best. There was a pinboard next to where the phone holder was attached to the wall and he rose from his seat to examine the eclectic mix of items pinned to it. He knew he was being nosy, but he wanted to know more about his reluctant hostess.

There were several photographs—Mia with stunningly long hair and two other women who bore a striking resemblance to her; arms entwined and heads thrown back as they laughed together at something. There was something so free and joyous in the image that Daniel wished he'd been the one on the other side of the camera capturing that tiny flash of perfection and preserving it for ever.

There was another more recent photo of Mia, this time with Madeline, touching glasses of wine together as they toasted each other. Mia was smiling in this shot too, but her expression was much less open and her hair was now shorn off in the mad pixie crop that she sported today.

There were postcards from a random selection of capital cities and scraps of paper pinned haphazardly between the photos, recipes torn from magazines, a scribbled list of tasks to be tackled on the house that daunted Daniel as he scanned down it, quotations for roof repairs and resurfacing the driveway. Daniel double-checked one of the amounts and then forced himself to turn away from the board, guilty at how nosy he was being.

Curious about the rest of the house, he headed out into the hallway, past the locked door to the upper floors, and poked his head into the first room on the right. The room was mostly empty, just an old Welsh dresser and a matching sideboard shoved back against one wall. The wooden floor scratched and dark with age was bare and the windows were lacking curtains.

With nothing to distract and soften the view beyond, Daniel's gaze was drawn inexorably to the writhing seascape and he moved without conscious thought until his nose was pressed up against the dirty glass of the French windows.

The memory of a long-forgotten poem rose unbidden. His dad had been a great one for poetry. A hard-working man, quiet—and some had thought him grim-faced and taciturn. Daniel had later realised this was a product of his dad's shyness though he had never found him so. A man with few opportunities who'd resigned himself to a life of manual labour, he'd been determined to learn all he could and made damn sure his son looked beyond his roots to stretch for the heights of whatever he chose to study.

Whenever he pictured his dad, it was always with a book in hand: poetry, biographies, history. He soaked up everything and Daniel had learned to read at his knee, a new poem to memorise every week. His favourite times were when his dad opened his huge atlas of the world, letting Daniel choose a page at random. Whatever location he landed on, they would study and explore. A smile played on his lips. They'd travelled the world together side by side at the dining room table.

Daniel lost himself in the rolling waves and the rhythm of the words as they ebbed and flowed through his mind like the white foam of the tide on the sands before him. He rocked back slightly on his heels—hands tucked into the front pockets of his jeans—and for the first time a little bit of peace and quiet stole into a corner of his heart.

This spot, this view had brought him a tiny step back to where he wanted to be. To whom he wanted to be. He wanted to be that man his father had envisioned as he plied his young son with knowledge and a love of learning, a love of exploration and wonder.

Daniel rested his suddenly hot forehead against the cold glass of the window as a wave of shame washed through him from the tips of his boots to the top of his head. A sudden gush of saliva filled his mouth, the sour taste of bile burning his throat. He wrestled with the handle of the French windows and burst out onto the scruffy patio. Lurching to the side, he doubled over, vomiting into the overgrown bushes that framed the door.

He heaved and heaved, feeling like he would turn himself inside out as the realisation hit of how disappointed his dad would be in the shallow, vain fool his beloved boy had become. For the first time, he was glad his dad had only lived long enough to enjoy the beginning of Daniel's success rather than being there now to witness his fall from grace.

He pushed himself upright, raising his arm to wipe the tears, snot and vomit from his face. A soft noise to his right caused him to whip his head around and Daniel closed his eyes against a fresh roll of shame as he realised Mia had finished upstairs and leaned against the open patio door, her head tilted to one side as she watched him quietly.

Chapter Four

Mia stayed still as she watched Daniel struggle not to fall apart before her. His chest heaved, lungs working like a bellows as the air sawed in and out. There was a smear of vomit on his chin, more down his dark sweater and across the sleeve where he'd scrubbed at his face.

She recognised the signs of an impending meltdown when she saw them; she had suffered plenty herself over the past couple of years. His obvious distress tugged at her. She didn't want this man, this intruder in her house. The rational part of her recognised that his presence wasn't voluntary, and she made a mental note to give Madeline a call later and voice her ire at the correct source of her dilemma.

Mia wanted to carry on as she was, hiding away and burying herself in the work to try and bring Butterfly House back to a semblance of its former glory. It was a Herculean task—even with the help and support of Madeline and Richard.

Her target for opening to guests was slipping further into the distance and part of her was glad of it. If the house wasn't ready, then she didn't have to be ready to deal with the outside world. Her grand plan to move forward with her life had turned into a different type of inertia. Perhaps it was time to act, time to take a chance and help someone else, and just maybe help herself at the same time.

Daniel raised a hand to cover his already shut eyes and his shoulders quaked. Moving before she was aware of what she was doing, she reached out to take his other hand, heedless of the unpleasant dampness of it.

'Daniel, come inside with me and let's get you cleaned up. It's all right, darling. It'll be all right, I promise.' She tugged gently on his hand and gave an encouraging nod when he dropped his big hand to blink at her through the moisture clinging to his lashes. The sparkle of his tears drew her attention to the stormy green colour of his eyes.

Walking backwards, she maintained eye contact as she led him through the empty room and back into the relative warmth of the kitchen. She guided him back to the table and he didn't resist when pressed into a chair. She dashed through to the dining room to close and latch the patio doors, her stockinged feet sliding across the wooden floor as she hurried back.

Pulling the kitchen door closed, she cocooned them in the warmth from the Aga. Daniel hadn't moved from the spot she had placed him in and Mia gave him a worried frown as she went over to the sink and turned on the hot water tap. She quickly rinsed her hands, washing off the vomit and snot and suppressing a little shudder. *Not the time to be squeamish.*

Retrieving a plastic bowl from under the sink, she filled it with warm water and fetched a clean towel from the drawer. After placing them on the table, she gripped Daniel's chin, turning his face towards her. He remained passive while she washed his face, letting her turn his head this way and that as she wiped away the traces of his outburst. She rinsed the towel out in the bowl, then cleaned off his hands with the same concentration, keeping her touch gentle, stroking his skin until he began to stir.

Daniel opened his mouth, no doubt to apologise for his behaviour, but she shook her head and tapped him under the chin to close his mouth. 'Arms up, Daniel. Let's get this nasty sweater off you.' Taking care not to let the dirty material touch his face, she eased the garment over his head and bundled it up with the dirty towel. Turning away, she shoved them into the washing machine, adding them to her grubby pyjamas and dressing gown. A quick twist of the dial and the soothing hum of the machine filled the air.

'You got a toothbrush in that duffel bag of yours?' Mia asked, pointing towards the big bag that lay just inside the back door. She waited for him to nod before digging around in its contents until she gave a little grunt of satisfaction as she located and retrieved his wash kit. 'You'll feel better once you rinse your mouth and clean your teeth; I always do,' she said trying to put him at ease.

Deciding a cold drink would probably be welcome, she fetched a can of Diet Coke and a bottle of mineral water from the fridge, before resuming her seat from earlier, one foot tucked beneath her in her habitual position. She'd regret it soon enough when the pins and needles started, but it was a habit she'd developed in childhood and never grown out of.

She watched Daniel rinse and spit, rinse again then dry his face and hands. He was braced over the sink taking deep breaths and the tension in his shoulders told her he was trying not to be sick again. Without any real thought, she crossed to stand behind him and rubbed his back softly. Making circles with her hand, she stroked the tense muscles until they yielded beneath her touch.

Stormy green eyes met hers over his shoulder and she twisted her lips into a semblance of a smile, though there was little true mirth in it. 'What a pair of fuck-ups we are,' she said bluntly.

Surprise widened his gaze, chasing away some of the desperate vulnerability she couldn't miss. She knew that look, knew it well, and it helped to crystallise her decision. 'I don't want to hear your sad story, Daniel. Nor do I want to tell you mine, so I'll make a deal with you. You can stay here for a week and get yourself together and in return I expect you to work on the house to earn your keep. There's a list of things to do as long as your arm. I wasn't joking when I said I didn't have a room fit for habitation. I'll get you a quilt and a pillow and you can crash on the sofa. Tomorrow you can pick one of the rooms upstairs and we'll clean it up so you have somewhere to sleep tomorrow night. That's my only offer—take it or take off.'

Mia hoped he'd take it. She knew what it was like to hit rock bottom and Daniel seemed close to that. It was time to move forward and she could manage a week. There were plenty of dirty, heavy chores on her list that he could help with. A bit of hard work might be just what he needed.

'Thank you.' His voice sounded rough, his throat clearly raw and dry. Mia stepped back, gathered the drinks and offered them to him. He reached for the Diet Coke, popping the tab and gulping at the cold, sweet liquid. She waited for him to drink his fill, wary in case it came back up, but he seemed more settled now that she had agreed to let him stay for a few days.

'A couple of the rooms upstairs are en suite so I'll sort the bathroom out while you sort the bedroom. Can you manage tonight without a shower? The only usable one is in my room and I just can't have you in there.' She turned away, needing to put some distance between them, muttering to herself as she resumed her seat. 'I just can't have you in my space.'

Mia crossed one arm over her chest and rubbed her other shoulder. The body language was defensive, but she couldn't help it. With each passing moment, panic rose. She wanted to rescind her offer, shove Daniel out the door and erect all her barriers again. *Danger! Keep*

Out! No Trespassing! She forced her hands down into her lap and tried to relax and keep her breathing calm.

'You've done more than I could ever have expected under the circumstances. I'm sorry to put you in this position.' His quiet tone sounded soft and sincere. With a rueful laugh, he continued. 'But apparently not sorry enough that I can bring myself to do the honourable thing and leave you in peace. I will do my best to repay you with a lot of hard work and I wouldn't dream of invading any more of your home than you are comfortable with sharing. A hot shower and a proper bed will be motivation tomorrow to get stuck in.'

Mia felt his eyes on her but didn't want to meet them. She crossed over to the kitchen window, pulling the curtains closed over the rapidly darkening sky. 'It gets dark so quickly this time of year.' She rolled her eyes at her inane remark; her back was turned so thankfully he didn't see her. The decision was made and it was time to face up to it. Hopefully they would find some neutral ground where they could both relax a little and adjust to the other's company.

She'd always been a feeder by nature, a nurturer. It was a source of deep regret that she and Jamie had not felt ready to have a child because at least then she would've had a piece of him to care for. They'd been young, eager to explore the world together, revelling in the selfish bliss of just their own company, not having to split their attentions on anything other than each other. They had their whole lives ahead of them, Jamie had said. No need to rush into a family.

A burst tyre and a slick, wet road had robbed them of their future; those dream babies that Mia had pictured holding would never fill her empty arms. 'Shit, *shit*, stop it, Mia!' She shook her head to dislodge the memories threatening to encroach.

Needing to hide for a moment to regain her compose, she crossed the kitchen and entered the narrow pantry that ran the length of the room. It was a treasure of a space. Sturdy, wide shelves down one side and a built-in wine rack at the far end. The bare stone floor helped to keep the temperature cooler than the rest of the kitchen, but was brutal underfoot this time of year, even with thick woollen socks on.

Mia grabbed the cob loaf wrapped in a muslin cloth and returned to the main kitchen space, wiggling her feet gratefully on the warmer floor in front of the Aga. She unwrapped the bread and tested its freshness. She'd baked it a couple of days ago, but the cloth had helped to keep it from drying out. Opening the fridge, she retrieved half a roast chicken, a pot of single cream and some stock. She placed them on the board and turned back towards the pantry. Daniel watched her, a slightly quizzical expression on his face.

'I thought I'd make some soup, nothing too testing if your stomach is still feeling a little rebellious. We'll both feel better for a hot meal, I think.'

She carried on past the table and back into the pantry to root in her vegetable basket for the bits she needed to thicken the soup and up the nutritional punch. Since moving to Orcombe, she'd made a conscious effort to eat well, having neglected herself for too long after Jamie's death. Cooking and baking had always been a source of comfort and enjoyment. Originally it had been a chore that she had learned through necessity thanks to her mother's negligence and her father's steadfast refusal to notice his wife's drink problem.

As the oldest of three, it had fallen to Mia to assume the responsibility for the day-to-day care of her two sisters. Each of them had taken on a different role to survive their upbringing. Kiki had been the pacifier, covering for their mother and making excuses for their father spending so many hours buried in his work. Nee had been the warrior protector of her elder sisters. A tiny bundle of spirit and fury from a young age, she was the one who verbally sparred with their father, driving him to distraction and the sanctuary of his study in her vain efforts to get his attention. Her exhortations to their mother to put down her glass and give a damn led to tears on both sides.

Together the girls had done their best to look out for each other but they had scattered to the winds as soon as they could. Mia and Kiki to young marriages; Nee to art school and more recently overseas. Mia glanced over to the pinboard at the postcard of Times Square lit up in all its seedy glory. She hadn't heard from Nee since that last card had arrived about three weeks ago and it struck Mia suddenly that she had no idea where her little sister was other than somewhere in Manhattan.

'I'm not a great cook, but I take instruction well. Is there anything I can do to help?' Daniel's deep voice broke through her reverie.

Mia blinked at him, trying to gather her thoughts before pointing to the cooked chicken. 'You can shred the meat from that if you don't mind; that would be a great help. Take it over to the table with you so that you don't get under my feet. I'm not used to anyone else in the kitchen these days.'

'But you used to have someone else in your kitchen?' Daniel prompted and Mia couldn't stop her whole body from stiffening.

She kept slicing and chopping, her hands working automatically as she reeled under an assault of memories. At least Jamie had never been in this kitchen. It was her own space, manageable most days. 'No sad stories, remember?' She jabbed her finger at the radio on the countertop next to her.

A commercial music station filled the kitchen with a rhythmic beat and Mia flicked the volume up a couple of notches, erecting a wall of sound that separated them. She chopped the vegetables with a practised hand, added them to a large saucepan with the chicken stock and set it to simmer on the top of the Aga.

Daniel bent to his task, stripping the meat from the carcass of the chicken, shredding it as he placed it on a clean plate. Mia paused to check his efforts before she returned to the stove, tapping a wooden spoon against the pan in time with the music as she checked the progress of the soup.

The music caught her in its rhythm and she swayed and sang along, waiting for the stock to boil. She couldn't carry a tune to save her life, but she loved to sing. Aiming for the high note in the chorus, she missed her target by a country mile. A soft chuckle behind her reminded her that she wasn't alone.

If her face glowed, it was the heat from the stove and most definitely not a blush.

Chapter Five

Daniel relaxed back in his chair and focused on Mia. He was surprised to find that he was hungry after his earlier disgrace, but the scents filling the kitchen soothed him and gave him a little more strength to push away the embarrassment threatening to rise again. And not just over his performance earlier. He'd have to call his client from yesterday and apologise for his unprofessional behaviour.

Over the last year, his agent had pushed him into more and more private sittings, trying to turn him into a half-baked celebrity snapper. Soap actresses, footballers' wives, and the idle rich had jumped at the chance of a personal portrait sitting with sexy, brooding Fitz, so bloody Nigel reckoned. He couldn't deny the money had been good, more than good, and the constant round of parties had been fun. Until suddenly they weren't.

Yesterday's client, a sweet girl engaged to her childhood sweetheart who'd been swept into the celebrity bubble because he could kick a ball, had borne the brunt of his hangover and short temper. When she'd shown him into the carefully staged room and spoken earnestly about learning about composition in GCSE art classes, something snapped inside him.

Storming out on a stream of curses, he'd gone straight to his favourite pub to try and drown his sorrows. The row with Giselle over failing to escort her to some stupid party had been the final straw.

Guilt sent an uneasy roil through his stomach. Somewhere along the way, he'd turned into the kind of self-absorbed wanker he'd first sneered at when arriving in London. *Don't think about it*. He wasn't ready to face a serious bout of introspection; he needed to use the week ahead to put some space between himself and the mess of his life that he had so abruptly fled from that morning. Hard physical work would be just what he needed. A couple of days to breathe, to sort out his head and get back on track.

Needing distraction, his eyes skipped to the long list of chores Mia had pinned on her wall. If nothing else, he would help her cross at least a few of them off. It would be good to do something productive and make his muscles ache from labour rather than his head aching from too much booze and the other rubbish he'd been shoving into his body over the past few months.

The phone, lying forgotten on the table in front of him, began to ring, startling Daniel. He looked at it with trepidation, wondering who was intruding on the little cave of solace he had found in the kitchen. Mia scooped up the handset and shimmied back towards the radio, turning the volume down a little as she answered the phone.

'Oh hey, Richard.' The warmth in her tone drew Daniel's attention and he met Mia's eyes as she pulled a little face and shook her head as she listened to whatever Madeline's husband had to say.

'Yes, I know, I know…you don't have to tell *me* she acted inappropriately, Richard. I didn't call her up and ask her to dump a random stranger on my doorstep.' Daniel flinched at that comment and Mia raised a hand in half-apology at him as she continued to hmm, and uh-huh and all those other noises that women universally made when they were on the phone.

'She had a feeling about what, exactly?' Sharpness entered Mia's tone and Daniel squirmed, feeling even more the awkward intruder. He moved away from the table towards the stove, trying to put some distance between them and give her some semblance of privacy.

He glanced over to Mia and pointed at the pot and the stove and mimed stirring it and she flashed him a thumbs up. Lifting the lid, he closed his eyes in appreciation, swaying just a little as the aroma of the soup filled his nostrils. His stomach growled as he gave the pot a stir and he tried hard to give it his whole focus and close his ears to the hushed tones coming across the room. It was useless.

'I don't need rescuing, Richard. I'm doing just fine… Oh okay, okay, yes you can call bullshit on that, but

I don't think I'm ready for company yet... No, *no*, you guys don't need to come over... I've told him a week, just a week and he's going to help out around the place.'

Mia crossed the room, phone still under her chin, and tapped Daniel on the arm. She pointed to the bread and then the knife rack before circling back around the table towards the phone holder on the wall.

'You know I can always use your help around here, Richard. Yes, and *Madeline* too, although she and I will be having words tomorrow... Uh-huh. Nine should be fine. I'll make bacon sandwiches to get us going... Yep, yep. Bye.'

Daniel placed a mountain of freshly sliced bread on the table, quickly followed by two steaming bowls, and was rewarded with a smile of gratitude from Mia. The phone call had upset the equilibrium achieved during their mutual preparation of the meal, the outside world inserting itself into the warm cocoon of the kitchen. He felt like he should apologise again for intruding, but the selfish part of him didn't want to give her an opportunity to ask him to leave.

The station on the radio switched to a mellower selection and he let the music and the warmth of the soup bring him down from the turmoil of the past couple of hours. Dipping his spoon into the hot liquid, he took a taste. It was perfect and he let go of everything as he let the soup nourish him body and soul.

His spoon soon scraped the bottom of the bowl and he grabbed another piece of bread to mop up every drop he could before leaning back in his chair, sliding down a little to stretch his long legs out. The warmth in his stomach spread through him, chasing away some of the hollowness and the remains of the shock following his earlier breakdown.

The previous jitters lurked still, threatening to rise if he let his thoughts stray to anything beyond the room around him. Especially if he thought too hard about the mess he'd left behind in London. He shoved them all into a corner and squashed them down, fixing his mind on the harmless task of counting things. There were twelve slate tiles to each row across the kitchen floor, fifteen rows in total. Eight cupboards, fourteen flowers on each curtain. Gradually the fluttery edges of panic smoothed away.

He'd have to deal with everything, but not just yet. A week, she'd said. Everything could be put on hold for a week. Forget Fitz, get back to being plain old Daniel Fitzwilliams. He'd wipe the slate and start fresh for this one week and try and figure out exactly who that was, or more importantly who he wanted Daniel Fitzwilliams to be.

***

Mia woke with a start and stared at her old friend, Mr Damp on the bedroom ceiling, trying to work out what had disturbed her. The second slam of a car door sent her straight out of bed and over to the grubby windowpane as she peered down to the driveway below.

She watched in disbelief as Daniel ambled out of the back door towards Madeline and Richard. They were all dressed practically in jeans, T-shirts and old jumpers. Mia glanced over at the clock on her bedside cabinet and squinted in disbelief at the position of the hands. *Five past nine?* What the hell? She never slept that late.

'Damn, damn damn!' Mia rummaged through her drawers, throwing old jeans and a long-sleeved T-shirt onto the bed before dashing into the bathroom, underwear in hand. She blinked and scowled at her reflection; the bloody Mohawk mice had been to visit in the night again and she had a big crease down one side of her face from the pillow. A quick wash, teeth scrubbed, hair vaguely wetted down and she rushed down the stairs, socks in hand and still buttoning her jeans.

She pulled up short at the closed, locked door at the bottom of the stairs before she remembered that Daniel had insisted that she shut herself in the night before.

'Not that I'm a raving maniac or anything, regardless of my behaviour today,' he'd said with a self-deprecating grin. 'But I am a stranger in your home and you are not used to someone else being here, you said. If you lock the door, you might rest easier.'

It had been a gracious thing to do, putting her at ease, and it had clearly worked given how well she had slept. For the first time in weeks there had been no nightmares. No waking up to the echo of her footsteps tapping on the cold tiles on that endless walk through the hospital corridor towards the room where Jamie waited for her, cold and lifeless. Pushing away the macabre images before they could take hold, she unlocked the door and let the sound of the living draw her away from the dead.

Mia entered the kitchen, pausing on the threshold to absorb the scene before her. Madeline stood at the Aga frying bacon, brandishing a spatula at Richard who was buttering bread and laughing at some rude comment he had made to her. Daniel leant against the back door, a cup of coffee in his hand, watching the couple with a wistful smile on his face. He looked less grey and haunted than the day before; perhaps they'd both managed a decent night's sleep. He stirred and the smile warmed as he sensed Mia's presence.

'Umm, Richard and Madeline are here,' he said and gave her a helpless shrug.

'So, I see,' Mia said dryly as she stepped further into the kitchen and moved towards Richard's open arms. She rested her head on his chest and let him enfold her in his fatherly embrace. Both he and his wife had waged a gentle, but insistent war against Mia's self-imposed isolation. She'd resented their endless cheer at first, but now she wondered how she would have survived the past few months without them.

'Hello, darling girl.' Richard pressed a kiss to her forehead. 'I've been dreaming about bacon sandwiches all night and we get here to find you still slugabed.' He chucked her under the chin and winked. 'You look better for it, still too pale for my liking though. I'm going to start force-feeding you Guinness if you don't get some colour back in those cheeks soon.'

Mia shook her head and stepped out of his arms to turn towards an uncharacteristically quiet Madeline. Tension vibrated from her as she concentrated on the bacon on the stove. Slipping her arms around Madeline's waist, she gave her a squeeze from behind. 'Meddling old bag.' She pressed a kiss to Madeline's cheek, feeling it twitch in a smile.

Mood lifting in an instant, the older woman leaned back into her. 'Everyone needs a meddling old bag in their life, my dear. Although we prefer the term "Fairy Godmother" if you don't mind. Now stop hanging off me; this bacon is done and Richard won't raise a finger until we've fed him.'

Mia let her go, crossing to the kettle to make a cup of tea as she let Madeline and Richard assemble a huge stack of doorstep sandwiches. They'd made the first steps towards healing the rift between them, although she still had no idea what had possessed the older woman to drop a stranger on her doorstep and run.

Letting her eyes drift to where said stranger hovered at the edges of their group, she felt a surge of sympathy at the uncertainty on his face. It wasn't his fault either. Holding out her hand she beckoned Daniel towards the table, nodding in encouragement when he hung back. 'Don't stand on ceremony, Daniel. If you don't get stuck in there won't be anything left.'

Not waiting to see if he followed, she settled into her usual seat. The smell of bacon filled her nose and her mouth watered in anticipation. Her tummy gave a little rumble and she clutched her hand to it, laughing along with the others. When was the last time she'd looked forward to eating? Too long ago. Accepting the plate and mug Richard placed in front of her, Mia grabbed the huge sandwich and bit down, closing her eyes as the crispy smoke of the bacon and the spicy bite of HP sauce hit her taste buds.

She opened her eyes to see Madeline watching her, a cloud of worry marring her kind gaze. Mia's heart swelled and she blamed the lump in her throat on swallowing too much of her sandwich at once. 'I don't know what I'd do without you,' she said quietly.

Madeline gave her a watery smile. 'That's not something you ever have to worry about, darling.'

Blinking away the prickle behind her eyes, Mia focused on her breakfast and sent up a silent prayer of thanks for such wonderful friends.

Chapter Six

Daniel chewed thoughtfully on his food—*everything in this house tasted amazing.* He watched the easy back and forth banter between Mia and the older couple as they ate and discussed the plans for the day, deciding which bedroom they were going to tackle and get ready for Daniel to use. From the conversation, it was clear that the rooms had all been cleared of furnishings and their contents moved to the large barn that nestled next to the garage at the end of the driveway. The plumbing and electrics had been replaced, but other than that the upstairs rooms lay untouched.

He thought about the cosy sitting room that he had slept in the previous night. The sofa had been a pleasant surprise, a huge sprawling L-shape with cushions deep enough he could stretch out his full length across them. The room had been dressed in warm creams and rich browns, with the odd splash of colour from the vibrant paintings on the wall and a few feature items including a tall pewter vase full of rich red poppies. The flowers had been silk, although it had taken a closer examination to verify.

Mia had told him it was intended as a space for her and that there would be a large lounge space for guests next door to what would be the dining room—the room with the impressive sea view.

It had been Richard's idea apparently to get Mia's personal spaces sorted out first, to make sure she had some semblance of a home while she worked to bring the rest of the house up to a habitable standard. Daniel was glad she had such good friends to support and guide her. It was clear from the open affection they shared that they had adopted Mia and viewed her as something close to a daughter.

The sweet, easy atmosphere around the table twisted his heart, reminding him again how much he missed his own parents, though the laughing couple bore little resemblance to the quiet, steady Fitzwilliamses. Chairs were pushed back, saving him from the welling emotions. Everything felt raw, scraped too close to the bone for comfort. He was relieved to be on the move.

Richard led him up to the first floor and ushered him into a large bedroom with bare, stained floorboards and the ugliest wallpaper he had ever seen in his life. Huge, garish orange and yellow roses beamed down from every wall, although there were strips missing where the electrics had been chased out and the wiring and fittings replaced. He grimaced at the blinding display and Richard clapped him on the shoulder. 'You should've seen the carpet that went with it, marmalade orange with a liberal scattering of mildew.'

Following Richard's instructions and armed with a steamer, scraper and face mask, he got to work whilst the older man entered the adjoining bathroom to tackle the tiling. It would take more than a day to get the room sorted, but Daniel was in no rush. The sofa was comfy enough and a strip-wash at the big sink in the kitchen would suffice if the bathroom wasn't usable.

Mia appeared, radio in one hand and two bottles of water in the other. She nodded in satisfaction at the progress Daniel was making and dropped a bottle of water at his feet before joining Richard in the bathroom. The strains of the radio and laughter soon drifted through the open door. There was no sign of Madeline, and Daniel wondered what she was up to as he turned his attention back to his task.

It was back-breaking work, and he soon discarded his jumper despite the lack of heating. He steamed, scraped and cursed his way down the wall and around the corner, piles of discarded wallpaper curling in his wake. His muscles ached a little from lack of use and his back would be a wall of pain later from all the bending and stretching, but Daniel didn't care. He had a definable task, a purpose for the next few hours, and that was just what he needed. The aches and pains would be a badge of honour for the efforts he put in this day.

Madeline showed up, a spotted cloth twisted around her head, keeping her hair off her face. There was a smudge of dirt on her cheek. She grinned and patted Daniel affectionately on the bottom after handing him a cup of tea. 'Aren't you doing a grand job, sweet boy? Take a break and enjoy your tea and I'll have a bit of a tidy through,' she said. Settling his hip against the windowsill with a happy sigh, he watched her stuff the rubbish into a black bag and let her soothing chatter wash over him.

She headed downstairs with the bulging bag, reappearing shortly after with two more mugs of tea, which she took into the bathroom. Cries of welcome from Richard and Mia echoed from the small room. Daniel listened to the banter and teasing and wondered when the last time was that he had felt comfortable enough around people to let his guard down like that.

It wasn't that everyone he'd met in London was a shark or a phony; he had a couple of good friends who weren't part of the art crowd, although thinking back it had been a few months since he'd spent anything like quality time with Aaron. His best friend had never been a fan of Giselle and the crowd she hung around with. As he'd been drawn further into her circle of wannabes and sycophants, he'd seen less and less of Aaron.

He'd tried to warn him about the rumours circulating about his party lifestyle, but Daniel had been in no mood to listen. Giselle had dripped poison in his ear, dismissing Aaron as too provincial, whispering he was just jealous of his success. And he'd let her feed his ego, drive a wedge between the two men. Isolated from the steady voice of reason, he'd been easy prey. Daniel sighed and tugged his face mask back into position. *Better add another name to the list of apologies owed.*

***

It was late afternoon by the time Mia waved Richard and Madeline off and she pressed her hands into her lower back to try and ease the stiffness in her muscles a little. She eyed the claw-footed tub in the corner of the bathroom and decided that a soak rather than the quick shower she'd originally planned on was called for.

After the initial tense start, things had smoothed out between her and Madeline. The right moment for her intended talk with her friend never materialised and she'd decided to let it go. There had been no malice in her actions, and Mia had to admit having someone else in the house had given new impetus to her plans. *Only a week.* The more she thought about it, the more it seemed like a good idea to help her ease into sharing the place with other people. She'd be a poor guest house owner if she didn't get used to having company around her.

It had taken some persuasion, but Mia had convinced Richard and Madeline that they should take a couple of days to themselves. She was so grateful for the time and energy that they gave her, but she still worried that she was taking advantage of their good natures. They weren't getting any younger and the tiling in the bathroom had been such a painful, painstaking job it had taken a lot out of her. Her friends were so dynamic and vibrant; it was easy to forget the thirty-year age gap between her and them.

She wandered into the dining room, wanting to catch a last glimpse of the ocean before the sun disappeared. Night fell so early during the dreary winter months. Madeline had been busy and the large windows sparkled inside and out, making the shabbiness of the patio and the garden beyond even harder to ignore.

Mia shrugged; it was too early in the year and the weather too cold and unpredictable to even contemplate tackling the outside work. Only the rare warmth of the winter sun that day had allowed Madeline to get outside long enough to wash down the windows but even then, Mia had found her half blue and hugging the Aga when she'd come down that afternoon to get more tea.

It would take at least another day for the sealant around the bathroom tiles to properly set and although the bedroom walls were finally free of paper, there was a lot of sanding and patching to do before the walls Daniel had uncovered were ready for painting.

That was his self-appointed task for tomorrow while she tackled the woodwork in the bathroom. The bathroom tiles were neutral enough they would go with anything and now the suite was going to be used by a man, Mia was beginning to rethink the colour scheme she had in mind. She'd always pictured her guests as couples or single older women and had planned the decorations accordingly. Her notes and the colour charts were in the kitchen; she would fetch them and give it some more thought whilst she had her bath.

She froze on the threshold. Daniel stood at the kitchen sink, a soft pair of cotton pyjama bottoms on, the matching T-shirt draped over the back of a chair. She watched in fascination as he tested the water in the sink then bent further forward, groaning a little as the movement stretched his lower back. She winced in sympathy. If his back was tight as hers it would be uncomfortable to lean so far forward, and he was a lot taller besides.

Maybe she should have offered him the use of a proper bathroom, but that would mean letting him into her little sanctuary on the second floor. He was too big, too *masculine*. She didn't want any man other than Jamie in her personal space, and that would never be possible again.

He dunked his head under the water, rubbed shampoo into his scruffy hair then dipped back down to rinse it clean. He groped blindly for the towel next to the sink and scrubbed vigorously at his hair. The movement sent the muscles down his sides rippling and she spun away, knowing she shouldn't be spying on him. She moved too quickly, bumping into the door frame with a resounding thump.

'Everything all right?'

Caught red-handed, and red-faced, Mia had no option other than to face the music. 'I'm sorry, I just came for my books,' she muttered. With a quick scurry across the room, she scooped them up and then turned tail and ran from the room.

Embarrassment and other things she didn't want to think about lent wings to her feet and she slammed the door to the upper levels closed with a resolute bang and a sharp snick of the key.

Mia rushed to her third-floor hideaway and closed the door behind her, leaning against it as she tried to catch her breath. How ridiculous to react in such a flighty, adolescent manner at the sight of a man's bare back. It had just been so unexpected and other than in films or on the TV, the only man she had seen stripped to the waist had been her husband.

Daniel was taller and broader through the shoulders than Jamie had been—his skin a deep tan where Jamie had been pale thanks to his sandy-haired, blue-eyed Scottish heritage. Not that she was going to start comparing the two men; Daniel was a temporary fixture in her life who would be gone in just a few days and the sight of his skin may have caused a few long-dormant hormones to stir briefly, but it was purely a biological reaction.

She ran her bath, adding a large dollop of muscle soak to the water, and flicked through the paint charts. The original plan for the room had been a warm, sunny yellow but now Mia wasn't convinced. She scanned the charts and paused on a soft, moss green and tapped the card thoughtfully.

Sliding into the hot water with a grateful sigh she sank down until the bubbles reached her chin. Flicking through the colours, she pictured various combinations in her mind's eye, trying to find the perfect match for each room in her planner. Her thoughts drifted next to the stacks of furniture out in the barn. She wanted to use whatever she could salvage from the original pieces that had been left in the house when she bought it.

Some had been beyond rescue and they had gone straight to the tip, but there was an oak bedframe and matching dresser that could be brought back to life with a generous amount of beeswax and some serious elbow grease. There was also a heavy wardrobe that didn't quite match, but might be brought into the grouping with the help of the right wood stain.

Mia dropped the charts on the mat next to the tub and closed her eyes as she rested her head back against the rolled edge of the bath. She let the warm water and her imagination conjure up the perfect room. If the colours she pictured matched a certain pair of stormy-green eyes, she didn't let her conscious self acknowledge it.

Chapter Seven

The next couple of days passed in a similar round of hard work, snatched meals and aching muscles. Daniel was relieved that he at least had access to a shower now the tiles had set and Richard had promised to come over that afternoon to help him move the bedroom furniture that Mia had picked out in the barn. A mattress had been delivered the day before from a local furniture store and was propped up in the hallway, still covered in its protective plastic covering. It would be nice to sleep in a real bed; the sofa in the parlour, though comfortable, was starting to lose its charm.

He dipped his brush back into the pot of pale grey gloss that Mia had chosen for the woodwork in the bedroom. It blended well with the green on the walls, and made a nice change from white, he mused. Mia and Madeline had exchanged several calls about the colour scheme and Madeline had apparently rustled up some curtains on her sewing machine that were 'just perfect' according to Mia.

Daniel couldn't understand how soft furnishings could be quite so exciting but had decided it was best to keep that opinion firmly to himself. A favourite song of Mia's came on the radio and Daniel paused, waiting for her tuneless accompaniment to start before he remembered that she was out shopping for bedding and other essentials to dress the room once the decorating had been completed.

It felt sometimes as though Daniel had been in Orcombe for weeks when in fact it was only the fifth day since his unexpected arrival. Only two more days until his deadline to leave arrived and he was determined to come up with a plan to extend his stay.

The colours in the bedroom could've been chosen specifically to match his taste and style and Daniel could imagine a couple of prints on the walls. He remembered the photos he'd taken in the garden of the quirky ornaments and he cleaned off the paintbrush with a cloth and left it to rest in a jar of cleaning fluid.

Taking the stairs two at a time, Daniel bounded down in search of his jacket and the camera he'd stuffed in one of the pockets. It said a lot about his state of mind that his camera had lain untouched since that first day. He found his coat hanging on one of the hooks in the mudroom between the kitchen and the back door and dug into the pockets, retrieving both his camera and his mobile phone.

He sat at the kitchen table and stared at his phone with distaste. He knew he needed to check it, to send at least a couple of texts to let people know he was okay. He switched it on and watched as the phone flashed up missed call after missed call and a raft of text messages. He ignored the voicemails and scrolled through his text messages with a growing sense of frustration and annoyance. Every message from Giselle was a rant—not a single expression of concern for him, only for herself and how his selfish behaviour had affected her.

She needed money; she needed him to take her to a premiere; she needed him to talk to some C-list moron about a portrait sitting. The whole diatribe just served to reinforce that getting away from her had been the right decision. The last message was a picture and he opened it and felt his gorge rise. She was naked from the waist up in a bed he didn't recognise. She was also not alone.

He tapped out a terse reply: *'Working on a project, will be away for the foreseeable future. I'm glad to see you've moved on. You can use the flat until the end of the month. Good luck.'* His thumb hovered over the send key for just a moment and then he pressed down hard. Their unedifying row in the street had been the beginning of the end as far as he was concerned and she'd given him the perfect excuse to finish things for good.

Feeling suddenly weary, he scrolled through the list of messages from his agent. Another set of demands and appointments. Time to stop being a cash cow to be milked dry of his last drop of talent and enthusiasm. He highlighted the messages and deleted them before tapping out a terse reply. *'Taking a break. Don't line anything up for me for the foreseeable future. I'll be in touch.'*

He opened his emails next, ignoring his burgeoning inbox, and fired off a note to his landlord advising him he would be away for the next few weeks and asking him to change the locks at the end of the month and send the new set of keys and the bill to Aaron.

A second email went to his best friend, who was also his accountant, assuring him that all was well but Giselle was out of the picture and he needed some time away to sort a few things out. His hand hovered over the keyboard for a moment before he typed out in a rush: *'I'm so sorry, mate. My behaviour lately has been inexcusable. You tried to warn me, but I was too stupid to see until it was almost too late. I'm down by the coast for a few weeks trying to clear my head. I'll give you a call soon.'*

He should call him now, but he was afraid he'd give the game away if Aaron heard his voice. He wasn't okay, not in the slightest. But he would be.

His phone started to ring before he managed to shut it down and he wasn't surprised to see Giselle's blank face flashing on the screen. He flicked the ignore button and switched off the handset. He had nothing to say to her.

Daniel rose and headed into the sitting room that would hopefully no longer be acting as his bedroom. He rammed the phone into the very depths of his duffel bag. Returning to the kitchen, he paused to wash his hands, feeling grubby after seeing Giselle's dirty little message. *How the hell had he ever ended up involved with her in the first place?*

He turned away from the sink and pushed the unpleasant thoughts away as Mia came bustling through the back door, her arms practically dragging on the ground she was so laden with shopping bags. He hurried across the room to relieve her burdens and she sank down into one of the kitchen chairs with a sigh and a stretch. She looked lighter, happier than he remembered seeing her, and he found himself beaming down at her as he placed the bags on the table before her.

'There are more in the car,' Mia said, a slightly sheepish look on her face. 'Once I got started, I decided that I really wanted to see the room as finished as possible. I know it's foolish when there is so much other work to do, but I think it is the way I want to do this from now on. Tackle a room and finish it completely before moving on to the next one. It might not be practical but I feel so energised after months of straggling from one bit of the house to another, never quite finishing anything. Does that make sense?'

Daniel was touched she cared about his opinion enough to ask and it struck him anew how hard it must be for her to try and pull this huge house into a semblance of order by herself. 'I think you need to do this in whatever way feels right for you. I'm happy to help if you can stand me under foot a bit longer. The work I've done over the past few days feels like the only positive and productive thing I've done in months. I don't want to push you, I know you said I could stay for only one week, but you can't possibly do this alone.'

Daniel trailed off as he watched her face tighten. *Shit, shit! Stupid idiot. Who was he to tell her what she could and couldn't do?*

He turned away to stare out of the little window above the sink. Ivy crawled across the glass and he made a mental note to get out there and cut it back in the morning. If he was still there, that was.

He sighed. 'Sorry, that came out wrong. You can do whatever you set your mind to; you have done *so much* already. All I've done is splash a bit of paint around the place. It's just that now I know how big this project is, I don't want to walk away and leave you to do it alone. You'd be doing me a favour if you would consider letting me stay on for a bit.' Daniel sighed and scrubbed his hands through his hair in frustration, knowing he sounded pathetic and desperate as he tried to force Mia to let him stay.

The silence stretched between them making his gut churn and bile burn in the back of his throat.

He risked a glance over his shoulder. Mia sat with her eyes closed and he watched her take a couple of slow, deep breaths. The tension in her frame loosened as she opened her eyes and sent him a considering look.

'I don't know what to say, Daniel. I don't know what the right answer is to give you. I didn't want you here; I didn't want anyone here, and yet having another person around to help fill the space has made me feel more positive about things. I just don't know whether it's fair to take advantage of you when you're clearly vulnerable. I feel like I would be exploiting you for my own selfish needs.'

Daniel gaped incredulously. She thought she would be taking advantage of him? He shook his head and gave a little snort of disbelief. 'Perhaps we should stop worrying about it and take advantage of each other.' He'd only meant to lighten the mood, but horror filled him when she paled and he shook his head frantically. 'Oh, shit, no, not that. I didn't mean it like that! I didn't mean that we should take advantage of each other sexually. Oh, crap, I just need to stop talking before you throw me out on my arse.'

***

Mia bit her lip and tried not to laugh. The utter horror in Daniel's voice was amusing and yet a tiny part of her hurt at the forcefulness of his denial. *What a contrary, emotional headcase she was. How could she be terrified he was propositioning her one moment and insulted when he clearly wasn't the next?*

Her animal hindbrain decided that it had been quiet for long enough and conjured up an image from the first night when Daniel had stood in almost the same spot he occupied now, stripped to the waist as he washed his hair at the sink. She remembered all too clearly how the light caramel tone of his skin had glowed warmly in the soft light, one small trail of water rolling down the centre of his spine. Mia closed her eyes and shuddered. Her animal hindbrain needed to shut the hell up. She loved Jamie; she didn't want to think about another man. She wasn't ready.

Mia focused again on Daniel and his shamefaced expression and offered him a rueful smile, hoping her face didn't look as hot as it felt. 'Don't forget the rest of the bags that are still in the car. I'll start carting these upstairs and then I'll see about making some lunch. Richard will be here soon to give you a hand with the furniture and he's bound to want feeding.'

The hopeful look on his face sent a wave of sympathy through her. Whatever had brought him to her doorstep—serendipity, fate, or just a well-meaning meddling friend—this half-broken man needed a safe place to stay. Madeline and Richard had reached out to her when she'd been at breaking point, perhaps it was time to give a little of that support back to someone else.

Opening the bags on the table, she began to sort through the contents. Pulling out the wrapped packages of new bedding, she stripped the plastic from them and put the stiff cotton sheets into the washing machine. There was nothing worse than the scratchy, itchy feel of them straight out of the packet. Daniel returned with an armful of bags, pausing to toe off his boots at the door. He looked like a kid at Christmas as he plonked the bags down with the others then peeked in the top of a few of them.

At this angle, she could see one or two silvery strands in the dark beard covering his chin. He'd trimmed it sometime over the past couple of days, cropping it short to just cover the skin of his jaw. His hair still tangled over his collar, no discernible style to it, but he was beginning to take some care over his appearance. He caught her studying him and a hint of speculation shone in his eyes. Feeling flustered, she made a performance of getting the washing powder and fabric conditioner from under the sink and set the machine going.

Once the sheets were done, she would make up his bed. The sage green cover held the hint of a jacquard pattern. Nothing too flouncy—he would look ridiculous in a flowery bed. Too dark and masculine for frills and frippery. The weight of his gaze rested between her shoulders and the air seemed too thin. Everything had been fine until he mentioned sex and now she couldn't stop thinking about him in that way.

She rolled her shoulders, trying to shrug off the uncomfortable feelings. That side of her had frozen up, like a fly trapped in amber, the moment she lost Jamie. She'd been happy to stay that way. A few friends had sent gentle hints over the past months, coded messages asking if she was getting out at all, the odd mention of a lovely guy they knew who was on his own. She'd ignored them all. Deep down she knew twenty-eight to be too young to write herself off the dating scene for ever, but it had felt wrong, like a betrayal of Jamie to even entertain the notion.

He'd be furious, of course, at the thought she'd put herself in eternal stasis, but she missed the feel of him beside her so much it had been easier to cut herself off completely. Having a man around the place was bound to stir things up. It didn't have to mean anything other than a simple biological recognition. Besides, Daniel didn't seem to be in a fit state for a relationship. Maybe he had a girlfriend, a wife even. There was no telltale sign of a missing ring on his finger, but not all men wore them.

Whatever, there was no reason she needed to act on any of these silly feelings—*biological recognitions, remember*. Yes, biology was to blame. She just needed him to be biological somewhere else for a bit until she could get herself back on an even keel. Fixing a cheery smile, she turned to face him, keeping her eyes focused just past his left shoulder. 'It'll be cold tonight; can you check the basket by the fireplace and stock it up with wood from the pile behind the barn?'

He leapt to his feet like a greyhound loosed from the trap. 'Sure, of course. I'll do that now.' He barely paused to shove his feet in his boots before clattering out of the kitchen. *Well, that's embarrassing.* Staring at the poor man like a mooning schoolgirl had obviously unsettled him. If they were going to be living under the same roof for a while, she needed to get a grip on her silly imagination.

Chapter Eight

Daniel took his cue and left the kitchen, glad to be able to put some distance between them. As soon as the denial had left his lips, he hadn't been able to think about anything other than what Mia might feel like in his arms, under him, pressed deeply into the new mattress as he explored her lush little body. He imagined how her shapely hips would cradle him softly, so unlike the clash of hip bones he'd experienced with Giselle.

He paced the scruffy patch of driveway outside the kitchen door, circling the car as he admonished himself for being such a rotten, dirty bastard. Mia deserved better than this; she deserved his respect and his friendship. That was all this was, all either of them needed it to be.

Gravel crunched and Daniel was relieved to see Richard and Madeline pulling up in their car. This was just the distraction he needed to get his head back to where it needed to be. Recalling his mission to fetch some wood, he loped to the stack and gathered a good armful. Madeline met him on the way back, all smiles, and he dutifully leant down to let her buss her lips across his cheek in greeting. Richard rested his hand briefly on Daniel's shoulder and Daniel's knees wobbled for a moment as the easy warmth and affection offered by the older couple soothed his battered heart.

He was amazed anew at how easily they had adapted to his presence and now he was apparently another lost waif that they had taken under their wings. He smiled gratefully as Richard took some of the logs from him and they followed Madeline into the kitchen.

Daniel paused on the threshold between his bedroom and the en suite, clouds of steam from his gloriously hot shower billowing behind him. His bedroom looked perfect, and it was *his* bedroom regardless of whether Mia realised it or not. The dark wood of the masculine bedframe gleamed richly. Madeline had polished the old furniture with beeswax and they had all been amazed at how well the wood had come to life under her ministrations.

The mattress had been a bitch to wrestle up the stairs, but it nestled perfectly in the frame, the mountains of crisp cream and green pillows scattered at the head of the bed just begging for him to sprawl amongst them. Brass-based lamps with dark green shades framed the bed on two old chests that he and Richard had unearthed in the Aladdin's cave that was hidden in the barns.

Daniel had promised himself another trip to the barns in the morning and this time he would take his camera with him. There were so many oddities that had caught his eye and he was eager to explore. He had an idea in his mind that he could put together a record for Mia of the progress of the work on the house. A private album that he would build for her as they slowly tamed the sprawling monster together. It was the first time in a long time that he was itching to get his hands on a camera and his internal instinct to frame and capture moments in time was stirring again.

He also wanted to explore the possibility of using some black and white shots of the pictures he had taken in the garden to decorate the walls of his room. If Mia liked them, he'd gladly put some other ideas together. The thought of his art gracing the walls of the house appealed to him.

'Daniel, dinner's nearly ready.' Mia's welcome call drifted up the stairs and galvanised him into action. He swiftly dried off and dragged on some loose cotton trousers, a T-shirt and the essential thick socks required to stave off the cold floors of the house, and then hurried down to the kitchen.

The ever-present radio was on and he paused in the doorway to watch Mia shimmy around the table as she placed cutlery and plates at what had become their usual seats. He often found himself watching her through the day as she got caught up in different songs. The uninhibited joy Mia clearly found in music drew his attention time and again.

Daniel winced at a particularly hideous chorus from Mia and put his hands over his ears to tease her as she rounded the table and caught sight of him. With an unrepentant shrug, Mia danced over to the Aga and lifted out a huge cast-iron casserole dish from one of the many mystery doors in the front of the stove.

The rich scent of beef stew hit Daniel's nose as he crossed to the fridge and retrieved two bottles of water. He felt the saliva pooling just under his tongue. Mia had been covered in flour to her elbows earlier, making dumplings that she had then dropped in the top of the stew. Daniel felt and heard his stomach growl in appreciation at the good meal to come. He grabbed a pot holder, placed it in the centre of the table and quickly stepped back as Mia lugged the heavy casserole over and placed it on the holder.

He took his seat and waited patiently as Mia filled his plate and then her own before she sat down opposite him. Daniel lowered his face closer to the plate and breathed deeply, drawing out the moment of anticipation before he dug his fork into his meal.

Daniel raised it to his mouth and blew gently, fragrant steam rising to curl in front of him, and he smiled across the table at Mia and raised his hand a fraction more in a gesture of acknowledgement and appreciation. The beef melted across his tongue and Daniel said a silent prayer of thanks to whichever serendipitous spirit had steered him towards this place in time.

The house truly was a haven, and the small comforts he received daily from his hostess in every meal she placed before him just reinforced his desire to stay. He imagined offering pre-dinner drinks to guests on the patio in the summer as Mia laid one of her heavenly meals out on the dining room table. Richard had pointed out the battered dining room table and chairs in the barns earlier that day, and Daniel wanted to examine them further.

The high-backed chairs had tapestry cushions on the seats, faded and threadbare. Richard had mentioned that Madeline had a project planned to embroider new covers, recreating the original designs. Daniel decided he would get them out into a decent patch of light and take a series of photographs to help Madeline.

***

Mia took another mouthful of her dinner as she flipped idly through her notebook. She hadn't decided which room she would tackle next although she thought that it would be best to stick with the first floor and get at least three more bedrooms completed. That would take them through March and hopefully towards some slightly warmer weather and they could then turn their attention to the main rooms on the ground floor. She was half-conscious that her thoughts on the work ahead were now being framed in her mind as things that *they* needed to do.

The original deadline of a week that she had set for Daniel was up in the morning and she had already decided not to mention it. They were rubbing along together fine and Mia didn't feel inclined to raise the subject again. She glanced across the table and wondered what had Daniel so deep in thought. His focus sharpened back from the middle distance and his mouth quirked, a flash of white teeth showing through the dark, close-cropped hair of his beard. She'd never considered herself a fan of facial hair, but the style suited his strong bone structure.

'I think we should take a day off tomorrow, Daniel. I need to have another look upstairs at the other three en suite rooms as I decide which one I want to work on next. I'll leave the master suite for the time being though. Now that we've finished your room, I want to revisit some of the designs I've been mulling over,' Mia said.

He gave her a funny lopsided grin, as though she'd said something to amuse him, but his answer was serious. 'That would work perfectly for me as I was hoping to explore out in the barn a bit in the morning. I saw some fantastic pieces out there and I want to take a few shots if that's all right with you?'

Mia was momentarily confused and then remembered the camera he'd been carrying when he'd first arrived. She wondered if photography was a hobby or something more.

'Sure, whatever you like,' Mia said with a nod as she rose from the table, gathering their dirty plates to begin the ritual of tidying up after their meal. Daniel got up to help her and switched the kettle on, both settling into an already familiar routine as they split the chores between them. The kitchen was soon clean and tidy and they each clutched a mug of hot tea. 'I might take this up with me, if that's all right?' Daniel said around a half-stifled yawn.

'Sounds like a plan.' Mia gathered her notebook and samples and ducked under Daniel's arm as he reached over to flip the kitchen light off. He followed her up to the first floor and she paused briefly to exchange goodnights before carrying on to the top floor. He turned towards his bedroom.

Mia stood at the large bay window and stared over the back garden and out to the sea beyond. They had been graced with a sunny day, although the wind was fierce and white clouds scudded across the pale blue sky. The sea was a stampede of white horses crashing into the dark sand.

Sheltered behind the thick glazing, the sun felt good on her face and Mia imagined sitting curled up in the window seat she was planning for the wide window area. There was a local joinery company based in the village—a father and son team—and they had already made an excellent job of repairing the rotten porch steps at the front of the house.

They'd quoted to repair the internal staircases and the work was booked in for April. They had also been full of helpful advice about refurbishing the wooden floors.

It had been down to them that Mia had decided not to replace a lot of the carpets once she'd had them ripped out and disposed of. Not one of the carpets had been worth salvaging. The few that weren't rotting away had been filthy and such a hideous collection of patterns and colours, Mia hoped never to see their like again.

Mr Robinson and his son Jordy were both calm, steady men and together with Richard, they'd helped Mia with the initial clearance and stripping of the furnishings. They were all of a type—the men in the area—something about being bred close to the sea, according to Madeline. It was hard to get an overinflated sense of one's own importance when faced with the vastness of the open water on a daily basis.

The doors to the main barn swung open, the movement catching Mia's eye. Daniel was exploring again. He loved the barn and spent any free time they granted themselves poking around inside. She watched in fascination as Daniel carried out each of the dozen heavy dining chairs, including the two carvers that graced each end of the vast, wind-out cherrywood dining table.

It was an original Victorian piece and Mr Robinson had nearly wept at the sight of its sorry condition. He was an old-school carpenter, taught by his father, who'd been a boat builder. He'd moved to Exeter to train under a master craftsman when he showed a natural affinity to shaping wood. His training had included French polishing and the table was waiting patiently under a waterproof tarpaulin until Mr Robinson could restore it to its former glory.

She watched Daniel pace around the chairs in the yard, snapping shots from all different angles, making sure he took plenty of close-ups of the faded embroidery seat covers. They were a cornucopia of flowers, birds, fruit—each one unique and although they blended as a group, there were several distinctly different styles as though stitched by more than one hand. Perhaps a fireside project for the women of a family who had once graced the house?

Mia unlatched and shoved up the large sash window in the centre of the bay and shivered as a blast of cold air rushed in. She burrowed a little deeper into the over-large Aran sweater, which was another of Jamie's items that she hadn't been able to part with. The sleeves were double-rolled to stop them slipping over her hands and it fell to her knees. She stuck her head through the gap and leaned out as Daniel took a few steps closer to the house.

'What exactly do you think you are doing with my chairs, Daniel Fitzwilliams?' she asked with a mock-stern tone to her voice.

'Richard mentioned yesterday that Madeline would be working on new covers for them and I thought it would help her to have a few pictures, that's all. You don't mind, do you? I checked the yard and made sure I put them in dry spots…'

Chapter Nine

Daniel trailed off as Mia ducked back inside slamming down the sash window behind her. Okay, clearly she did mind. He placed his camera on the barn steps and returned the chairs carefully to where he'd found them before securing the main doors. He picked his camera back up and hurried towards the house. He toed off his boots in the mudroom, already well trained to the 'no shoes in the house' rule.

Slipping and sliding across the wooden floors, he raced to the first floor. He cornered into the back bedroom and dropped to his knees in horror in front of where Mia was curled up under the bay window, rocking back and forth as fat, salty tears rolled down her cheeks. She closed her eyes and pressed them into her bent knees at his arrival, as though she didn't want him to see her.

Feeling completely helpless, he crouched down. She was trying to say something, but he couldn't catch her words, which were muffled in the jumper and punctuated with sobs and gasps. Her distress was a palpable entity and it clutched at his heart. His instincts strained to gather her into his arms, but her defensive body language warned him off so he settled for a tentative hand on her back, which he moved in slow circles.

He didn't speak and didn't try to make sense of what she was trying to say, he just rubbed his hand around and around until the storm of her weeping lessened and finally eased to a few hiccups and gulps. He let his hand slide up to gently cup the nape of her neck and let it rest there.

Daniel let her settle until her breathing was back to normal before flexing his fingers, the briefest of coaxing movements. She scrubbed her face across her wool-covered knees and then inched her head up a little. He bent his head down close to catch her eye and she let out a whoosh of breath and a shaky laugh before speaking. 'I'm sorry, you didn't do anything wrong. I had no idea Madeline had plans to remake the covers for the chairs. Such a silly thing to set me off, but it's more often the kindness of others that gets to me. I am pretty much inured to sad things after more than two years of blind grief, but when people do nice things it knocks the wind right out of my sails.'

'Grief? You lost someone, didn't you? Your husband? That's the sad story that you're so determined not to share.' Daniel felt Mia's almost imperceptible nod through his hand as he slid it up from her neck to cup her head and draw her closer to him. She resisted for a moment before her body went limp and she clambered into his lap.

He sat back, stretching his long legs in front of him, back braced against the wall, and squeezed her to him. She felt just right, and another little piece of his scattered self clicked back into place. They'd been joined at the hip for the past few weeks and he was finding it more difficult to imagine leaving Orcombe and this hidden treasure of a house. Waking up without a view over the cove didn't bear thinking about.

There was nothing sexual in their embrace, a simple giving and receiving of comfort. It occurred to him he might be the first man to hold her like this since she'd lost her husband. A primitive and possessive part of him hoped it was true before his veneer of civility chased off the inappropriate thought. The primitive part gave a grunt of disdain and slunk off to its corner to wait patiently for the rest of him to realise that Mia was his. Civility rolled its eyes and assured Daniel that his feelings were entirely honourable, brotherly in fact. She shifted in his lap and civility fled as her bottom nestled a little too close for comfort.

Daniel bit down on his tongue and turned his thoughts outwards, giving all his focus to the woman in his arms. Perving on a grieving widow might be a new low, even for him. He rubbed his hands in soft, smooth circles on her back and let his body relax a little more, encouraging her to do the same. He turned his head to the side to rest his cheek on the soft down of her hair.

Feeling awkward over his inappropriate feelings given the source of her upset, he cast around for something neutral to distract them both. He spotted the notebooks and samples scattered beside them and, still holding Mia in place with one arm, he reached his other hand over to draw the books closer to them.

***

Mia raised her head from where it rested against Daniel's chest as his movement stirred her back to attention. The sheer comfort of his warm body and the slow, steady rhythm of his heart beneath her ear had soothed the ragged edges caused by her sudden breakdown. She didn't want to move and he seemed in no hurry to let her go as he flipped through one of her notebooks, pausing when a swatch of material or picture caught his attention.

She must look a fright. She was not a pretty crier—had yet to meet a woman outside the big screen who could do the sparkling tears and perfect lip quiver. Her face always turned blotchy with her eyelids swelling until it looked like she had two translucent slugs balanced on her face. Lifting her sleeve, she rubbed it across her cheeks to dry the last of her tears then settled back against Daniel.

Her gaze drifted over the well-thumbed images in her notebooks as she thought again about her plans for the empty room around them. 'I'd like to be able to bring the beach in here. Does that sound silly? I want it to feel like the outside is inside; the walls should be the clear blue of the sky on a summer day. I'd cover the floor in soft rugs in shades of sand; the bed would be a darker blue with huge white pillows like clouds or the tops of the waves. The furniture will be white pine, and I'd add jars full of shells and bits of driftwood resting in the corner and along the windowsills. I want there to be a huge window seat here, a daybed, with the same dressings as the bed so guests can sit here and look out across to the sea.'

Mia leaned forward to grab her notebooks and Daniel moved his legs to accommodate her until she ended up sitting between his raised knees, back still to his chest. He peered over her shoulder whilst she showed him the colours on the paint charts.

'Have you thought about draping the bed, creating one of those canopies maybe? If you use a soft, sheer material it could be really effective and capture that cloud-like theme you were talking about.'

Mia glanced back over her shoulder. 'This is nice, you know? Having someone else to bounce ideas around with. It helps. I was so mad at Madeline when she dumped you on my doorstep, but I'm grateful now.' She hesitated a moment then spoke the simple truth in her heart. 'I'm glad you're here.'

Daniel pressed a light kiss to her temple, barely a brush of lips against skin, but it lit her up inside like a Christmas tree. She sat up straighter—embarrassed at her reaction, feeling a little pang of regret when he dropped his arms from around her. Wanting to hide the rosy glow warming her cheeks, she busied herself gathering together her notebooks. Just like that, the spell broke and their perfect, peaceful shared moment vanished.

Mia swallowed a sigh of regret and knew that there was no-one but herself to blame. The kiss had been innocent, a fraternal gesture of comfort, and she'd made it into something else by her foolish reaction. She bit her lip, risking a quick glance at him as she rose to her feet, books clutched in front of her like a paper shield. The bay window framed him where he sat with his arms hooked around his raised knees. A frown creased his forehead, drawing his dark brows down to hood his eyes. The green of his irises seemed to change with his moods and they were growing stormy again as though something had disturbed him.

Plastering a bright smile on her face, she took a backward step towards the door. 'I think I'll go and do some shopping, strike while the iron is hot and the decorating muse is upon me, you know?' she babbled, the intensity of his expression stirring anxious feelings in her tummy. Why didn't he say something?

Mia edged further towards the door, feeling like a snared rabbit in the ferocity of Daniel's gaze. 'Um, right, so I'll maybe put the kettle on and have a cup of tea before I go. Do you want one?'

He shook his head, the furrows on his brows lifting. 'What? No. No tea. I'll get back to the barn and finish those photos for Madeline.' A hint of colour spotted his cheekbones and she couldn't bear the strained atmosphere a second longer. Spinning on her heel, she ducked out of the door, heading up to the sanctuary of her room rather than the kitchen. She needed to wash her face, and if she stayed upstairs for a bit, she wouldn't risk bumping into him on his way through to the barn.

She threw herself down on her bed and buried her head under the pillows. Try as she might, she couldn't block out the thought running around in her head. She *liked* Daniel. Flipping onto her back with a groan, she stared up at the damp patch on the ceiling. 'What the hell have you gone and done, Mia Sutherland?' she muttered to herself. But she knew the answer. Somewhere along the line she'd begun to fall for him. Now she recognised it, she would be able to put a stop to it. His friendship was too important for her to risk on a silly crush.

Feeling considerably better after a wash and brush-up, Mia hesitated on her way to the car. The barn door was open and she could hear Daniel moving things around. Driving off without saying goodbye would be rude. Cursing her good manners, she unlocked the car, tossed her bag onto the passenger seat then took a deep breath before crossing the yard to the barn.

The relative gloom compared to outside left her blind for a few seconds, so she stopped just inside. Her eyes adjusted to the change in light. The scrabbling noise of Daniel wrestling with the huge tarpaulin pinned over one of the rear windows drew her attention.

He let out a muttered curse as he barked his shin on one of the many crates littering the floor and she winced. Wondering if she would be more help or hindrance, she watched him adjust his grip on the covering. A sharp tug on the stubborn material and it pulled free from its anchor point in a cloud of dust that sent him staggering back as a flood of light poured into the barn.

'Careful!' She held out a hand when he almost tumbled backwards over an old, moth-eaten chair. They'd done her a favour although the hideous floral pattern must have given the poor creatures indigestion.

He shoved his sweaty hair from his forehead, leaving a thick streak of dirt on his skin. 'Feeling better?' He tried to approach her, but the tarp had tangled around his body and he couldn't seem to kick free of the weight of the material. Mia moved forward to help, but he held his hand up to stop her. 'I wouldn't come over here. This thing is bloody filthy.' He shoved and twisted until he finally untangled himself in another cloud of dust and dirt. He scrubbed his hands on the front of his sweater and closed the distance between them. Mia took an involuntary step back.

'Off out then?' He nodded at the keys dangling between her fingers.

'Wh...what? Oh, umm, yeah, just into town to grab a few bits and pieces. I want to follow up on some of those ideas we talked about for the back bedroom...' Her words trailed off as she remembered that moment of innocent happiness sitting between his raised knees looking at colour cards and material swatches in her notebook. Barely an hour had passed since then and yet her world axis had lurched into an entirely different orbit.

Covered in dust, a huge streak of dirt across one cheek, which had a sweat trail cutting through it from his temple to his throat, he'd never looked sexier. The contrast between their sizes struck her. It would be so easy to step forward and let him wrap her up in his warm arms. Her upper body swayed forward unconsciously and he took a step nearer as though drawn like a magnet before stopping abruptly. She hovered, helpless for a moment then spun on her heel and rushed from the barn, not stopping until she was cocooned in the safety of her car.

'Shit, shit, shit!' Mia banged her hand on the steering wheel in frustration as she fumbled uselessly with the other hand, trying in vain to get the key into the ignition. She pressed the back of her skull into the headrest and closed her eyes. Taking a deep breath, she held it before exhaling slowly to calm down.

She was acting like a fool, she knew, but the feelings Daniel stirred in her were so unsettling. He was a good man, thoughtful, kind, and she couldn't deny good-looking too. She'd been on her own for so long, maybe she just missed being with someone and she'd latched on to him because he was there.

Until she could sort things out in her head, it would be best to ignore the idea of a connection. To act before she was sure would be disastrous, and he deserved better. A bit of distance and distraction would do them both a power of good. She opened her eyes, tilted her head so that she could see to guide the key into the ignition and fired up the engine.

She drew in another deep breath to find her centre as she tugged her seat belt across her body and engaged it firmly into the slot. She would not drive whilst upset; she owed it to Jamie's memory to not risk an accident. Another breath and a quick flick of her eyes to the rear-view mirror assured her Daniel was still in the barn and hadn't witnessed her foolish behaviour. She eased her car into first gear and bumped along the driveway and away into town.

Chapter Ten

Daniel wiped his paintbrush on the rag hanging at his waist before dropping it onto the newspaper beneath his feet. He stretched the kinks that had worked into his back over the past few hours of stooping awkwardly to paint the skirting in the beach room. That was what both he and Mia were calling it and it was starting to come together.

Jordy had been in to measure up and was working on a frame for the daybed that would fill the bay window. The base of the bed would incorporate shelves, which Mia planned to fill with books and also with random treasures gathered from walks along the shoreline.

A trip to the local junk emporium had yielded a bag of shells, which she'd glued around the frame of the large pine mirror they planned to hang over the bed, facing the window. The bedroom furniture was all made of a similar basic pine, which Mia had painted white and then distressed to give a bleached out, weathered effect.

The skirting boards and picture rail were coated in brilliant white gloss and the walls above the rail were duck-egg blue with a deeper azure shade covering the lower half. The floorboards had been stripped and sanded, a hellish job with a beast of a machine they had hired from the local DIY merchants.

It was filthy out. Daniel eyed the glowering clouds scudding across the sky as another fierce squall rattled rain against the window. On days like this, it was hard to imagine the vista would ever reflect the soft summer calm of the beach room colour scheme. The weather had closed in almost a week ago and they were both feeling a bit stir-crazy. Neither had spoken of their embrace, but a simmering tension lay between them.

Trying to ignore his attraction to her proved useless and he couldn't stop finding little excuses to touch her, hoping to see an answering need in her eyes. There was nothing overt or sexual in his actions: a pat on the hand to thank her for another glorious home-cooked meal, a gentle brush of shoulders as they surveyed the design notes for the room, a paint smear wiped from her cheek. He needed to touch her, to reassure himself the ethereal little woman was real. That his presence in her life and her home wasn't a fever dream.

His gaze moved across the rear garden towards the barn, drawn again to the plans that were slowly forming in his mind's eye.

The basic structure was sound and the large windows that faced towards the beach were a marvel once he had uncovered them. A huge run of light, the entire length of the wall. He could see the place divided into working units, perfect spaces for creative studios. He knew of at least a dozen of his artistic contacts in town who would relish a clean, quiet environment to recharge their batteries. The ever-changing sky and seascape would be a source of inspiration.

Daniel was a prime example of what could happen if someone with an artistic temperament didn't take good care of themselves and their talent. He hadn't discussed it with Mia yet, but he would soon. He wanted to talk to Aaron about the project too, get his input and assistance in putting some numbers together. His best friend's younger brother, Luke, was an architect who was developing a solid reputation, stylish without the desire to over-engineer everything. If he could get them both down for a weekend to look over the barn and take some measurements, maybe Luke could make a start on drawing up some design concepts.

The building was certainly tall enough for a mezzanine floor, which could accommodate living space for the artists using the studios below. Daniel had more than enough money to cover the costs of the conversion and he hoped he would be able to persuade Mia that it would be a positive companion to her more traditional guest house.

A small creative enclave would be a draw to the more discerning guests and would perhaps offer an opportunity for an accompanying gallery to display some of the pieces created. There was a run of disused garages adjacent to the barn, which could be converted into a gallery or a small shop.

The more he thought about it, the more the excitement fluttered in Daniel's belly. Part of him wanted to sprint down to the kitchen where Mia had escaped to do some therapeutic baking and blurt out his thoughts. He wanted to sit at his usual spot at the table and watch her soothing movements as she mixed and kneaded the most basic of ingredients into a mouth-watering selection of treats.

He was already addicted to her cooking and with every day that passed the feeling grew that fate had steered him to the exact place in the universe that he needed to be. He was also terrified of moving too soon on his plans for the barn. And for her. If she understood how much he wanted to make a permanent place for himself both at her table and in her life, she would run a mile.

Daniel also understood that what he needed and what Mia needed would not necessarily end up being the same. The last thing he wanted to risk was the friendship developing between them. Whilst he might want more one day, he was not prepared to lose what they had if Mia could not move past the loss of her husband.

A tap on the door turned him from the rain and his musings as Mia nudged the door open with one hip. She entered the room with a laden tray in her hands. Two steaming mugs of tea and a plate of shortbread biscuits brought a smile to his face as he realised that she was choosing to take a break and spend time with him. A small step perhaps but it warmed his heart just the same.

Flour dusted through Mia's hair, which stuck up in all directions as usual. She had an unconscious habit of shoving at her hair, as though it hung in her face, even though the pixie crop she sported meant that it never did. He wondered how long ago she had cut her hair and whether the gesture was a hangover from days when it had fallen around her shoulders as in the picture pinned to the corkboard in the kitchen.

Daniel cocked his head slightly and tried to picture her that way; he loved the short style she wore now as it left her face open and highlighted the sharpness of her bone structure. Her warm eyes dominated her face. Young women often used curtains of hair to hide behind, flipping and fiddling with it in ways that drove a man to distraction, and not in a good way.

Giselle had long blonde hair that she ironed flat until it hung around her face like a blank, bland curtain. Daniel had hated it. It had been everywhere he looked in his flat: in the shower, in his brush, on every suit he owned. She'd shed worse than a bloody cat.

Daniel pushed the memory away and reached for one of the mugs on the tray, raising it in toast to Mia before inhaling the steam and taking a quick sip. The brew was strong enough to curl his toes and he took a bigger gulp and enjoyed the pleasure-pain of the slightly too hot burn spreading through his belly.

Mia bent to place the tray on the floor and his body twitched at the sight of her heart-shaped bottom curving before him. He turned quickly towards the window and stared blindly out at the lashing rain, willing his libido to settle down. *Friends, friends, friends*, he chanted to himself.

'What about friends?' Mia said. She took position next to him, clutching her own mug of tea as she surveyed the miserable weather before them. She stood close enough that their shoulders were practically touching and Daniel raised his mug to his mouth, brushing her arm with his, unable to stop himself. He kept the motion ultra-casual, catching his breath when she leaned towards him until her head rested against his shoulder. It was the first time she had initiated contact between them.

'What about friends?' she asked again and he realised he had spoken aloud before.

'Oh, I was just thinking about my best friend and his brother, you know, wondering how they're getting on.' It sounded weak to his ears, but Mia appeared to take it at face value.

'Have you spoken to anyone since you came here?' Her voice was soft, and Daniel couldn't quite get a measure on her tone.

'I've sent a couple of texts—to my agent.' He hesitated then took the plunge. 'To a some-time girlfriend of mine to break it off.' At least she would know he wasn't attached, should that information be of interest to her. He rushed on. 'I also sent an email to Aaron. He keeps an eye on my money and I didn't want to worry him when I took off. He was the one I was just thinking about actually.'

'Agent?' She lifted her head, eyes bright with interest. She didn't mention the girlfriend and he couldn't tell if that was a good or bad thing. *Stupid idiot.*

'Umm, yeah, sounds more glamorous than it is, but I'm a professional photographer. Was, I should say, before I burnt myself out and fell off my perch. Wound up on your doorstep, puked in your hedge; you know the rest.'

Daniel felt his face warm as he remembered the disgrace of his first arrival. What a bloody mess he'd been. He still felt a little rough around the edges and although he'd taken a ton of shots around the house and the barn, he still wasn't feeling his muse. He was trying to keep a record of progress for Mia and still had it in his mind to put together a bit of a portfolio for her. Another thing he hadn't mentioned to her. Those things were starting to add up.

***

She studied the man beside her. The oh-so casual mention of an ex hadn't escaped her attention. Was he fishing to see if she was interested? Should she snap up the bait? Daniel's warm, masculine presence had lifted some of the self-imposed burdens from her shoulders.

She wasn't incapable of making decisions, but having someone to act as a sounding board helped enormously. Especially when that someone bought into her vision of the house, and could see past the wreck it was to visualise the home it would be. He didn't care

100

what job she gave him to do, in fact he volunteered for the nastiest tasks. He had even fought a heroic battle to finally tame the evil floor sander, for which Mia would be ever grateful.

It was nice to have someone to cook for as well. It spoke to the nurturing part of her soul and it gave Mia a soft glow of satisfaction every time Daniel smiled or passed comment on the meals she prepared for him. As though he could read her mind, Daniel nudged Mia's arm gently. 'Did you bring that shortbread up here to torture me or are you going to share?'

Mia glanced up into green eyes that seemed to delve deeper than she wanted and she fought the natural urge to duck her gaze away. She watched the dark pupils expand to swallow some of his irises and froze like a rabbit when he leaned in closer. Her eyelids shuttered down and then up as she waited for the brush of his lips and blinked in surprise when Daniel planted a kiss on the tip of her nose. 'Don't try and distract me with that limpid gaze, woman, surrender the biscuits!'

Mia didn't know whether to be disappointed or relieved that Daniel had broken the tension of the moment. She huffed a laugh and grabbed the plate of shortbread up, clutching it protectively against her body, her arm shielding the plate. 'Mine, all mine, big man,' she taunted and then squealed when he closed in on her until she was trapped in the corner of the room.

Daniel backed her further up, bracing himself over her with a hand planted against the wall on either side of her head. He pressed in closer, hovered over her mouth a moment, and she caught her breath again. Raising his hand, he traced a finger across her brow, down her cheek then lower. He circled the slight indent at the base of her throat. The caress lit her on fire and she longed for him to close the gap between their lips and lay claim to her mouth.

'There are things you can tease a man about, Mia, and things that are no laughing matter.' She heard the catch in his voice and felt a corresponding shiver at his husky tone. She was right there, primed and ready for him, and every cell in her body called out to him to touch her.

Kiss me, Daniel. She held the thought in her head as the moment stretched to infinity between them—an impasse neither seemed willing to break. Feeling like her body would explode with tension, she knew she had to do something. Mustering the courage, she urged herself to lean towards him to press her lips to his.

Daniel moved before she did, running his finger down the centre of Mia's breastbone. She shuddered again and opened her mouth to speak, to encourage his touch when his fingers suddenly lifted and he grabbed a handful of the shortbread and stuffed as much as he could in his mouth at once.

She could only gape and clutch the empty plate as he gave her an outrageous wink then backed away towards the window to recapture his tea and wash down the mouthful threatening to choke him. With a glare of mock indignation, Mia spun on her heel and stomped her way back down to the kitchen. Daniel had given her an out, and they both knew it.

The phone rang as Mia placed the plates on the table for supper, surprising her as few people called other than Richard or Madeline and they had left less than an hour earlier. They'd finished the beach room finally, and she needed to decide what to do next. Move on to another room, or start the boring, but essential larger decorating jobs like the hallway and first floor landing areas.

She gave a half shrug towards Daniel as she crossed to answer it, assuming it was one of those ubiquitous PPI sales calls. She lifted the handset to her ear expecting the usual automated voice.

'Eunomia.' The slightly distracted tone as much as the use of her full name identified the caller.

'Hello, Dad.' She braced herself. George Thorpe wasn't one for an idle catch-up.

'I thought I'd better give you a call and let you know that your mother is a bit under the weather.'

Under the influence more like. Mia bit her lip against the unkind, if truthful thought. 'I'm sorry to hear that. What did the doctor say? You promised me you would take her to see him.'

'Oh, well. I was going to, but you know she doesn't like a fuss and I've been tied up with this paper I've been working on. It's a fascinating treatise on the development of religious worship on the island of Delos.' Mia closed her eyes while her father rattled on about his work. If he paid half as much attention to his wife as he did to the long-dead ancient Greeks, things might be better between them.

'Did you clear out the drinks cabinet like we discussed?' Her parents' resolute determination to ignore the reality of Vivian's alcoholism had been the subject of several difficult conversations between Mia and her father. She was also conscious that she was washing her dirty laundry in front of Daniel but it couldn't be helped.

George's sigh gusted in her ear. 'The contents of the drinks cabinet aren't going to be a problem. Your mother took a bit of a tumble and she's in the hospital with a badly broken leg. She'll be there for at least two weeks.'

Mia pressed her forehead against the cool wall and tried to calm her racing heart. 'Oh, God. Is she all right?'

'They're taking good care of her.' *Which wasn't a proper answer at all.* Her father took another audible deep breath. 'So I was wondering if you might come home for a bit. To visit your mother, of course. But, I thought you'd give me a hand taking care of the house. The doctors say she'll need assistance with her rehabilitation afterwards.'

Guilt settled hot and heavy on her shoulders. 'I can come home for a visit, of course. But I can't stay long. There's so much to do here and you'd be better off getting a nurse or a proper home help in.'

Mia raised her eyes to meet Daniel's, wondering what he thought of the side of the conversation that he was privy to. She probably sounded cruel, but the thought of getting sucked back into the George and Vivian show was more than she could stand. Her parents had spent years locked together in a web of regret and resentment. Just the thought of walking back into the unhappy home of her childhood made her stomach queasy.

'How can you be busy? You've got no job. Your mother needs you. *I* need you. I have lectures to give and an important dinner with my colleagues next week. I need you to cater for it and act as hostess in your mother's absence.' *Ah, now we're getting to the heart of it.* Her father's career came before everything, as usual.

'I am sure your colleagues will understand if you postpone under the circumstances.' There was no getting out of it; she would have to go home. 'Can you give me a couple of days to sort things out here?'

'If that's what you need, I can muddle through to the weekend. You'll at least help me make the arrangements? You are so much better at the practicalities.' That was true. With their father wrapped up in his work and their mother self-medicating with gin, it had fallen to Mia to take care of her sisters and run the house.

'I'll speak to Kiki and see if I can stay with her.' Staying with her sister and the git she called a husband wouldn't be a picnic, but she'd get to see the kids and maybe get a chance to talk to Kiki at the same time.

'Will you stop using those ludicrous nicknames? You and your sisters all have perfectly good names.' There was no point in pursuing the old argument so Mia ignored the sharp retort. Their father had named them after the *Horae*—a trio of minor Greek goddesses, fathered by Zeus. The teasing at school had been painful, but served as another cord to bind the three of them closer together.

Mia watched Daniel gather their cooling plates of food and slide them into the lower shelf of the Aga to keep warm. He pointed towards the door and raised a brow, clearly offering to give her some privacy. She shook her head and held out her hand towards him, relieved when he crossed to her side and gathered her small hand between his own. He chafed her knuckles gently with his thumb.

Mia stared absently at their joined hands as she listened to her father go on and on about how busy he was, how hard it was for him to cope with work and hospital visits. How vital the dinner was to the future grant plans for his department. She wasn't prepared for the bombshell when it landed. 'And of course the staff at the Royal Brook are taking great care of your mother.'

At the mention of the hospital where she'd had to identify Jamie's body, her legs gave out and she found herself slumped on the floor, staring up at Daniel. With a worried frown creasing his brow, he knelt beside her. The oxygen she hadn't missed from her lungs came rushing back and the first sob shook her whole body. A worried squawk came from the handset dangling between her fingers. She tried to speak, tried to take a calming breath, but grief rose like a wave, rolled her over and dragged her into its salty, bitter depths.

She barely resisted as Daniel eased her fingers free of the handset and exchanged a few quiet words with her father before hanging it back up on the wall. Strong arms banded around her back as he picked her up and carried her towards the kitchen table. He found a seat, tugged her down into his lap after him. His warm arms curled around her, cocooning her, and Mia let him press her face into the crook of his neck.

His hands circled around her back and up to her shoulders, massaging gently, soothing the tension from her body. Mia pressed her nose deeper into the space between his neck and shoulder, inhaling deeply, allowing the familiar warm, masculine scent of this man to fill her senses as she drenched his neck and shoulder in her tears.

Chapter Eleven

He hadn't got the full gist of the conversation between Mia and her dad, had tried hard not to listen to something obviously personal and painful. Hot, wet tears slipped down between his collar and his neck, soaking his skin, and he clenched his jaw against the virulent anger stirring in his gut. He wanted to smash something, grab up a sword and slay the dragon who'd caused this precious woman so much hurt. He tightened his arms around her back.

A harsh sob ripped from her throat and Daniel pushed away his feelings. This wasn't about him. Mia needed him to be a man and take her pain. Even if every drop of salt seared him to the bone, he would take her tears and be the shoulder she needed to cry on.

'I've got you. It's okay, love; let it all out.' He cupped her head, pressing her face into his shoulder. 'Is it your mum?'

'Yes, no. She's...it's the hospital...and Jamie...I'm sorry...' Her voice rose on a wail of such pain it hurt him to hear it. They'd been rubbing along so well together he'd almost forgotten about the invisible barrier of her husband between them. There was no way he could compete with the love she still held for him. He hadn't even been in the running.

Shattered, he squeezed his eyes tight against the sting of his own tears and laid his cheek upon the top of her head. 'Shh. Don't be sorry; don't ever be sorry for how you feel,' he murmured. Something he needed to remember too. She was a woman worth loving, even if they would never be more than friends.

On and on, the storm of her grief battered him and he held firm, giving her an anchor until she subsided into a series of hiccupping sobs. She shivered, burrowing closer to him, and he rubbed her arms to try and soothe the goose bumps forming. He stood gingerly, tucking his hands under her thighs to take her slight weight. Mia wrapped her legs tightly around his waist and pressed closer, clinging like a monkey, and Daniel adjusted his grip until he knew he could hold her safely.

He didn't speak as he slowly climbed the stairs to the first floor and turned towards his room. He didn't want to invade Mia's space without invitation and she had always been protective of her room on the top floor; besides, he knew where everything he needed was in his own room. Forgoing the light switch, not willing to let go of his precious burden, he kicked the door wide and navigated to the big bed. She didn't speak, but sat on the edge at his gentle urging. He bent to slip off her shoes. The blouse she wore had rucked up around her middle.

A quick rummage in his bedside drawer produced a soft T-shirt. It was an old favourite band shirt from his youth, the pattern barely visible anymore and the cotton washed so often it was as soft as butter. He unbuttoned her blouse, left her bra in place and pulled the T-shirt over Mia's head. 'Stand up for me a minute?'

Her movements robotic, she stood. The blank stare on her face worried him more than the hysterical weeping from before. Taking care not to touch her bare skin, Daniel unfastened her jeans and helped her step out of them. He tugged back the thick quilt and then stopped and turned to Mia, cupping her face gently in his hands as he raised her face to look at him.

'Do you want to sleep here tonight, or would you rather go up to your room?' he asked.

'Here, please,' she whispered. 'Here with you.'

That wasn't what he'd meant. Not at all. The sofa downstairs had served him well enough and he'd planned on tucking her in and leaving her in peace. If company was what she needed right now then it was the least he could offer, given how much she'd done for him.

He pressed a soft kiss to her forehead and urged her towards the bed, scooting her across the sheet as he climbed in beside her and drew the quilt up over them. Mia curled in to him, and he pulled her closer, shielding her body as though he could protect her from the pain she was suffering. She nestled in against his shoulder like a kitten seeking warmth. He lay back and stared upwards, the light from the bathroom casting shadows across the ceiling.

'I didn't mean to lose it just now. Mum's in hospital, the same one where they took Jamie, you know, afterwards. I told you last time it's the strangest things that set me off.' She shook her head to ward off the tears gathering in her throat. 'Anyway, things with Mum and Dad have never been easy. I think they must have loved each other once, but when I look at them through grown-up eyes they seem such an odd match. He's a scholar, career-focused and obsessed with all things ancient Greek. She drinks.'

There was so much pain wrapped up in those two words. Shame washed over him. How many people had he hurt like this in his own pursuit of oblivion? She needed to know. 'I drank. Took stuff too. Nothing too hard, pills, a bit of blow now and then. It started as a way to handle the attention, a quick shot or a sniff to calm my nerves. Became a bit more than that, but everyone around me was doing it so it felt normal. If I hadn't left town when I did, I'm not sure where I might have ended up.'

'Do you miss it?' Her soft question startled a bark of laughter from him.

'Christ, no. It's the thing that scares me most about the idea of going back to London. I don't know how to live that life and not get sucked back into it.'

***

She could feel him trembling against her, sense the fear in his voice. What had it taken for him to make such an admission? He'd shown no signs of needing a drink, and she knew them all by heart from watching her mother. The nervous check of her watch, the glances flicked towards the drinks cabinet as the afternoon ticked past to an hour deemed acceptable for alcohol. The not-so-funny jesting remarks. 'The sun's past the yardarm. It must be five o'clock somewhere.' And five o'clock became four, then three, then a quick tipple with lunch, a nip of sherry at eleven, a splash of vodka in the breakfast orange juice.

She couldn't cope with another alcoholic in her life. 'Promise me you'll say if that changes.'

'I swear, if I even think about a drink, I'll find a programme. I don't want to be that man, Mia. Fitz is the past, a character I played for a while, but he isn't me.'

He was filling up the dark empty corners of her heart, piece by piece, and Mia had to make him understand what she was feeling before things got any more complicated between them. She didn't want to be a pity project, a way for Daniel to make himself feel better by taking care of her. If he was looking for a cause to champion, he'd have to look elsewhere. If they were going to make something of the growing bond between, it would need to be on equal footing. She would have to do her part and take care of Daniel and his needs as well.

'I was thinking today, before the phone call, when I was making dinner,' she started to speak and then sat bolt upright. 'Damn, you put the plates in the oven to keep warm and we've left them in there.' Mia started to scramble for the edge of the bed, but he stopped her with a gentle touch.

'Stay here in the warm and I'll go and sort them out. If it's still edible I'll bring it up or we'll be starving later. Can you manage a bite to eat?' Mia nodded and sat back against the pillows.

'You don't have to wait on me, Daniel. I'm really okay; I can help.'

'Indulge me, please? I'll be two minutes.' Good to his word, he was soon back with the two plates of pasta on a tray with some cutlery and a large bottle of water, cold from the fridge. Once they stirred the food, it was fine as she hadn't stinted on the cream sauce, and they sat together in the bed sharing the water between them as they ate.

'So, you were thinking when you were cooking...' Daniel prompted.

It was crunch time. 'Oh. Yes, well. I was thinking about how much I like you being here with me. I'm not saying I want anything to happen between us.' She blushed and felt a little ridiculous when he grinned at her.

'You sure know how to boost a man's ego.' The teasing tone set her at ease.

'I'm not saying I don't either. I just...' She huffed out a breath. 'I don't know what I'm saying.'

'I don't think either of us are in the place to be making big steps beyond friendship. I like being around you, and I want to stay here with you. I want to see you achieve your dreams here.' He glanced away then quickly back. 'I'll be honest, I think about what might be. A lot.'

She stared down at the remains of her pasta. 'Me too.'

'I know it's overstepping the mark, but I can't help myself making plans for the future. Whatever may or may not happen between us, I want to stay. This house feels like the first home I've had in years. I want to stay. With you. As friends, if nothing more. I've even got some ideas for converting the barn.'

Mia knew she probably looked dumbstruck as she stared open-mouthed at Daniel. It was almost as though he could read her mind as his words echoed perfectly her own feelings. 'I want the same thing, whatever else happens here, I want us to always be friends, Daniel. I feel like we came together at a moment in time when we both needed the other so badly without even realising it. You have become so special to me in just a few weeks and I can't bear to think that we might spoil this by rushing too far ahead or striving to feel something that just might not be there for us. I think we need to promise to be honest with each other, no matter what we fear the other person might say because it is only by staying true and trusting each other that we can hold this together. Do you agree?'

Mia reached up to cup his bearded cheek and he turned his head to press a kiss into the centre of her palm.

'Yes, I agree. I also think we need to start sharing some of those sad stories, but not tonight and not all at once. The dark should be for whispering about our

114

dreams and hopes for the future. Let's save the tough stuff for the daytime, okay?'

It was such a sweet idea that it appealed deeply to Mia, to keep their most intimate times a haven, knowing that she could lie beside him and be safe and warm and not have to face anything upsetting or difficult. A time to plan and look to the future. It was perfect.

'So tell me about these plans of yours.' She settled back against her pillow and let him tuck the quilt under her chin as if she were a child. He drew back to his own side of the bed, leaving a clear space between them. He mimicked her position. Snug as two bugs in a rug, as her mother used to say when she still used to put Mia to bed. She closed her eyes and took a deep breath, and then listened with her heart open as Daniel described his fledgling ideas for converting the barns.

***

'The air here is different, even the sky looks different. I didn't realise how much the darkness of the city was getting to me until it was almost too late. You end up living this life that isn't yours, if you're not careful, and then you lose that part of you that your creativity and artistry needs to survive and thrive. I was so full of hope, so full of ideas and excitement when I moved to London. My pictures reflected that positivity. All my themes were of things to be celebrated.'

Daniel paused, trying to find the right words. 'I need to show you my portfolio and then you would understand.' He sat up intent on fetching his tablet, but she stopped him with a light touch on his arm.

'Save that for later. You were talking about the difference here away from the city and how it makes you feel. What does that have to do with your plans for the barn?' She rolled onto her side, tucking her hands beneath her cheek.

He settled back down and turned to face her, heart racing a mile a minute. He'd thought for sure any hopes of a relationship with her had been dashed because she still grieved for Jamie, but she'd offered him a lifeline with her shy admission. Now was not the time to push it though. They would have plenty of time to explore things between them if she liked what he said next.

'I want to convert the barn into a studio, well, a collection of studios really. Something to cater for different artistic disciplines. A pottery studio with all the equipment: a wheel, a kiln, drying racks and display cases. A photography studio with a dark room for the old-fashioned types and a top-of-the-range computer and printing set-up for us digital addicts; one for a painter to use, one for a sculptor.

'The light in the barn is fantastic and the view across the beach to the sea would be inspirational to the most jaded of eyes. The gardens here are fascinating too. I love them as they are—so much to explore, so many hidden secrets to capture on film, on canvas, in clay. I just think it would be fabulous to be able to offer an exclusive retreat to people. Somewhere they can tuck themselves away and recuperate, recharge their batteries and maybe rekindle their muse if they are struggling like I was.' He cut himself off with a laugh at the saucer-eyed expression on her face. 'Yeah, I've been giving this a lot of thought.'

'It never occurred to me the barn could be anything other than an eyesore and a dumping ground. I've always known I'd have to tackle it at some point, but trying to deal with the house has been overwhelming enough.' She nibbled her lower lip, a single line etched between her brows—her thinking face, as he thought of it. *And when had he started giving names to her different expressions?* She spoke again, distracting him from the thought. 'I can see the appeal of the idea, but I never planned on turning the place into an artist's retreat.'

A note of uncertainty crept into her tone and Daniel plunged on, hoping to sell her his vision. 'It's such a beautiful place; it would be perfect. I want to invite my friend Aaron down to visit and check it out further. He's the one with a head for figures and his brother's an architect. I want to get their input and ideas, see if Luke can take some measurements, maybe put together some sketches. I'd make sure it wouldn't interfere with the guest house. They would be pretty self-contained with the little apartments on the mezzanine floor, although you might get a few begging at the back door once they smell your cooking.'

'You plan to have them sleep there too? You wouldn't be expecting them to stay in the house?' Mia sounded surprised and he wanted to slap himself for being a fool. She'd obviously thought he wanted to take over everything.

'God no, the guest house is *yours*. I wouldn't presume to interfere with your plans. The barn is huge, plenty of room to put in a first floor. That was the idea, studios down below with maybe a staircase connecting to a loft type apartment above. The artists can totally retreat if they wanted to, although I would hope that people would mingle a bit in the summer if we had a barbeque or a bit of a beach party. Get everyone together and all mixing. Maybe put a few bits of art around the house to decorate and we could offer them for sale if anyone was interested. We could even set up a small gallery in time if there was enough interest. A gallery and a tea shop to draw the holidaymakers in the season and something to offer the locals off-peak.'

Mia started laughing as Daniel raced on a mile a minute. So yeah, he was miles beyond just a few artist studios, but he could see it in his mind's eye and excitement fizzed in his gut like champagne bubbles.

'You're mad, you know?' She was laughing, though, much to his relief. 'The dream I had for opening a guest house seemed unachievable only a couple of months ago and now here we are thinking about adding an artist's retreat, an art gallery and a bloody tea shop! It all sounds marvellous, but I barely have enough in the budget to finish this place.'

Oh, hell, he was really mucking this up. 'The cost of anything you agree for the barn would come out of my pocket, not yours. I'll buy or lease the space from you, with a proper contract and everything. Once I became flavour of the month, people paid quite ludicrous sums for my work and even more for a personal sitting.'

A flicker of guilt over that last disastrous sitting jabbed him in the belly. 'I have more bloody money than I know what to do with and no-one and nothing in my life that was worth a damn penny of it until now, until this.' He sounded desperate to his own ears and knew he should back off, but he needed this, needed something physical to show for his almost thirty years of existence other than a few pictures and a failing reputation.

The frown on her forehead smoothed out and excitement gleamed in her eyes. 'It's a great idea. I love it and if you can afford to make a go of it then you have my blessing. We'll have to finish the beach room if you are going to invite your friends to stay. You can put one in there and one in here, if you don't mind giving up your room for a couple of nights?'

A weight he hadn't been aware of lifted from his shoulders and he wanted to drag her into his arms and hold her tight, but it seemed too intimate given their location. 'That would work. The sofa did me fine for the first week. I can camp out on it for a couple of days while the guys are here. Are you sure you don't mind me inviting them down?'

'I don't mind.' She laughed. 'I actually don't. I've been cocooned in this place for so long, I forgot what it was like to enjoy the thought of company. Once we've finished the beach room, we could look at converting one of the other rooms on the top floor for you to use. Once we have paying guests, you won't want to be on the same floor as them; you'll never get any peace. And I like the idea of having you close.' She said it so calmly, it took him a moment to register the significance. In opening her private space to him, she was offering him a permanent home. A place to belong and set down roots.

He swallowed hard on the lump in his throat. 'If you're sure?'

'We'd have to share the bathroom, and only the bathroom for now, but if you don't leave the seat up it should be fine.' Her jaw cracked around a huge yawn. 'Sorry.'

He smiled and tucked the quilt around her. She hadn't made any move to return to her own room and he liked the idea of keeping her close, even if it was just for one night. 'Don't be. Let's get some sleep and tomorrow will be a better day.'

She wriggled around, turning from one side to the other, taking more and more of the quilt with her each time she shifted. *Maybe sharing a bed wasn't such a great idea.* Waiting until she finally settled, he risked a surreptitious tug on one corner to claim just enough of the duvet to cover himself and turned on his side to face her. He bit his lip against the urge to laugh. There was little more of her visible than the top of her head. ''Night, pet,' he murmured.

''Night Daniel,' she replied from the muffled depths of the bed.

Chapter Twelve

A sharp pain digging in her ribs woke Mia and she tugged at the tight band of her bra. Her knickers had formed an uncomfortable wedge in places unmentionable, and it took a moment of confusion before she remembered why she'd fallen asleep in her underwear. She froze, one finger hooked in the elastic of her pants, and held her breath. Slow, even sounds came from her left and she peeked over the top of the quilt. Daniel sprawled on his back beside her, one arm flung above his head and a hairy leg hooked over his side of the covers.

His chest rose and fell in an easy motion, the T-shirt he'd kept on moulded to his frame. Broader than Jamie through the shoulders, she noted, followed by a quick wash of guilt. She shouldn't be comparing the two of them. There should be *no* comparison between the man she'd loved for ten years and this relative stranger.

The bathroom light shone dimly in the early-morning gloom, evidence neither of them had stirred in the night. Feeling awkward, although they'd done nothing more than sleep together, she inched out of the bed and slid to the floor in a crouch. Not wanting to risk waking him, she collected her jeans and tiptoed towards the door.

An errant floorboard creaked beneath her foot and she stopped, one leg raised like Wile E. Coyote trying to sneak up on the Road Runner. Daniel snuffled, rolled on his side and *thankfully* went back to sleep. A huge snore rent the air and she used the sound to cover the low click when she opened the bedroom door. Taking care to stay quiet, she scurried down the stairs and closed the kitchen door behind her with a sigh of relief.

Cold tiles nipped at her toes, so she scrambled into her jeans and stuffed her feet into her cosy boots. A quick peek through the kitchen window showed the first pink-red streaks of a dawn that promised a fine day. She made a cup of tea, poured it into a travel mug. Bright it might be, but the air still held a sharp nip so she bundled up in her coat and a hat and carried her drink outside.

Overgrown shrubs and bushes formed strange shapes in the early-morning light. She picked her way carefully towards the steps leading to the beach to avoid any brambles waiting to snare an unwitting foot. She could hear the sea before she saw it, the dark water merging too closely with the sand to make out. It was close to high tide, so she chose a spot up near the small dunes edging the beach and sat with her legs crossed.

Pale pinks, soft oranges and a deeper red striped across the grey sky, the colours brightening with each passing minute. The ocean grew visible next, leaving lines of foamy bubbles to be swallowed up by the next rolling waves. Clouds seemed to boil from the horizon, edged in crimson and shades of fuchsia. Letting the wonder of nature fill her eyes, Mia sipped her tea and gathered her thoughts.

Sneaking away from Daniel's bed seemed a bit cowardly and she hoped he wouldn't be offended to find her gone when he woke. From a safe distance, she could admit to herself it hadn't only been guilty feelings over Jamie that had driven her from the warmth of the sheets. Being next to Daniel had felt right and it scared her. After Jamie, she'd never thought she might care for another man again, and she wasn't quite ready to let Jamie go.

Sunday mornings had been her favourite part of the week. Long, lazy hours spent reading the papers, grazing over breakfast and snuggling back down for sweet caresses. They'd grown up together, first and only lovers, finding their way around each other's bodies until they knew every spot to draw a gasp or a sigh.

What would it be like to let someone else that close? What if she didn't like the way Daniel touched her, what if he proved a better lover than Jamie? She wasn't sure which would be worse. *Stop it. Stop it.* There was no point in torturing herself over things that might not even come to pass.

The pale disc of the sun crested the horizon, chasing away the blaze of colours into the pale blue of full morning. A chill crept into her bones from the damp sand, soaking through the layers of her coat. Not quite willing to drag herself away from the view, Mia raised the cup to her lips, surprised to find it empty. Seagulls swooped and danced in the sky overhead, their raucous cries breaking the silence. A shiver ran through her, the cold striking deep enough to force her into motion.

She needed to call her dad, finish their conversation from the previous night, and Madeline and Richard would be along soon as well. Time wouldn't stop for her; she knew from bitter experience that life went on whether she was ready for it or not. Things changed and a new direction lay open before her.

Daniel was a fixture in her life now and she couldn't imagine living here at Butterfly Cove without the sound of his deep voice calling down the hall to her. His warm presence at her table had become a necessity, making her smile as he scoffed down whatever meal she put before him with the same alacrity and gratitude whether it be a ham sandwich or a full Sunday roast. His plans for the barn were exciting too; nothing she would have ever thought of herself. She scrambled up, eager to see the place from the new perspective he'd given her.

The door to the kitchen creaked, drawing her attention towards it, and she waved Daniel into the room when he stuck his head through the gap. She turned her attention back to the phone. It was still early, but her dad liked to get to his office before students started knocking and ruining his train of thought. She pictured him behind the big oak desk, which would be covered with precarious stacks of papers and books. His study at home had been worse, a no-go zone for them as girls in case they made a mess of the filing system only he seemed to understand.

'I didn't mean to upset you,' he said again, sounding thoroughly miserable. Always more comfortable in the past than the present, the dusty remains of long-dead poets and scholars were his purview.

She sighed, knowing it was hopeless to wish for anything different. George Thorpe was too set in his ways to change. 'I know, Dad. It was just that the mention of the Royal Brook caught me off guard. I haven't been there since the accident.' She swallowed hard and continued briskly. 'Stupid little things like that set me off, but I'm okay.'

Silence greeted her and she could imagine him rubbing the lenses of his glasses on the front of his jumper as he tried to find something to say. 'I didn't think,' he managed in the end, sounding forlorn, like a small boy scolded for some foolish transgression.

'Forget it, Dad.'

'I can see why visiting your mother would be hard. They're taking very good care of her and it would be more useful to both of us if you saved your trip until she comes home.'

Mia sagged against the wall in relief. 'And you'll postpone your dinner?'

'Oh, yes. Good job you reminded me. I'll send the email now.' She heard the clattering of his fingers on a keyboard.

'All right. Will I call you in a few days then?'

'Yes. Fine.' He hesitated, then cleared his throat. 'You're a good girl, Eunomia. I'm not sure I ever told you that enough.' Surprised how choked up she felt over his comment, Mia rang off.

She'd been half aware of Daniel moving around in the room behind her, but now she stared at the phone in her hand, not quite sure how to approach him. He saved her the trouble, turning her to face him with a gentle hand on her shoulder. He brushed a quick kiss against her temple.

Turning back towards the table, he took his customary seat and she could see he'd laid everything out for breakfast. She watched him pour tea into the mug in front of him then unfold the morning paper he must have retrieved from the front doormat. He looked at home. *As it should be.*

***

The next weekend dawned fine and dry and Daniel was grateful for the respite from the recent rain. He waited at the station, memories of his own journey down from London playing through his head. He wondered again what would have happened to him

127

had Madeline not been in the same carriage as him. He shuddered to think at where he might have ended up, and scrolled through his phone to his browser to look for a local florist.

He found a number for one in the main town and racked his brain for Madeline's address. Luckily the florist was the same one that Richard used and he was apparently a huge romantic as he had an account with them. The florist even gave Daniel some advice on which were Madeline's favourite flowers.

On a whim, he ordered a dozen roses for Mia, and settled on mixed shades of pink after another helpful hint from the florist. White or cream was for weddings only and red was such a cliché, apparently. They'd been taking things steady since the night of her breakdown, but a few tentative steps closer to the intimacy he grew ever more certain he wanted. He craved every connection with her. Nothing major, nothing they couldn't walk back from without hurting each other. Simple things like when she'd rested her feet in his lap while they watched a film one evening. The peck on the cheek they used to greet each other in the mornings now.

Daniel reeled off his credit card details as the train approached. He thanked the florist as he raised his hand in greeting when he saw Aaron and Luke step onto the platform. He grinned and returned the bear hug from Aaron and shook hands with Luke.

'You scared the crap out of me, Fitz! Don't disappear on me like that again.'

'It's Daniel now, not Fitz.'

Aaron blinked once, then nodded. 'About bloody time too. Welcome back, mate. I missed you.' He tugged Daniel into another hug, thumping his shoulder a couple of times in the way men do rather than express too much emotion.

Daniel tried to process his friend's response as he bent down to pick up his bag. He felt sick at the mess that he had abandoned in his wake and guilty that he had essentially dumped his most loyal friend to live the high life. Yet here he was, with almost no complaints, ready to pick up where they'd left off. Daniel had used and abused their friendship and there would need to be a lot of restitution soon.

He dropped the bag and it was his turn to gather Aaron in for a tight hug. 'I'm sorry, mate. Truly I am. I've been such a selfish bastard.' Daniel swallowed hard around the lump in his throat as Aaron stepped back but kept his hand on the back of Daniel's neck and looked him straight in the eye.

'It wasn't a problem, Fit...Daniel. Sorry, that's going to take a bit of getting used to. I've been worried about you for a while now and I was just glad that you had got out of town for a bit. That lifestyle was killing you and I couldn't find a way to make you see it.'

Daniel shook his head and wondered again about fate bringing the right people into your life when you needed them. It had certainly done the trick when he and Aaron had ended up in neighbouring rooms during their first year at university.

Both new to London, they had little in common other than proximity and not knowing a single person in the city. Daniel, the gruff Northern lad from a loving, working-class background. Aaron, the outgoing West Country boy with a bumpkin's twang hiding a sharp brain and plenty of heartache. They had bonded over stock North-South divide jokes and taking the piss out of each other's accents. A few ill-spent evenings followed by some extremely rough mornings and they had become fast friends. Best friends.

They reached the car and Daniel helped them stow their bags in the boot. 'I really appreciate you guys coming down here. I know I've been a shitty friend, but I'm getting myself back together I hope.'

Aaron patted Daniel on the arm as Luke crawled into the back seat. 'As I said, you weren't right for a long time and I knew it but I didn't know what to do about it. I had my own stuff going on and it was easier to drift away when you got in with that crowd. It wasn't my scene but I should've tried harder to get you out of it rather than just backing away. Let's say we both could've been better friends there for a while and leave it at that, okay?'

Daniel felt a bit choked up and he grabbed Aaron for another quick, hard hug.

'Pack it in, you two love birds,' Luke yelled out the window. 'I want to meet this woman who's turned you on your head, Daniel, and get on the right side of some of that great cooking you've been boasting about. The sandwich I had on the train was rank.' As if to punctuate his point, Luke let loose a large belch and grinned unrepentantly.

He was still playing the annoying little brother, even at twenty-five. He'd been the bane and the pride of Aaron's life since the day his step-mother had brought him home from the hospital. Daniel knew all about the problems Aaron had been through with his stepmother and it was to his eternal credit that he'd never allowed it to sour his relationship with his half-brother. Aaron adored Luke and he hero-worshipped him in return. Their closeness had been a source of envy to Daniel at first, being an only child, but the two men had just drawn him into their lives and he was beyond grateful for that.

The three of them laughed together and chatted about Daniel's ideas for the barn as he drove them back to the house. They rounded the corner of the drive and he pulled up as the back door opened and Mia stood on the doorstep in her usual huge jumper and jeans. She smiled shyly as first Aaron and then Luke swooped on her with hugs and kisses before Daniel shoved them both away and stepped in front of her, arms folded like a bodyguard. 'Oy, keep your hands and your lips to yourselves!' Things might still be up in the air between him and Mia, but he'd be damned if either of these two charmers would swoop in and steal her from under his nose.

Mia gave him a shove in the back then ducked around him. 'Why don't you go and check out the barn and I'll put the kettle on. Tea will be about fifteen minutes.' She disappeared into the kitchen and Daniel pointed the brothers in the direction of the barn. Luke rummaged in his pocket for a notebook and his laser measure as he strode purposefully towards the ramshackle building. Aaron followed at a more leisurely pace, taking his time to examine everything around him, including turning back to survey the imposing structure of the main house.

'It's incredible here. I can't believe how clean the air is after London.' A touch of envy tinged his voice.

Daniel watched Aaron wander away from the barn to stop halfway across the scruffy rear lawn as he saw the break in the hedge and caught sight of the beach and the rolling sea beyond it. He smiled as he watched the joy suffuse his friend's face. The whole place was working its magic and Aaron was hooked—he could tell.

'Christ, mate, it's paradise.' Aaron's words were thrown back over his shoulder as he loped across the grass towards the inexorable pull of the sea beyond.

Chapter Thirteen

Mia turned her back on the three men at the table as they threw ideas back and forth, discussing the correct level of light for each of the studio areas, colour schemes and textures for the floors and walls. The discussion was dizzyingly fast and the noise was something she was just not used to. She found it quite unsettling to be in such a masculine atmosphere again. Jamie had been one of four brothers and when they got together it was like they spoke their own language, often leaving Mia a little alienated.

It was so different from being one of three girls. Largely ignored by their mother, they had been left to their own devices unless they managed to draw the ire of their father. They had basically raised each other and had dwelled in a fantasy world of lost maidens rescued from fearsome beasts by handsome, but very politely spoken and entirely harmless, heroes. The reality of boys, in all their awful smelly, wonderful, disgusting glory was a shock from which Mia was never sure she had quite recovered.

The boisterous exchanges behind her now were a bit of an intrusion on the quiet solitude of the house, and Mia felt equal parts annoyed at them and guilty with herself for wanting to deny Daniel the time with his friends. He had a beautiful laugh—a deep rich baritone, which rolled through her and curled her toes. It was nice to hear him so positive and excited about the potential for the new venture of fixing up the barn. She just wished they could be positive in a slightly quieter fashion.

Mia rolled her eyes at herself and set about making tea and coffee for everyone. She stared towards the window. The black night was impenetrable and the window reflected the room behind her. Fifteen minutes had turned into three hours and dusk fell quickly this time of year. She watched the men talking and teasing each other until Daniel raised his gaze as though conscious of her eyes on him. She smiled in what she hoped was a reassuring manner but she obviously missed her mark because Daniel frowned and rose from his seat to cross the room and stand behind her.

He placed a warm hand on her shoulder and met her gaze in the reflection of the glass. Mia smiled more warmly, feeling more settled and secure under his touch, and she raised her hand to cover his.

'All right, pet?' Daniel was still frowning a little and Mia couldn't stand that she was putting a dampener on his mood.

'Really all right, Daniel,' she whispered and patted the back of his hand. 'It sounds amazing already. Aaron and Luke seem to be full of good ideas.'

Daniel snorted and squeezed her shoulder. 'They're certainly full of something,' he muttered then laughed out loud as a balled-up tea towel struck him on the back of the head.

'Cheeky sod, we dropped everything to rush down here and help you, worried half to death about what sort of state we would find you in and look at you! Shacked up with the most gorgeous girl, who not only looks beautiful, but also cooks like a dream and is the nicest person I think I have met. We had visions of you with your hair turned grey and bones poking out, but you're fit as a fiddle and happier than I've seen you in at least five years.' Aaron's words were spoken in jest but there was a trace of the worry and stress he must have felt when his best friend had all but vanished off the face of the earth for weeks.

'Shacked up?' Mia raised an eyebrow at Daniel's reflection in the window.

He held his hands up in protest. 'Nothing I've said. The lads have put two and two together and made five.'

'You sent her flowers, roses even. What the hell are we supposed to think?' Luke pointed out, not unreasonably.

She caught Daniel's eye again. 'I love them,' she mouthed and his lips quirked up in a shy grin.

His face became serious as he turned back to his friends. 'I'm sorry, Aaron. I don't know what else to say to you other than that. I had to get away from London—you're right, it was killing me.' The bleak expression on his face made Mia want to hug him, but that would only add to the speculation from the others about their relationship.

Aaron stood and slung his arm around Daniel's shoulders. 'Don't worry about it. Seriously, mate, you look better than you have in a long time and I'm just pleased to see you getting back to yourself. If you do feel the need to redeem yourself then you could tell me some good news. Something along the lines of Mia having a sister—as glorious as she is.'

'Two sisters,' Luke interjected.

Mia laughed, turning towards the kettle to finish making the drinks. 'I do have two sisters actually and they are the ones who got the looks in our family.' Mia glanced fondly towards the pinboard on the wall where her favourite picture of the three of them was displayed.

'The bad news is one is married and the other is living it up in New York. Although knowing her, she's probably starving in some garret trying to capture that authentic artist vibe.'

She thought it best not to mention that Kiki's husband Neil was an enormous arsehole who physically abused her sister in addition to a constant barrage of emotional bullying. She'd tried to talk to her so many times about it, but Kiki refused to acknowledge it, to the point of threatening to cut all contact with Mia if she raised the subject again.

After losing Jamie, the thought of her sister—almost her twin having been born less than a year apart—cutting her out of her life was too much for her to bear. Mia had maintained a reluctant silence on the matter and hoped that Kiki would one day find the strength to face the problem and deal with it.

Nee's answer to their difficult childhood had been to fly the nest as soon as she possibly could to go to art school. She produced some incredibly dark pieces that Mia knew were her way of funnelling the frustration and upset of her childhood experiences. They were powerful and terrible in their beauty and they broke Mia's heart every time she saw one of them. Nee had gained a bit of a cult reputation, which had led to the offer to study in America. She had been gone like a shot, seemingly needing as much physical distance from the past as she did emotionally.

Mia thought back to the period before Nee had left for the States; Kiki had just had her second child, Charlie, and Mia and Jamie had travelled back to their home town to stay with his parents and see Kiki and her new baby. Their mother had turned up at the hospital, clearly drunk at ten in the morning. She had become hysterical when Mia had refused to let her anywhere near the baby. Jamie had ended up calling Mia's father, who had arrived at the hospital with the family doctor. Vivian had been swiftly interred in a clinic for a couple of months whilst her 'nervous condition' was treated.

Mia had cried on the phone to Nee about how awful it had been. Mia and Jamie had extended their stay by a couple of weeks, taking Kiki's older child, Matthew, to stay with them at Jamie's parents'. The new baby was sick and Kiki had struggled to cope with her and a lively two-year-old. Matty had wanted to play with his new baby sister and couldn't understand why she and their mummy kept crying all the time. Neil had been worse than useless, refusing to take any time off work to help his wife, insisting that as she did nothing else, the least she could do was manage to look after the children.

It had been a difficult and chaotic time and now that Mia thought about it, she realised that she had not listened to Nee during the fraught conversations they had over what to do about their mother, their sister, their niece and nephew. Mia and Nee had sadly reached the conclusion that they were powerless to do anything about any of it. Nee had been working on an exhibition for her finals and Mia had insisted that she stay in town and focus on that, determined to protect her baby sister from as much of the horror that was going on at home.

Then Jamie had died and she hadn't had time for anything or anyone else. She'd let Nee drift away. Now Mia needed to talk to Kiki, find out what she knew of their little sister's new life in New York and then track her down. She'd neglected her sisters for far too long.

***

'The weather looks promising so I might try and distract them with some hard labour in the garden.' They'd been rained in for twenty-four hours and Daniel was starting to regret inviting his friends to stay. It was foolish to be jealous, but Mia and Luke had been holed up in the far wing, running through the various design concepts the architect had drawn up. Every laugh from that direction had distracted him from the endless task of painting the first-floor landing. Aaron had smirked at every huff and sigh he'd made so he'd got his own back by making him paint the skirting boards.

Mia glanced up from her notebook. 'Better wait until Madeline arrives. She's my self-appointed Head Gardener. I don't know a hydrangea from a hawthorn, but she swears there is hidden beauty somewhere under the weeds.' She put down her notes and folded her arms. 'According to local history, the gardens were famous in the area for attracting insects and wildlife. That's how the beach got its nickname—Butterfly Cove. I assumed it was an act of whimsy by one of the previous owners, but apparently not.' She didn't sound convinced.

Daniel sat back in his chair, trying to imagine the scene. He recalled the half-buried statues hiding in the undergrowth and wondered what other treasures they might find lurking. He'd need to make sure he took his camera with him to capture some before, during, and after shots.

If Madeline was coming, then Richard was bound to join her. Quieter than his wife, he was no less enthusiastic about helping Mia transform the place and Daniel had quickly come to admire his dry wit and steady presence. Once everyone else was busy in the garden, he might try and steal him away for a few minutes to talk about the barn. His stomach gave a little nervous roll. He hoped Richard would approve of the project.

Having the older man was a blessing and a curse. His dad's death had happened just as things had taken off for Daniel in London and the booze had helped to numb the pain. Properly sober, the hours spent doing repetitive tasks around the house allowed his mind to wander and his thoughts strayed constantly to the stern, reliable man who'd taught him so much. How his dad would have loved the idea of taking something broken down and giving it new life. *Oh, Dad.*

The sound of footsteps clattering down the stairs heralded the noisy arrival of Aaron and Luke. Grateful for the distraction, Daniel hurried to put the kettle on, giving his burning eyes a surreptitious rub on his sleeve as he did so.

The silence seemed to go on and on, driving Daniel's nerves close to breaking point. Richard had listened without interruption to his ideas, and now wove his way around the piles of old furniture littering the barn, pausing now and then to flick through the scribbled sketches and notes in his hand.

Say something. Daniel opened his mouth, lost his courage and turned away. Dusty velvet caught his eye and he raised an old oilcloth to reveal an elaborately gilded chaise longue and matching footstool. It was one of the items on the list Mia had given him for the next room she planned to work on. Needing to dissipate some of the nervous energy filling him, he picked up the stool and carried it out into the yard.

He returned inside, to find Richard standing next to the chaise. His neutral expression revealed nothing of his thoughts. He nodded at the piece of furniture between them. 'Need a hand with this?'

Was he really not going to say anything about the barn? Perhaps Daniel had been too forward in seeking his opinion, presuming on a friendship the other man might not reciprocate. He swallowed his disappointment and forced a smile. 'Yes, please. Mia has some fancy plans for a boudoir, apparently.'

They carried the heavy chaise out to the yard and placed it next to the footstool. 'Anything else we need to fetch?' Richard asked. Feeling thoroughly miserable, Daniel handed him the list and trudged after him back into the barn.

Richard dragged a dust sheet off a matching pair of floral armchairs and sank down into one, nodding to the other one. 'Before we get started, I think we should talk about your fancy plans, don't you?'

Apprehensive at his stern tone, Daniel took a seat. 'You don't approve.'

'That's not what I said, son. Why don't you tell me a bit about what brought you here? Madeline says I should mind my own business, but Mia is our heart and soul and I won't have you filling her head with flights of fancy only to let her down.'

Daniel propped his elbows on his thighs and stared at the floor between his feet. What could he say? If he let Richard see everything inside him, then he would have to admit his failures to himself at the same time. He didn't want to look back; he wanted to move forward. *But if you keep hiding from the past, how will you ever get over it?*

A warm hand came down on his back and Richard's voice sounded close to his ear. 'Talk to me, Daniel. Let me help you, son.'

The words poured out—every ugly hidden thing from the past few years. The drink, the drugs, the faceless girls and his own stupid arrogance. Like lancing a boil. He spoke of his fears. Of the bone-shaking terror that he had burnt out his gift, thrown away the God-given talent his dad had been so proud of. His dad. *Oh, his dad.* The tears came next, gut-wrenching sobs that shook his entire body. And through it all, that strong hand never moved from his back.

Calm at last, he moved on to his hopes for the future. 'I want to help people like me. Give them a space to breathe, a safe place where nothing matters other than their art. I'm not the only one, I'm sure.' Now he thought about it, he could recall the glazed and dazed expressions of at least a dozen other artists he knew. That same jaw-gritting determination to cope because it was what you needed to do to get on. To get noticed, to be a personality rather than letting the work speak for itself. How many youngsters fell by the wayside because they couldn't hack it? How much talent was lost to the harsh competitiveness of the art world?

'And Mia?'

He glanced up at Richard through red-raw eyes. 'I love her. Body and soul. But in the end, it's not up to me what happens between us. Butterfly Cove is my home now. I'll work side by side with her and take only as much of her as she is willing to give me.'

Richard patted his shoulder. There was no censure in his eyes, just a warm, familiar twinkle. 'That's all I needed to hear. Come on, let's see if we can find the rest of the stuff on the list.'

Feeling lighter than he had in months, Daniel scrubbed his face with his hands then stood up. He'd said it out loud. Admitted what he'd been feeling for a while. He was head over heels in love with Mia Sutherland. Sending up a silent prayer that she might one day return his feelings, he followed Richard's lead and began to search through the heaps of junk to find the things she wanted.

Chapter Fourteen

The sun warm on her back, Mia stretched and wiped her brow as she surveyed the decimated border in front of her. The weeds had run rampant and although she would never have much of a green finger, she had followed Madeline's instructions to the letter about what to cull and what to keep.

Mia looked across to where Luke was cursing and doing battle with the old lawn mower for the third time that day. He had seemed happy to turn his hand to every task Madeline gave him. She couldn't see Aaron, but the noise of an electric hedge trimmer pinpointed his location somewhere deep in one of the overgrown thickets.

Daniel and Richard were still in the barn. They'd been in there for a long time, only appearing now and then to haul out various pieces of furniture Mia had earmarked for the next bedroom. She had decided on an exotic boudoir theme after discovering a beautiful chaise longue under an oilcloth in the back of the barn.

It would be a room to tempt and delight the senses, full of different, luxuriant materials, scented candles and lush greenery.

The name in her notebook was the harem room and she wanted the space to be one of utter indulgence, something for couples to use. The room was in the back wing of the house, which would offer some privacy to the occupants. Mia was toying with the idea of turning the room between it and the beach room into a sitting room so that it was a completely private haven for whoever rented the space.

She decided to speak to Luke about it, see if he could come up with some alteration ideas to expand the bathroom so she could install a small steam cabinet as well as a shower and a large bath. She looked across again and smiled at his crow of triumph as he got the stubborn old petrol mower going again.

They had been blessed with a bright day but the sun wouldn't last for too much longer so Mia headed towards the house to prepare dinner. She waved at Luke and pointed towards the kitchen so he would know where she was. She kicked off her muddy boots in the doorway.

Dinner was a calm, quiet affair and no-one objected when Mia placed a pack of cards on the table with the pot of tea and some shortbread afterwards. A quick discussion established a couple of games they all knew although it soon became apparent that there was some familial licence in the rules they each played to.

An easy hour passed and Mia felt much more relaxed with these men in her home. Aaron started to yawn as he surrendered his final hand. 'I'm bushed. All this sea air and honest work is doing me in. I've never been ready for bed before 10 p.m. before.' He laughed around another jaw-dislocating yawn.

Luke looked wide awake despite his exertions in the garden so she fetched her notebook and started to discuss her plans for the harem rooms with him. He dived head first into the distraction and they headed upstairs whilst Daniel promised to clean the kitchen. Aaron retired to his bed.

Luke surveyed the three rooms that would comprise the suite and started scribbling furiously in his own notebook. Mia sat quietly with her hands curled around her knees, which were drawn up under her chin. He was a live wire and when he set his mind to something his level of concentration and focus was a little daunting. Mia shivered as she tried to imagine being the sole focus of that much energy. She decided that it was too intense for her.

Daniel was so much more matter of fact about things. He was a good foil to her more sensitive nature. Mia watched the wild blond curls of Luke's hair fall over his forehead again and he shoved them away in an unconscious movement. He was an impressive man, thick through the shoulders, like his brother, in contrast to Daniel's taller, more slender build. They were all men who would make a woman feel safe and sheltered.

Mia stood up and stretched her aching body. The work in the garden was starting to take its toll and she wanted a soak in the bath and half an hour with a good book. She patted Luke on the shoulder and left him to it with an instruction that the space was his to do with as he pleased. He flashed her a sweet, shy grin before he bent back to his sketches and calculations.

She paused on the landing and saw that the lower floor was in darkness and only a soft light was spilling down from the third floor. She urged her weary, sore legs up the stairs to find Daniel clad in a T-shirt and jogging pants, sprawled in the middle of his bed with all the pillows propped beneath him.

He had certainly made himself at home in the little bedroom next to hers. A laptop rested across his knees and clothes hung over the back of a rocking chair he'd come across in the barn. The iron-framed bed he sat upon was a sea of flowers and lace; she ought to buy him some more suitable bedding. The green set had been washed and left on the bed downstairs for Aaron to use so Daniel had ended up with one of her spare sets. He made a dark shadow amongst the frilly pillowcases and flowery duvet cover. The contrast made her smile.

She leaned against the door frame. 'Everything all right?' There were dark shadows under his eyes, and he'd been subdued over dinner.

He lowered the screen on his laptop and smiled at her. 'Yes, fine. Just uploading a few of the pictures I took today.' She noticed then the camera connected by a cable to the computer.

'Ooh, will you show me?' She hovered on the threshold, eager to see but not wanting to invade his privacy. He hesitated just long enough for her to feel awkward before patting the quilt beside him.

'Sure.'

'You don't have to…'

He shook his head. 'I'm being daft; don't mind me.' He turned the laptop towards her, showing an image of Aaron holding Luke in a headlock. The brothers were laughing, caught completely off guard, and the natural joy Daniel captured in the image drew her closer.

'It's wonderful.' She perched on the edge of the bed and he set the screen down between them.

'I thought I might send it to their dad. He was always good to me whenever I went for visit.'

'I bet he'll love it. Jamie's parents always moaned about not having enough pictures of him and his brothers once they grew up.' Daniel stiffened beside her and she cursed herself for bringing Jamie's name up.

'You must miss him, terribly,' he said, eyes fixed hard on the laptop.

'I do. But it's getting better every day.' She touched his arm to make him look at her. 'You being here is making it better.' Her fingers tingled with awareness, and she stroked the fine hairs on his forearm.

'Mia, I—' Colour suffused his cheeks, disappearing into the dark hair of his beard. What would it feel like if he kissed her? Scratchy or soft? Overwhelmed with curiosity, she leaned forward and pressed her mouth to his. His lips parted beneath hers, a soft groan escaping, which she captured as she opened for him. He took control, curling a big hand around the back of her head to hold her in place as he explored her mouth in slow, leisurely strokes.

Her head spun, and things long dormant stirred low in her belly. She gripped the back of his arm tighter, somehow afraid she would float away without an anchor to hold her down.

He broke the kiss on a gasp of air. 'Go to bed, love. Before I make you regret this.' His smile was sweet in contrast to the glittering need in his eyes. Thankful he had enough sense for them both, she slipped off the edge of the bed and scampered to the safety of her own room.

***

He shoved the laptop to one side and flopped onto his back, chest working like a bellows. Fists clenched at his sides, he counted slowly to twenty, willing the fire in his veins to calm. It took more willpower than he knew he had to lie still instead of sprinting after her. The kiss was a gift. A sweet, sexy gift he didn't want to throw away by going too fast.

She hadn't come to his room with the intention of seducing him; that much had been clear by the surprise on her face. The taste of her lingered on his tongue and he forced himself to count again, reaching fifty this time before he got himself under control.

The groan and clank of old pipes startled him and he opened his eyes as he listened to the water hiss

149

through them. Her little bathroom lay just the other side of the wall. His wash kit perched on the window ledge in there mixed together with the myriad bottles and tubes all women seemed to accumulate. He'd felt a bit strange going into her room but it was the only working bathroom on the top floor. At least he'd kept his eyes to himself, crossing her bedroom as quickly as possible whenever he went in there.

An image of Mia slipping into the roll-topped tub filled his head and he buried his head in the pillows with a groan. Being so close to her was torture. With a sigh, he sat up and threw his pillow towards the foot of the bed in frustration. He needed a distraction. Dragging his laptop back over, he did his best to focus on the images on the screen rather than the ones in his mind.

The ache in his neck from leaning forward too long forced him to stop in the end, and he put the laptop into shutdown mode and stowed it on the bedside cabinet. There was no sound from next door, and he frowned trying to recall if he'd heard the bath emptying. He strained his ears for some sign of movement next door, but heard nothing. He was being stupid; she must have got out while he was focused on his work. Crawling under the covers with a tired sigh, he clicked the lamp off and shut his eyes.

Bollocks.

Daniel threw back the quilt and crept quietly from his bed and down the hall. The door to Mia's bedroom stood slightly ajar, soft light shining through the gap. He peered through, hoping she didn't catch him acting like some Peeping Tom. The bed lay undisturbed, so he nudged the door a bit wider and took a careful step into the room. A neatly folded pair of pyjamas sat on the foot of the bed. 'Mia?'

No answer. He crossed to the bathroom and tapped lightly on the door. 'Everything all right?' What if she'd slipped over and banged her head or something? Filled with trepidation he turned the handle, raising a hand to his chest in relief at the sight greeting him.

Mia lay in the tub, head pillowed on a folded towel, fast asleep. A few stray bubbles lingered on the surface of the water. He crouched beside the tub, keeping his eyes on her face rather than the blurred outline of her body. 'Hey, sleepyhead,' he murmured.

Long dark lashes blinked slowly at him. This close, he could see the ring of dark grey edging the deep brown of her irises. A frown creased her brow. 'Did I fall asleep?'

'Mm-hmm. Come on, you must be freezing.' Keeping his eyes averted, he stood up to grab a bath towel from the rail and held it out to her. Water sloshed and the drain began to gurgle as she pulled the plug and climbed out. He engulfed her in the towel and rubbed her dry with more vigour than finesse.

Satisfied once her skin was pink and glowing, Daniel fetched her pyjamas, leaving the room again to let her dress in private. He glanced around the bedroom, not sure whether he should leave or wait for her to emerge. Deciding he had trespassed enough, he took a step towards the door. The soft gleam of the bedside

151

lamp caught the edge of a silver-framed photo and he paused. He couldn't make out the detail, but the pose of the couple and their outfits told him it was a wedding picture. A black and white photo stood next to it and he blinked in disbelief. *It couldn't be.*

He walked around the side of the bed and picked it up. The picture was of a woman's delicate hand cradled protectively in a larger, masculine grasp. The man's thumb was caressing the thick wedding band on the woman's ring finger. The hands in the photo were not young, but creased and spotted with age and the ring she wore was scratched and nicked. It was a beautiful, simple image of enduring love. In the bottom corner of the image was a familiar scrawled word, *Fitz*.

'Oh, you're still here.' Mia padded over to his side, smiling as she saw the picture in his hand. 'Jamie gave it to me on our wedding day.'

'It's mine.' He croaked, unable to tear his eyes from the image.

'What do you mean it's yours?' She peered over his shoulder then up into his face. '*You* took this?' He didn't blame her for sounding incredulous. It seemed an impossible act of serendipity, but there was no denying it. The picture was from an early collection he'd done, a study of different hands. You could tell a person's life story by their hands his dad had always reckoned, and the collection had been an homage to him.

'Jamie said he wanted our own hands to look like that together one day. But some things are just not meant to be, I suppose.' She eased the frame from his hands and placed it carefully on the table, staring at it for a long moment before turning back to him.

'Do you believe in signs?'

He shook his head. He'd always been of a practical nature. Dreams and portents were flights of fancy to be captured through his lens, but that's where they stayed, frozen in a single moment in time. She raised her eyebrows at him and he saw something in her eyes. 'But you do?'

She shrugged. 'I don't know, maybe. Or maybe I'm just looking for something to help me find the right answer.'

She looked so forlorn, like a little girl lost in her striped pyjamas and her hair all tousled from the bath. He took her hand, rubbing her fingers, marvelling at the contrast between the softness in their skin. 'And what's the question?'

Dropping her head forward so it rested on his chest, she heaved a huge sigh. 'You're the question.'

He dropped a kiss on the top of her head, then took a step back before he did something foolish like tug her down onto the bed with him. 'Maybe you should sleep on it and see if the answer's any clearer in the morning.' *God, he hoped so.*

She gave him a nod, opened her mouth to say something and ended up smothering a huge yawn instead. That was his cue to leave her in peace. He placed a kiss on the top of her nose and lifted the bedcovers. 'Let's get you tucked in.'

Mia climbed into bed and settled onto her side. She stared up at him. 'I won't keep you dangling for ever. I just need to be sure.'

'Don't rush. I'm not going anywhere, love. If, and when, you're ready, I'll be around.' He hoped she understood he meant every word.

Chapter Fifteen

Mia was alone in the house when the phone rang. She had baking to catch up on and it was nice to take a breather from the men and have a bit of quiet time to herself. This constant indecision over Daniel was driving her to distraction. Goodness knows what he must think of her blowing hot and cold, but every time she thought she'd made up her mind some little chink from the past cropped up to unsettle her again. She dusted her hands clean on a tea towel and tucked the phone beneath her chin.

''Lo,' she said into the mouthpiece, looking down and brushing ineffectually at the flour on the front of her T-shirt.

'Mimi,' the voice on the other end of the phone quavered.

'Kiki-Dee? What is it, darling? Are you all right?' Mia's voice was sharp with concern at how sad her sister sounded.

'Oh, Mia, can you come up please? I think Mother's really ill this time. Dad is totally useless, refusing to see how bad things are. Neil is at the end of his tether and the kids have got some hideous D&V bug Matty picked up at school. And trying to organise this bloody dinner is the last thing I need. I'm... God, I'm just... Can you come? I need you, Mimi.' The sobs choked off the end of her entreaty.

'Hush, darling. Hush. Of course, I'll come. I was waiting for Mother to be released from hospital. Hang on, what dinner are you talking about? Dad said he would cancel it.' She couldn't believe he was going ahead with it and expecting Kiki to help him.

'He was going to, but Neil was so cross about it because he was banking on Dad to help him secure funding for his next grant.' Kiki's voice broke again and Mia tamped down the anger building, knowing exactly how much pressure that bastard Neil would have heaped on his wife. It had been the same since he'd stuck a ring on her finger.

He seemed to resent anything that took her time away from him, including his own children, which was something that Mia had never understood. They were two of the sweetest little souls it had ever been her delight to meet and she hated that she didn't see them as much as she wanted to.

Neil made every visit so unpleasant and Mia hadn't been in a fit state since Jamie had died to spend proper time with them without risking getting upset and upsetting them in return. Matty had not understood why Uncle Jamie was suddenly no longer around and it had broken her heart anew when she realised little Charlie was too young to remember him at all.

She pressed her forehead against the cold wall and listened to her sister sob into the phone. Kiki had always been the softest of them, the one who'd taken most to heart their dad's inability to care for them and their mother's drunken scorn. Neil had seemed a good match at first. Calm and seemingly enamoured, his flattering attention had been a balm to Kiki and she had soaked it up and slaked her desperate need to love and be loved with him. Mia had become concerned and then outright opposed to their relationship as Kiki slowly subsumed what little bit of herself was left and moulded herself into the image of the perfect wife that Neil demanded.

Sadly, it was soon apparent no matter what Kiki did, it was not quite good enough. How many times had she tried to explain to Mia why it was her own fault that Neil wasn't happy with this or that minor thing? Mia had begged her not to marry him but by that stage, her sister was so far under his thumb she wouldn't listen.

Then there had been the awful dinner party that Jamie and Mia had been invited to as a celebration of their engagement. It was clear from the moment they arrived that Neil hadn't wanted to host them and he had picked at and criticised Kiki until Mia was ready to climb over the table and throttle him. Only Jamie's hard grip on her thigh under the table had held her in her seat, but she hadn't been able to keep her mouth shut and had eventually told Neil not to fucking speak to her sister like that.

Neil had stormed out and Mia and Jamie had been ushered to the door soon after by a frantic Kiki who kept telling them over and over that it wasn't his fault. He was tired and so busy at work and it had been Kiki's selfishness for insisting on holding the meal that was to blame. Poor Neil was under pressure from the grant committee who were a bunch of short-sighted fools because they had rejected his latest project for funding.

She had been in tears as she practically shoved them out the door and ran to soothe Neil's pathetic ego. Mia had cried all the way home, the only way she could relieve the pressure of her frustration at the mess of her sister's life. Jamie had been the voice of reason, calming Mia and reminding her that her behaviour wouldn't have helped Kiki and that he was sure her sister understood why Mia was upset but that she was in such a low place that she couldn't see a way to get herself free of it.

Mia had taken a bouquet around the next day and been utterly horrified at the bruise on her sister's face.

Kiki had trotted out some excuse about slipping on the stairs and catching her face on the bannister but Mia had known that Neil had punished Kiki because of her own outburst. She had left her sister's house in a rage and had stormed straight over to the university and into Neil's office.

She'd warned Neil that if she ever saw another mark on her sister it wouldn't be the police he would have to worry about because she would do for him. She had been completely serious and from then she saw no evidence of violence on her sister, although the verbal abuse had continued. She wondered now if he'd just made sure to hit Kiki where the bruises wouldn't show. It didn't bear thinking about.

Mia made soothing sounds into the phone as the thoughts and memories swirled in her head. Eventually the storm of weeping subsided and she had a chance of being heard. 'Listen, Kiki Dee, I'm sorry I've left you in the lurch. I spoke to Dad and thought everything was under control. Can you hold on for twenty-four hours so I can sort something out?' She'd swallow her doubts and stay at her parents' place if she had to, but it would be a last resort.

There was a pause from the other end as Kiki drew in a few sniffling breaths and then she asked the obvious question. The one Mia had been avoiding. 'What about Bill and Pat? Can't you stay with them? I'm sure they'd be glad to see you.'

The mention of Jamie's parents froze her blood. Not because they had been awful to her since their son's death, the complete opposite. They had given her the love and support that her own parents had frequently failed to offer. They would understand and probably be happy to help with the kids for a couple of days as they had always been pleased to spend time with them before.

But now there was Daniel, and Mia didn't feel right about asking them for help when she was starting to move on. 'I'm not sure that's a good idea, Kiki. Things are a bit complicated at my end these days. I'll talk to you about it when I get there. Just hang on a little bit longer and I'll be there to help you, I promise.' Kiki hiccupped as she tried to keep her control and Mia promised to call again in the morning once she had sorted her arrangements out. They ended the call with their usual endearments.

Mia closed her eyes and took a deep breath. It looked like the time for hiding out and looking after only her own needs was over. The world outside was beckoning her forward and for once she felt strong and centred enough to face it. First she needed to speak to Daniel and see what he wanted to do. She felt a bit weird about leaving him alone in the house, but then she supposed it was because she had only ever pictured them there together.

She thought again about Bill and Pat. It had been too long since she had seen them and perhaps it was time to sort that out too. She picked up the phone and screwed her courage tight as she dialled their number.

'Mia, lovely girl, is that really you?' The bright greeting was enough to lift Mia's heart and she found herself smiling as though Pat would be able to see her.

'Hello, Ma, how's things? Sorry it's been so long since I called.'

'Hush, lovey. Bill and I understand perfectly how hard everything has been for you. Are you okay though? Nothing wrong is there?' The warmth and caring enveloped Mia even from a distance and she said a silent prayer of thanks that she had such wonderful surrogates in her life in Pat and Bill and now also Madeline and Richard.

Mia quietly explained about what had been happening with her parents and the state that Kiki was in trying to manage everything. She didn't have to go into all the gory details as Pat had held her through many crying sessions when she had been younger and was still trying to come to terms with the fact that her parents just didn't love their daughters the way other parents did.

'Do you want Bill to drive down and fetch you, darling? You know he wouldn't mind a bit.' There was a muffled exchange as Bill obviously heard the comment and wanted to know what was wrong.

'No, no, I'll probably come up on the train and if you can pick me up the other end, that would be great. I'll hire a car when I get up there if I need one.' Following assurance that she had a friend who could drop her off at the station at this end and a promise to text with the train times, Mia hung up and headed out to explain to Daniel that she would be away for a few days.

Mia pressed her face to the window of the train and watched the trees and fields rush past. Daniel had been brilliant about everything and had even offered to leave the house and go back to London whilst she was away. It wasn't until he had made the offer that she realised how much happier she would feel knowing that the house was being looked after. She trusted Daniel and the others implicitly.

She promised him she would be fine and said she would prefer he stayed and got on with the plans for the barn. With any luck, Luke would finish up his sketches for the harem suite and she would have something new to get stuck into when she got home. Now things were progressing, she was eager to get the house whipped into shape. They might even make it in time for the summer season.

It also made more sense to leave the car there so Daniel wasn't stranded. Madeline and Richard had called the night before and she had explained what was going on. They had promised to come over and help Daniel. Madeline had sounded pleased to have someone to fuss after and take care of. Mia couldn't believe how blessed she was with her friends and she knew that whatever happened over the next week, she had a solid base to return to. Butterfly Cove finally felt like home and the thought of what she was leaving behind would sustain her over the days to come.

Chapter Sixteen

Her in-laws were full of hugs and kisses, swooping down on the station platform and gathering her close like a long-lost daughter. It was their open affection and easy manner that Jamie had inherited and between them they had helped Mia to soften and relax her defensive shields.

They had three other sons and a brood of grandchildren, which had helped to cushion the loss of Jamie just a little. The family had rallied around and pulled Mia into their warm love and shared grief, which had helped for the first few weeks, but then she had found it too hard. Their constant presence had merely served to remind Mia of what she had lost rather than offering the solace of what she still had. Distance and perspective had helped her with that, though, and she was glad that Bill and Pat insisted on remaining a presence in her life, although a restrained and slightly distant one as that is what she had needed at the time.

It struck Mia then that she had been quite selfish in her desire to withdraw and hide and she was so grateful that they had decided to keep their door (and their arms) open to her. They had just reached the car as she turned and clutched Pat a tight hug.

'I love you, Pat, you and Bill.' Her voice was husky around the tears she was suddenly holding back. 'I'm sorry I ran away but I just had to. I'm sorry if that hurt you but I hope you can forgive me.'

Pat pulled back and clasped Mia's face tightly in her hands. 'One of the greatest gifts our Jamie gave us was you, Mia. You are as precious to us as one of our own and we completely understand why you needed to distance yourself. We missed you horribly and we just hope that you won't vanish on us again. We're dying to hear about the house and we are definitely on the list to be your first paying guests.'

Bill moved up behind them and curled his arm around Mia's shoulders, pulling her close and pressing a long and heartfelt kiss to her temple. He was a quiet man most of the time but still demonstrative and Mia felt warmed through to her toes by his solid support. She would need them over the next few days, but she knew they would never let her down.

Mia's mobile phone trilled in her pocket and they all stepped away whilst she looked at the screen. Bill placed her bag in the boot of the car and Pat ushered her into the back seat whilst she read the message from Daniel. He was claiming that Madeline was smitten with Aaron and Luke and didn't know whether to adopt them or elope with them. Mia smiled at the silliness and she looked up and caught Bill's eye in the rear-view mirror.

'That's a smile that only a man can put on a girl's face,' he said with a wink as he manoeuvred the car into the traffic.

The shock of his comment left her winded and Mia turned her hot face towards the window. She had been wondering how to broach the subject of Daniel with them. She had decided that it was something that needed to be discussed during her visit. She had never been one for lies or deceit and they had always been so decent to her that anything else felt terrible.

'I didn't mean to embarrass you, sweetie. I'm just an old fool for prying; pay me no mind. It would just do our hearts good to know that you weren't all by yourself down there. We know how much you loved our boy. We also know how he would've hated to see you so lonely and sad. If you've found some happiness, then it would please me no end.'

Mia turned back to meet his eyes as they sat at the traffic lights. It was one of the longest speeches she could remember Bill giving and she loosened her seat belt so that she could lean forward between the seats in front.

'Are you sure, Bill? I would hate to hurt you or have you think I was disrespecting Jamie's memory. It just sort of happened. I never planned it, never looked for it and now I seem to be deep into something without really knowing how I got there.'

Pat turned in her seat with a smile on her face and just the hint of moisture in her eyes. 'Tell us all about him, Mia.'

Mia sat back in her seat and explained how Daniel had come to be in her life. She paused often in the narrative as she sorted it through in her own mind. Things had become so intense so quickly and there had been so much emotional upheaval in just two short months that it was good to get some perspective on the situation.

The next few days would give Mia and Daniel both the chance to think things through and make sure that they weren't just swept up in the need for someone, anyone, to relieve their loneliness and misery respectively. Mia was coming to terms with her feelings but she was suddenly glad of the space to chew everything over in her mind.

She didn't want to talk about it with Kiki too much, worried that her own happiness would offer such a stark contrast to how bad things were for her sister. It would feel like she was rubbing her face in it, having met another good man after Jamie when Kiki was still tied to her own mistake. Although perhaps it would finally stir Kiki into doing something about her situation. Mia so wanted to drag her and the kids away from it all. Steal her away to Butterfly House to rest and heal and recuperate. It was something to consider. She would make the offer if she got the chance.

Pat and Bill were so delighted about Daniel and genuinely interested in hearing about him and the house that Mia chatted about him all through their evening meal. Pat had given her eyes a wipe when Mia had explained about Daniel being the artist who'd taken the photograph Jamie had given her. It had been an iconic moment during the wedding, at the end of his speech, so everyone in the family knew of its significance.

Bill and Pat declared themselves thrilled with the situation and extracted a promise from Mia that they could come down at Easter for a break to see how the house was progressing, meet Daniel and help where they could.

The talk turned more serious as the evening wore on and her in-laws were adamant that Mia should persuade Kiki to let Charlie and Matty come and stay with them for a few days. Mia shook her head, amazed again at their infinite capacity to love and protect her and her family.

Mia climbed the stairs with Pat whilst Bill did his rounds, checking all the windows and doors and switching out the lights. They paused on the landing outside what had always been Jamie's room and the one they had shared on their visits home. 'Would you rather stay somewhere else, darling? I never even thought about it but you can use one of the other spare rooms if you would prefer?'

Mia shook her head. 'If you don't mind then I think I would really like to stay here. So many lovely memories are just the other side of that door. It's time I gathered them back around me. It's strange but spending time with Daniel has helped me face my memories of Jamie, and I can think of him with a lighter heart again. I'm thinking more about our life together than the loss of it for the first time. Does that make sense?'

Pat smiled through her tears and gathered Mia close to her. 'He loved you so, Mia, always swore that you were the light of his soul. From that very first day that he met you. He came home from school with the stars in his eyes and told me that he'd met his future wife that day.' Mia smiled through her own tears and bade her mother-in-law goodnight.

She slipped into the familiar space and leaned back against the door. She didn't need to turn on the light; she knew the layout as well as her room at home. Mia stripped her clothes quickly and crawled under the quilt. She automatically lay on what had traditionally been her side of the bed and turned over to face the empty space that had held her first love.

The tears flowed hard and she tugged one of his pillows down into the bed and curled around it, giving in as the familiar scent of the fabric conditioner that Pat always used opened the floodgates to the past. It was a smell that she would always associate with Jamie and this house, this bed, and she wept until the worst had passed.

She knew now that it was best to roll with the storm when it hit, holding it back always made it worse when she finally slipped control of the reins. This way it was spent quickly and calm would return sooner. She cried until a particularly harsh sob made such a huge bubble of snot burst out of her nose that it made Mia laugh at the sheer disgustingness of it.

She rolled onto her back and flipped on the bedside light, fumbling for the box of tissues that the ever-mindful Pat had already placed there. After a good blow, which would have put a herd of elephants to shame, Mia calmed her breathing and rolled off the bed. She found her wash kit and pyjamas in her bag and slipped into the clothing and quietly out of the bedroom. She moved across the landing to the main bathroom.

She scrubbed her face hard and cleaned her teeth, feeling much better as she poured herself a glass of water. She hesitated in the hall, as Bill stood shadowed in the master bedroom doorway. 'All right?' he asked quietly and Mia gave him a nod and an honest, if slightly watery smile. He narrowed his eyes at her as he took stock before nodding his head once and then retreated, closing the door behind him.

Mia crawled back under the covers, mobile phone in hand. There were another couple of chatty, funny texts from Daniel and she replied with a brief message that she was fine, a little blue, but glad she was there. The phone beeped, signalling a reply.

I miss you
I miss you too x
Sleep tight <3 xxx
You too xxx

Mia placed the phone on the bedside cabinet and turned the light off. She switched the damp pillow next to her for a fresh one and cuddled into it as she played her favourite memories of Jamie through her mind. She stared into the backs of her eyelids and built her favourite images of him.

He was turning back to look at her, always a bit ahead of her due to his long legs and swift step. That was how she so often pictured him. Half turned, hand stretched out towards her, urging her to catch up, his sandy hair blowing in the breeze and his eyes squinting in the bright sunlight. Always in a hurry, her Jamie, it had been a source of constant good-natured niggles between them.

He was too fast, she was too slow; he needed to just wait a minute, snails were overtaking her; hurry up! Just wait! To anyone else it might have sounded like an argument but it was one of those private exchanges that every couple had. Their own code, which really said: 'I love you; I'll never leave you behind.'

'I know. I love you; I'll follow you wherever you lead.'

Mia pressed her face closer into the pillow that she clutched close. 'I love you,' she whispered aloud. 'I'll always love you, Jamie, and I will always be grateful for the way you rescued me and showed me what it was to love and be loved, to be part of a proper family. I'm sorry we didn't get to continue our journey together until we could take a picture of our hands together, old and aged, marked like you wanted. I'm sorry we won't ever have sandy-haired babies and that your parents won't ever get to hold them and love them as they would have wanted to. I'm sorry for everything, but I'll never ever regret that you found me and showed me how to be the person that I always wanted to be.'

The image of Jamie in her mind sharpened into perfect focus as he laughed and beckoned her towards him. With an answering whoop of joy, Mia ran towards him and he enfolded her in his tight embrace. 'I love you, Eunomia Sutherland. You are the light of my soul, the song in my ear, the sun on my face. I always knew from that first day I saw you that you would only ever be loaned to me for a little while. I always knew that you would go on without me; that's why I was so desperate to catch you and keep you whilst I could. Be happy, Mia, hold me close in your heart, but not too tightly that there isn't room for anyone else.' He kissed her hard before he gathered her hand and they walked along the shoreline together.

In that weird way of dreams, they were on the beach at Butterfly Cove, even though Jamie had never been there. Dream Mia didn't have time for rationalisation. She was just glad to be beside him, their hands clasped, trousers rolled to the knee so that they could splash in the chilly waves that lapped the shore. They walked for hours, talking and reminiscing, and the beach stretched on endlessly. No matter how far they walked, the house stayed just on the horizon. They paused and Jamie gathered her close again. They stood wrapped in each other, their breath in unison, their hearts a matching rhythm, and Mia felt whole again.

Eventually, Jamie leaned back and kissed her softly and oh so sweetly. 'Time for you to go now, my love,' he whispered and Mia looked around to see that the steps leading from the beach to the garden were just behind her.

Slightly in shadow but his shape unmistakable, Daniel stood there, hands in his pockets as he waited patiently. Mia turned her head back to Jamie and he nodded and smiled and gestured with his head towards the steps as he took a step backwards. Mia reached for him but he just shook his head and continued to move away from her.

She looked down and her feet were sunk deeply into the sand, holding her in place. She glanced back up frantically and cried out as Jamie was barely visible in the distance. There was a warm presence at her back and she knew it was Daniel. He wrapped his arm around her chest and pulled her back to lean against him. A door banged in the distance.

Mia gasped and her eyes flew open, staring up at the familiar ceiling. She closed her eyes trying to slip back into the dream, to catch another glimpse of Jamie but it was gone. Mia wiped the damp from her cheeks and listened to the creak of the stairs as her in-laws moved around the house. Clearly her subconscious had decided that she needed some closure and had conjured the perfect scenario; although the fact that she had been handed like a baton from one contestant to another in a romantic relay made her snort at herself.

Pat was busy scrambling eggs when Mia entered the kitchen. Mia was showered and dressed, a little pale beneath her make-up, but feeling at peace with things. Pat looked over and Mia could see that her face was a little puffy also. They shared a smile of warmth and understanding but didn't speak of what had passed. They ate breakfast together and discussed the best way forward for Mia.

'I'll have to go to the hospital and see Mother, make sure that she's all right. Well, as all right as she can be. I think I'll go and do that first thing.' The last thing she wanted was to go within a mile of the Royal Brook, but now to be in the area and not check up on Vivian would be unforgivable. 'And after, I'll go over to Kiki's and see if I can persuade her to let me bring the kids back here.'

'Do you want us to come with you, dearest?' Bill was frowning in concern over the top of his paper. 'I don't want you going there alone.'

Bless his sweet heart. He'd gone with her last time. Held her hand, offered to go in alone and do the identification, but she'd felt the need to see for herself. Had carried a tiny seed of hope the police and everyone had got it wrong and Jamie was just lost somewhere, not lying on a cold slab. *Don't think about it.* 'I'll be fine, Pa. Quick in and out and then I'll be on my way.'

He frowned. 'Well, as long as you're sure?' The doubt in his voice said he was anything but, but at least he let the matter lie there.

Chapter Seventeen

Daniel sat at the kitchen table and watched Luke and Aaron both scrape the last of the gravy from their plates with thick slices of bread. Madeline was bustling around looking as pleased as punch to have a brood to take care of and Richard sat at the head of the table with a fond smile on his face as he watched his wife lift an apple crumble from the Aga. The sweet fragrance filled the room and Daniel felt his mouth water, even though he was already full to bursting from the second helping of stew that had been heaped on his plate earlier.

They had all worked hard that day, heaving stacks of furniture from inside the barn into the open air of the yard. Richard had suggested they get as much out into the light as possible so they could examine the pieces for rot and damage and to then group pieces that would work together. It had been a clear, fresh day and although they were filthy by the end of it, Daniel was sure that Mia would be pleased with the results. Luke had already selected a few pieces that would suit his plans for the back wing although he was remaining remarkably tight-lipped about exactly what those plans were.

Daniel couldn't help but smile as Madeline ruffled Luke's hair and patted Aaron on the cheek as she took their empty plates from the table and replaced them with bowls of steaming crumble and custard. He looked over at Richard and was surprised at the sadness on his face, so he leant forward to catch his eye. Richard shook himself slightly and forced a smile.

Daniel stood up from the table and casually nodded towards the back door. 'I'm going to stretch my legs for a couple of minutes before I try and tackle pudding.' Richard stood quickly and followed him, looking relieved of the chance to escape the cosy scene.

They strolled across the garden, hands in pockets, not talking in the way of men. They paused at the top of the steps that led down to the beach and Daniel drew in a great lungful of fresh, salty air. He still couldn't believe that he was here in this idyllic place and he made a mental promise to himself to not take the situation for granted.

The wind was picking up and there was a slight sting of sea spray in it. He turned and leant against the side rail and Richard turned to mirror him on the other side.

Keeping his head facing towards the water, Richard began to speak in a low voice. 'We could never have children. We tried for a few years but Madeline couldn't keep them. Not that I blame her at all, it's just one of those things. After the third time, she nearly bled to death and I went and got a vasectomy whilst she was still in the hospital recovering. I couldn't bear the thought that I would lose her and she eventually forgave me for it. It might have been different if we were of your generation. The advances in medical science are extraordinary from when we were your age, but we can't change that. When I see her with you boys, with our Mia, it fills my heart with such joy and yet I can't help mourning the loss of the family we could never have.'

Daniel stood quietly as he watched Richard blink hard, the moisture on his cheeks not entirely from the sea spray.

'I miss my dad, Richard. Miss him and Mam so much. I was so lost when I came here. I think Madeline saved my life when she gave me a lift that day at the station. I know how much Mia values you both and I want you to know that I already feel the same way. I don't know what will happen between us—you know what I want to happen, of course, and I'm hopeful she wants that too. If things work out, then maybe one day we'll be able to give you that family.'

Daniel watched as Richard drew a shuddering breath and turned to face him with a huge smile on his face. 'It would be the icing on the cake, son.' They stepped together and Daniel allowed himself to lean against Richard as they embraced. It felt good to be held and supported and he knew that it would mean a lot to Richard that he was looking to him for such support and strength.

He thought again about how close he'd come to throwing everything away on a cheap buzz and a life of false friends and hangers-on. His muscles ached and he had paint and varnish stains on his hands and yet he couldn't be happier. He'd even had his camera back out again today, capturing the stacks of dusty and damaged furniture sitting forlornly in their odd groupings in the yard. He still had it in his mind to put together an album for Mia, a memory piece of the work that had gone into transforming Butterfly House from a sad wreck into a vibrant and beautiful home.

He hoped that they would one day be able to show it to their children as a part of their history, telling them the story of how their parents had met. He knew he was getting way ahead of himself but these secret dreams of his heart were growing day by day.

Mia had been honest about going to stay with Jamie's parents and part of Daniel was terrified that she would decide she wasn't ready to move on from the past or that with a bit of distance perhaps she would find Daniel lacking in comparison to her lost love.

They'd kept in touch via text messages and he had deliberately kept his light and amusing, afraid that he would let his burgeoning feelings loose otherwise.

He didn't want to speak what was in his heart until Mia was back home and he could gauge her reaction. There was also the risk she would run a mile and he needed to be face to face with her so that he could persuade her not to.

He stood quietly in Richard's arms and allowed these doubts and fears to wash through him. Richard squeezed his shoulder tightly and Daniel raised his head to meet the older man's concerned gaze.

'You'll do right by each other, son. Just be honest with her and with yourself. If thirty years of marriage have taught me anything, it's that the secrets and unspoken doubts will spoil things. Nothing good ever came from trying to shield your partner. Trust her with your dark places.' With another squeeze on his shoulder, Richard steered them both back towards the warmth of the kitchen where Madeline and her delicious crumble awaited them.

They entered the cosy glow of the kitchen. The wave of warmth made Daniel shiver. It was strange how sometimes you didn't realise how cold you were until after you got somewhere warm. Aaron was tapping away on his phone and Luke and Madeline were huddled together, foreheads almost touching as they perused some of the sketches Luke had put together for the suite. Madeline glanced up to wink at Richard briefly before she turned her whole attention back to Luke.

Daniel was glad that she had drawn his friend out. She had that way about her that made people surrender under the onslaught of her sweet determination. Like a fragrant, linen-clad steamroller, Madeline just kept on coming until she flattened your barriers. She was the perfect foil to Luke's mother—Aaron's wicked stepmother. Daniel had met her a few times when he'd accompanied Aaron on trips home during half-terms and holidays. They had ventured north to his own parents more frequently and Daniel understood why. The no-nonsense, unconditional love he'd had waiting for him was so unlike the brittle cold war that was waged daily at the Spenser home.

It was an age-old story of love that never quite lived up to expectations. Cathy had wanted Brian Spenser since the first moment he had sat down at the table that she and her best friend Trisha had been sharing in the Student Union bar at university. Brian had only had eyes for Trisha, and she had fallen for his easy charms hook, line and sinker. As soon as they had graduated, he'd whisked Trisha away to a life of wedded bliss in Somerset and there they had stayed.

Their perfect life had only been further enhanced by their perfect baby boy and Cathy had smiled and seethed her way through the christening, godmother to a baby that in the darkest reaches of her bitter heart should have been her own. It had been tragic when just a few years later, Trisha had been diagnosed with breast cancer. An evil disease that had eaten away her body, but not her bright, beautiful spirit. Cathy had put everything aside to help her friend in her last few weeks.

It was only natural that Brian should turn in his grief to the friend who had supported them both, who knew them both so well. Cathy had offered him the comfort of her body. She did everything to show Brian how perfect a replacement she could be for Trisha, taking such great care of Aaron, giving him all the love that he needed as the poor little boy tried to understand why Mummy wasn't there anymore.

It had been for Aaron more than himself that Brian had finally submitted and married Cathy. He'd tried to hide it, tried to love Cathy as she deserved but too much of his heart had died with Trisha. Aaron was the blessing in his life, the picture of his mother, and the more that Brian doted on him, the more resentful Cathy became.

She fell pregnant, determined to provide a better child for Brian, one who would draw his love away from Aaron and towards them, towards her. She had never understood that Brian had an infinite well of love when it came to his boys and he had adored them both in equal measure.

Thwarted again, the dreams of perfection that she had built in her mind were in tatters and Cathy blamed Aaron for everything. If he had just not been there, reminding Brian of Trisha every day, then Cathy knew Brian would love her the way he was supposed to. The way the hero did in books, the way Brian always had in her twisted fantasy life.

She'd only ever seen the superficial veneer of Brian and Trisha's life together. The brave face that all couples show to the world. Married life was hard. They'd had their ups and downs like all relationships, but they had worked together to find their common ground and built a strong foundation upon it. Cathy had never seen the tears, the silences, the misunderstandings that are a part of all family life, so she compared her small disappointments to a false idol of perfection that had no basis in reality.

Aaron had been too young to understand at first. He only knew that Mummy was in heaven, an abstract idea that seemed to him like a special holiday place that only grown-ups got to visit. He loved Cathy because she had been so warm and comforting, holding him when the dreams were bad and letting him cry on her shoulder. Daddy let him cry too, but he tried not to do it too often in front of him as he didn't like to make Daddy even more upset.

He tried to be a good boy for Cathy, to clean his teeth and tidy his room. He painted her pictures and made her cards to say thank you and at first she had delighted in his efforts. That had started to change about a year after Daddy had married Cathy and Aaron had turned five.

Slowly, but surely, Aaron started to be a bad boy, to get things wrong and make Cathy angry; although he never understood quite what it was that he did that was so bad. Cathy said he had been bad, told Daddy he had been bad, and Aaron had to try harder to be good.

When Luke came along, Aaron had been pleased because Cathy didn't have time to tell him off and find fault so much. She was too wrapped up in the new baby and Aaron loved Luke for lots of reasons, not least because he made Daddy smile more.

The pattern had continued throughout his childhood; Aaron could do no right, Luke could do no wrong and Brian just loved both his boys. Luke had followed Aaron around from the moment he was first aware of him, initially with his big brown eyes and then on his belly as soon as he could crawl. Like a magnet, his first hesitant steps had been towards his big brother and Cathy had yet another reason to hate him.

It was a testament to their father that his determination to treat both boys as equals had helped to negate the poisonous games that Cathy played. Aaron had realised by the time he was around nine that there was nothing he could do to please her, but he never stopped trying. He stayed out of her way as much as possible and focused on his dad and his baby brother.

He was not a natural rebel. That eagerness to please had stayed with him so he diligently made Cathy Mother's Day cards and picked pretty flowers that he thought would make her smile. The cards would be hidden on the mantelpiece behind a vase; the flowers went unwatered and soon graced the compost heap. The report cards he bought home full of praise and high marks were glanced at without comment, unless there was a chance for Cathy to point out a weakness, some small failing that she would latch on to and raise for weeks on end.

Aaron was gifted at sports and his dad had urged him towards team games where he could make friends and shine. Rugby was a firm favourite and Dad and Luke had bounced around on many a muddy touchline, cheering him on. Luke had of course wanted to follow him, and had happily laughed down the fact that although good, he was never quite in his brother's class.

The escape to university had been a relief. Aaron was too old by then to sit quietly whilst Cathy twisted another one of her barbs into his psyche. Luke had started to notice and jumped to Aaron's defence, making things worse as Cathy saw this as more evidence of wrongdoing on Aaron's part.

Luke had always submitted peaceably to his mother's smothering attentions. He had been cosseted and spoiled by her from day one and yet somehow he had remained a stoic, happy child. He loved his mum and dad, but Aaron was his number one and he'd never let him down. Always been there to offer a steadying hand, fend off the bullies and teach Luke everything from how to tie his shoelaces to how to talk to girls.

When Aaron went away to university, Luke had been lost for a while, not quite sure which direction to turn in now that his lodestone was absent. His father had stepped in and provided the guidance that he needed to steer a straight path and Aaron had made sure to keep in contact every day until Luke had settled down again.

Luke had latched on to Daniel as a natural extension of his brother and had followed them to London, to the same university that they had graduated from. His frequent trips into London to visit Aaron had triggered his love of buildings and architecture. Luke had roamed the streets for hours, seeking out the old and the new: the graceful airy charms of the Georgian town houses and the concrete monstrosities of the experimental Sixties and Seventies. He had explored them all and loved them all for the stories that they whispered in his ear.

Daniel stayed by the kitchen door, his attention on Aaron who was seemingly lost in the scrolling world of his internet connection, but Daniel knew better. Like a hound on point, Aaron was focused intently on the interaction between Madeline and Luke, alert for any hint of spite or unpleasantness.

Daniel wondered if Aaron himself understood just how wary of women his upbringing had made him. There had been some mild flirtation with Mia, but only because Aaron knew that she was taken and therefore no threat to his heart. Unlike Madeline. She could bust Aaron's shell right open and give him the kind of maternal affection the man was aching for but would never admit to wanting.

Daniel wondered how long the scars of the past would stand against the tide of love that carried Madeline through life and he decided that Aaron didn't stand a chance. He was glad that he had brought his friends to Butterfly Cove and was determined to drag them back as often as possible under whatever spurious excuses he could concoct. These friends of his needed a safe harbour too.

Chapter Eighteen

Her parents had always been good at maintaining an outward façade, their public face so different to that behind closed doors. She was sure that some of her father's colleagues suspected that there was more than met the eye. No-one could be quite as delicate as her mother allegedly was, although they nodded sympathetically when she had to go home early because she had a dizzy spell. It was usually the quarter bottle of vodka in her purse that made her head spin, but most times she would make it through the main course before succumbing to one too many trips to the bathroom.

Mia paused at the nurse's station. She was outside of visiting hours but hoped for a sympathetic hearing. A bare-faced lie about having been away and rushing back as soon as she could earned her a pat on the shoulder. A kindly nurse ushered Mia into the private side ward her mother was in. She swallowed hard and braced herself before crossing the threshold. Her mother looked small in the bed, propped up stiffly with too many pillows, her plaster-encased leg raised in a sling to keep the weight off it.

She hadn't seen her since Jamie's funeral when a furious Nee had shoved her into the back of the car and driven off with her after a visibly drunk Vivian had staggered into a floral display in the crematorium and knocked it over. It had just been another horror in a day of epic shocks and horrors, and Mia had been too distraught to care much. Those who had mattered on the day already knew all her family's secrets and she didn't have the energy to care about the opinion of those who hadn't.

Mia stepped closer and studied her mother, looking for the beauty beneath the swollen eyes and broken veins on her cheeks. Vivian had been a stunner in her heyday, turning all the boy's heads, including studious, unworldly George Thorpe. He had been totally captivated by her, obsessive and relentless in his pursuit, according to one of her mother's rambling reminiscences. Vivian had only agreed to go on a date with him because he wouldn't leave her alone and she hoped to let him down gently. He'd been so attentive and flattering that Vivian had been caught up in his image of her as this siren, this creature of myth that was drawing George to his doom.

He had been so unlike her other boyfriends and his outlandish comparisons of her to goddesses and heroines of the past had fed her ego to bursting. Her parents had encouraged the match, glad that their daughter had found a serious, worthy man and not some rake who would fleece her considerable inheritance.

Before she knew it, Vivian was married to George, pregnant and living in a small house that was attached to his junior teaching position at the university. No servants, no parties or holidays while he was busy climbing the academic career ladder. Worse still, not having had a lot of money growing up, George had fastened his grip firmly on her money and tied it up in investments and savings bonds.

Vivian's new allowance barely covered her regular hair appointments—never mind the shopping sprees she'd been used to. George didn't understand why she needed so many clothes. Who was she dressing up for? Who was she trying to impress? Terrified that Vivian would be lost to him, he desperately tried to change all the things about her that had attracted him in the first place.

Vivian wasn't a scholar; she was a beauty. It was all she was, all she knew how to be from a young girl when she had been dressed up and primped and presented to her parents' friends like a perfect little doll. She didn't possess much of a personality or wit; no-one had ever had any expectations of her other than as a decoration and Vivian didn't know how to do anything other than be pretty and spend her time doing all the things that went into making her pretty.

The more paranoid George became, the more distant he grew, and Vivian had no defence against it, having only ever been cosseted and spoilt. She sought solace in her evening cocktails, which soon became lunchtime martinis and then bucks fizz or vodka and orange with breakfast.

She had never bonded with Mia. Suffering from a mild case of the baby blues and not used to being the responsible party in any situation, she had been totally out of her depth. She had never wanted to be bothered with the baby and could only lament at the changes to her body. The other two girls had followed; Kiki less than a year later had been a complete accident—something Vivian made a point of mentioning over the years. Nee had followed some three years after. At that point, Vivian had moved to her own room and refused to let George near her again.

She had been a distant figure throughout their childhoods. A succession of housekeepers had kept them clothed and fed and settled into a routine, but there was no-one to kiss a scraped knee or check their homework or soothe them after a bad dream. Vivian had spent more and more time in her room and George had spent more and more time at work, his distance from his wife extending to his girls as he sought solace in his studies. His reputation grew until he had become one of the foremost scholars of ancient Greece in the country.

'Hello, Vivian,' Mia said quietly and her mother blinked and tried to focus on the intruder in her room.

'Who's that? Alice, is that you?' Mia moved closer and leaned in so her mother could see it was her daughter and not her own sister.

'No, it's Mia; how are you, Mother?' She rarely called her by that title, her mother preferring Vivian as they grew up. She hadn't wanted her own age to be judged by that of her children.

'Oh, Mia, where have you been? Where's that lovely husband of yours?'

Mia glanced upwards and suppressed a shiver. It seemed like Vivian had finally drowned her memory in the bottom of a glass. 'Jamie's dead. He died more than two years ago in a car accident, remember?' The words came out harsher than she intended, and she softened slightly at the confusion on Vivian's face.

She perched on the edge of the bed and took her mother's hand. 'How are you feeling, Vivian? What happened to your leg? Did you take a tumble?' Her mother started to thrash on her pillow and Mia leaned closer and pressed a hand to her shoulder, trying to still the restless movement.

She watched helplessly as Vivian's face crumpled and tears spilled over her cheeks. 'He pushed me; Georgie hates me so, he pushed me, he pushed me,' she muttered and Mia reared back in shock.

A nurse bustled in at that moment without even a knock on the door frame. She strode over to the bed and fiddled with the drip that was plugged into the back of Vivian's hand. 'Pay her no mind, now. Your poor father, it breaks his heart when she comes out with such things. She doesn't know what she is saying half the time, sees people from the past he reckons. People she hasn't seen since she was a girl. She calls me Katherine; your father says she was her best friend, but they haven't seen each other in years. Try not to let it upset you. The doctor says it might just be the shock of the fall.'

Mia tried to gather her wits about her as the nurse rambled on. Was it true what the nurse was saying—that her mother was just talking nonsense? Or had her father somehow been the cause of her accident? It wouldn't be the first time Vivian had taken a tumble due to the amount of alcohol in her veins and her father had never raised his hand to his wife. Not that she'd even seen. She watched as the nurse fiddled with the gauge feeding the drip on her mother's hand and Vivian soon began to calm. Her lashes fluttered close across the paper-thin skin of her face and her grip on Mia's hand slackened.

Mia rose and gathered her bag and jacket, desperate to be out of the blank impersonal room and away from the smell of antiseptic and illness. She briefly considered kissing Vivian's cheek, but only because she knew the nurse would expect a show of daughterly affection.

Mia was past pretending that all was sweetness and light in the Thorpe family. It was time to stop caring so much about the judgements of strangers. She thanked the nurse for making Vivian comfortable and took her leave. It was time to face the second unpleasant visit on her schedule.

Mia dropped her head wearily onto the kitchen table and knocked it against the wood a few times in frustration. It had been a horrendous day and she knew it wasn't over yet. Bill placed his hand on the top of her head for a moment before he carried on past and flicked the switch on the kettle. He was of the old-school opinion that there wasn't much that couldn't be improved with a nice cup of tea.

Pat was upstairs trying to settle Matty and Charlie into the same spare room they had stayed in whenever they had been at Bill and Pat's before. Matty was very quiet and Mia knew that she would need to try and have a talk with him sooner rather than later. The poor boy had barely spoken since Mia had arrived to find Kiki in floods of tears because she had managed to burn the meal she was cooking and because she'd had almost no sleep for forty-eight hours because the kids had been so sick. They were still under her feet having only just recovered from the stomach bug they'd been suffering from.

Charlie had latched on to Mia like a limpet, only releasing her grip long enough to be put into the back of Mia's hire car. Matty had not protested when Mia told him to go and put a few clothes together and find his and Charlie's toothbrushes.

Mia had managed to get Kiki to stop crying long enough to comprehend that she was taking the kids for a couple of days. She'd told Kiki to find the menu so that Mia could order a takeaway for supper in the hopes that Neil would be partially assuaged by the fact that there was something to eat when he got home from work.

Kiki had mumbled a few protests about the children needing to be back at school the next day but Mia put her foot down. It was Thursday already so missing Friday wouldn't be that big a deal and she would keep them at Bill and Pat's until Sunday evening so that Kiki could get some sleep and get the house sorted out.

At the reminder that it was Friday the next day, Kiki had paled in horror over the impending dinner party. Mia had agreed to go back to Kiki's the next morning and help her with the planning. She hated Neil and couldn't give a damn about him or the bloody party, but Kiki looked ready to break so she had grit her teeth and promised to be there.

Mia knocked her head against the table again and knew that she didn't have any choice in the matter. She would have to speak to her dad and take over the running of the party for him. Her phone buzzed in her pocket, causing Mia to startle and bump her head more firmly on the table. She sat up, rubbing her forehead as she fumbled her phone from her pocket.

It was a text from Daniel and Mia suddenly longed to hear his voice. 'I'm just going to make a quick call, Bill, and then I'm going to need you and Pat to help me with a council of war.'

'Who's the enemy?' Bill grinned viciously at her, seeming pleased with the prospect of going into battle with anyone who had hurt his girl.

'My brother-in-law and his fellow arselickers from the university's history department,' Mia said, her voice dripping with sarcasm.

'No-one who matters then, lovey. No-one who matters a jot.'

Mia laughed out loud, her burdens suddenly lighter and more manageable. Bill was right, Neil and his cronies didn't matter. Only Kiki and the children did and she would do whatever was necessary to help them.

'Mia, love, what a lovely surprise to hear from you. Are you all right?' The reassuring rumble of Daniel's voice was another balm to her weary heart as she made herself comfortable on the back step. It was cold out, but the late afternoon sun was warm on her face as she closed her eyes and raised her head like a flower seeking nourishment.

'A difficult day, Daniel, but I don't want to talk about it just yet. Tell me what you've been up to. I just want to listen to your voice for a few minutes.'

There was a brief pause and she knew that Daniel was wrestling with himself, wanting to push her for more detail but trying to respect her request. A soft sigh of acquiescence ghosted through the phone and he proceeded to tell her about the latest events at home. His deep voice lulled her as she pictured the scenes he described.

Her beautiful kitchen came into her mind's eye. It was her favourite room in the house, the hub around which everything else revolved. When she was lost in her cooking, Mia felt complete. It had been down to her to take care of Kiki and Nee, to make sure that all three of them had a decent meal at least. Their father ate mostly at work and provided there was a light supper waiting for him, he didn't care who had prepared it.

Mia often wondered whether her dad understood how disengaged his wife had been, and for how long. Perhaps if Mia hadn't tried to cover things up then he might have done something about it earlier. Perhaps not. It was simply unfortunate circumstances that her parents had been so wholly unsuitable a match and the children were just innocent victims caught in the fallout of their unhappy marriage.

Mia could be mostly philosophical about it when she had some physical distance from everything, but just now the ghosts of past disappointments were crowding close. It was also becoming clear to Mia that Kiki was far from okay and that her marriage was becoming increasingly difficult to bear.

A tiny part of Mia just wanted to get away from it all and hide away back at Butterfly Cove. Surely it was past time she was responsible for everything and everybody? Surely she had suffered enough of her own pain and it was time for Kiki to stand on her own two feet? Almost as soon as the thoughts formed, Mia felt sick and treacherous. She sounded like her parents: selfish, childish and self-centred.

Mia had been fortunate in her choice of husband and both Jamie and his parents had shown her what proper family life was meant to be like. Kiki had thought she would be safe and sheltered with Neil. He had seemed strong and in control. It was only once it was too late that Kiki had come to realise that Neil was weak and spoiled. A small-minded bully who needed to push others down to boost himself up. Kiki was a ready-made gift for him to exploit. Desperate for love with no real sense of self, she'd been wide open and vulnerable to his flattering attentions.

With a sigh, Mia pressed the phone closer to her ear and let Daniel bring her what comfort he could from so far away.

'So, what are you wearing?' he rasped and Mia burst into gales of laughter.

'Have a heart, pet. A man has needs, you know?' Daniel tried to sound hurt, but there was no disguising the laughter in his voice. His silly ploy had the desired effect and dragged Mia at least partially out of her sour mood.

'I'm going to be here for a few more days, at least the weekend, maybe longer. I'm back at Bill and Pat's and I've got the kids with me. Kiki is...' Mia felt her throat catch and she swallowed hard and tried again. 'Kiki's in a bad place and I need to do what I can to help her. I've got to sort this dinner out for Dad, much as it pains me to do anything to help Neil and his stupid friends.' She paused and then decided to share the selfish thought she'd had earlier.

'I don't want to be here; I don't want to deal with all this shit. I just want to come home and lie in bed with you and weave our future plans. Oh hell, Daniel, I'm such an awful sister to feel like this but I just can't seem to help it.' Her last words were barely a whisper and she bit hard into her lip to stop any more spilling out.

'Hush now, hush, darling. There is nothing wrong with feeling the way you do. We're all pretty selfish at heart. We all struggle and strive for the things we want and feel disappointed when we don't get our own way. You didn't hesitate when Kiki called you, did you? You dropped everything and ran to help her. Even though it meant dealing with some of your own pain by seeing Jamie's parents, you did it without complaint. Well, maybe a little bit of complaint, but that's what I'm here for, sweetheart. I'm in it for the good and the bad. Look at what you did for me. You didn't want me and my mess interfering with your life, but you didn't turn me away.'

Mia nodded along with Daniel's words. He was right and she was being silly. Feeling guilty for not doing more to help Kiki in the past. This time she would make it right; she would fix what was wrong with her sister.

'Do you want me to come up? The guys have got to head back to town this weekend ready for work on Monday so I can close up the house and come to you if you need me.'

Oh, how tempted Mia was to jump at his offer. If Daniel came up then she could lean on him, let him carry the burdens of her past. She didn't want to be the responsible adult; she wanted to be the needy child. She opened her mouth to say *Yes! Yes, come and sort this mess out for me*, but she didn't. She closed her mouth and drew a deep breath. Daniel had his own issues to deal with, his own past and secrets and messes to resolve, and it hadn't been many weeks ago that he'd been brought low by the weight of it all.

Mia had never been one to shovel her burdens onto another person, not even with Jamie. He'd given her his love and support, but she hadn't depended on him, had never depended on anyone other than herself to make things right. She was the big sister, the coper, the manager, and that wasn't about to change now. Mia would not surrender herself up to another person that way. Her mother had done it, so had Kiki when it came to it, but not Mia.

Stubborn, mouthy, interfering: all labels her brother-in-law and others had thrown at her in scorn. All parts of her personality she carried with pride.

'I'll be all right, Daniel. It makes me feel good to know that you would come to me if I need it, but I'm really okay. This is really okay, well it's not, but I'm going to make it okay.' With every word, her voice grew more determined, more certain. 'I would rather you stayed there and carried on working on the house. Hold our dreams fast for me, Daniel. Hold them tight and keep working towards them and that will give me the strength that I need.'

'If you're really sure?'

'I am.'

'Okay then, now back to my previous question: what are you wearing?'

Chapter Nineteen

Mia sat propped up in bed, grateful again that Pat and Bill had a brood of grandchildren so they had naturally swung into action dealing with Matty and Charlie. Bill had distracted Matty with card games and riddles. Pat had breezed around the kitchen with Charlie glued to her hip, recognising that the little girl felt a bit lost and in need of lots of kisses and cuddles.

Mia had been happy to rattle around, putting together a simple supper for the children and a more elaborate meal for her in-laws, the least she could do to say thank you. It was a credit to her mother-in-law that she recognised Mia's need to be helpful and had surrendered her kitchen, happy to find whatever Mia needed, set the table, rinse dishes. Play the supporting role.

The children had been settled into the bedroom next door. It was set up with a couple of single beds as well as a cot and it was full of toys and games.

Glow stars on the ceiling and a night light by the door helped to settle the children down and Mia had happily read them stories until they had drifted off.

Bill and Pat had planned a trip to the local wildlife park for the next day; it would keep the children occupied and give Mia the chance to focus on Kiki and the dreaded dinner party at her father's. Mia was planning the menu, a few options for each course as well as a vegetarian alternative. She was wondering whether her father would appreciate the humour in a pastiche of the archetypal seventies' dinner party when a noise at her door caught her attention. She had left the door slightly open and she could see a shadowy outline.

'Matty, darling, is everything all right?'

The door pushed open wider and her nephew stood there, clutching his sister's chubby little hand and shifting his weight from foot to foot uncertainly. Mia put her notepad on the bedside cabinet and lifted the edge of the quilt up, shifting across as she did so. She smiled and patted the warm bit of the bed invitingly, nodding her head in encouragement.

'We're not supposed to get out of bed, but Charlie had a bad dream and she didn't remember where she was.' Matty spoke softly, his eyes cast down as though waiting to be scolded.

Mia looked over Matty's lowered head at his little sister who seemed perfectly fine if a bit sleepy.

'I was feeling very lonely,' Mia said as she held her hand out towards them. 'You would be doing me a big favour if you would come and keep me company for a bit.'

Matty looked up shyly and Mia forced herself to hold her smile at the worry she saw in the little boy's eyes. She wondered if it was Neil who had made his son so afraid to seek comfort in the night. She could not imagine Kiki would ever turn her children away.

'Come on, you two. I'm letting all the heat out; jump up now.' That last little bit of encouragement was all that was needed before Mia was overwhelmed by two wriggly, chilly little bodies that tried to burrow in as close as possible. With a bit of shifting around, including Mia lifting Charlie across her, she soon had one child tucked on either side of her and they snuggled deeply under the quilt.

Charlie sighed, clutched a handful of Mia's top, and dropped off almost immediately. Matty lay there, very still, but Mia could tell that he was still awake. She turned her head and pressed a kiss to the top of his head.

'What's up, doc?' she said softly and was rewarded with a little giggle. It had been a favourite phrase of Jamie's and the way he had always greeted Matty. Matty turned on his side and curled his little arm across Mia's middle, resting his head in the crook of her shoulder.

'Do you miss Uncle Jamie?' he whispered and Mia felt her heart clutch.

'I miss him every day, darling. Every single day.' She took a deep breath and screwed her courage tight. Matty clearly had something on his mind and she would have to eat her own pain to help him through.

'Do you miss him, Matty? You know that he didn't mean to leave us, don't you? That it was just a horrible accident?'

'Daddy said that Uncle Jamie would be glad.' Mia bit the inside of her cheek, hoping that Matty had misunderstood something he had overheard rather than it being another example of Neil's cruelty and spite.

'Uncle Jamie would be glad about what, darling?' It was a battle to keep her voice gentle and even.

'Glad about being free from you, Aunty Mia, but I don't understand what he meant. He said you are a hairy dean. What's one of them? You don't seem hairy to me.' Matty sat up and stared quizzically at Mia and she swallowed hard as a bomb exploded in her brain.

'I think your daddy said that I am a harridan, which isn't true. Your daddy thinks I speak too much and should be quiet and nice like your mummy. I'm not very good at keeping quiet though, Matty, but your Uncle Jamie never minded that.'

'I wish Daddy wasn't so loud. He makes Mummy cry when he tells her off. She thinks I don't see her, but I know that she cries. Her face gets very white and her nose goes all red.'

It was one of those horrible moments when Mia hated that she was the grown-up and she would have to pick her way carefully through the minefield the conversation with her nephew had become. 'Is Daddy loud a lot, Matty? Is he loud at you and Charlie or just Mummy?' Mia clamped down on her anger, determined to let this poor little boy have a safe place to voice his worries and fears.

'He gets loud if I've done something wrong, like if I don't get top marks in a test or if I make too much noise when he is trying to work. He doesn't like it if Charlie cries and he blames Mummy for not looking after her properly. I don't get things wrong as often as Mummy does. She's stupid. I don't think she is stupid—she always helps me with my homework—but Daddy says she is stupid. That's what he calls her, like it's her name.'

Mia swallowed hard against the bile that suddenly burned in the back of her throat. She felt physically sick at the images that her nephew was painting of his life at home. He was only seven years old and already being damaged by Neil's abhorrent behaviour. She placed her hand on the back of Matty's head and urged him to settle back down against her. She stroked his soft, sweet hair lightly and tried not to let him see how angry she was.

'Don't worry about anything, sweet boy. I'm going to help your mummy tomorrow.'

Matty sighed and snuggled closer. Mia muttered under her breath: 'And if your daddy thinks I'm a hairy dean, he ain't seen nothing yet.'

Mia raised her hand to her sister's front door, hesitated, then knocked harder than she'd originally intended. There was nothing about today that she was looking forward to but delaying the inevitable was pointless. The door swung open and Mia flinched at her sister's pale, pasty face. Her eyes were bloodshot and swollen and her waist-length hair trailed lank and greasy down her back. Kiki attempted a watery smile, which got stuck somewhere along the way, and Mia stepped around her and inside the house, pushing the door gently shut before she gathered Kiki into her arms.

Kiki seemed to lose all ability to hold herself up as she melted into Mia's arms, leaving her no choice but to lower them both to the floor. Kiki buried her head in Mia's lap and sobbed. The wracking shudders of her body shattered Mia's heart as she bent low over her sister's head and stroked her back. She whispered quietly to Kiki, told her how much she loved her, how sorry she was that she had left her alone, that it would be okay now. In the end that was all she could repeat over and over: 'It'll be okay now.'

The storm passed as quickly as a summer squall and Kiki soon quieted. Mia continued to soothe and stroke her sister until she finally raised her head and loosed an undignified sniff, which made them both giggle weakly. Mia pressed her forehead to Kiki's and drew a deep breath. She'd always believed it was better to lance a wound than leave it to fester and she had a feeling these would not be the last of her sister's tears that day.

She pulled back to clasp her sister's face and stare into her eyes. 'All right for a minute? Let's get the kettle on and work out what needs to be done today.'

Kiki tried to draw a settling breath, coughed and made a second, better attempt. She nodded and pushed herself to her feet, clasping Mia's hand and drawing her up. Kiki kept hold of her hand as they entered the kitchen and she sank into the nearest chair, as though that small effort had overwhelmed her again.

Mia patted her hand before freeing her own and bustling around the kitchen, putting on the kettle and brewing them both an industrial-strength cup of tea. There were days when Mia wished she had developed a taste for coffee but she had never accustomed her palate to the bitter brew. She plunked the cups down on the table and drew her notepad and a pen from the depths of her shoulder bag. She pushed one of the mugs up against Kiki's fingers until she wrapped them around the hot mug and then nodded once.

'Okay, let's get started...'

'The kids?'

'They are okay. We had a sleepover in my bed and they are fine. Bill and Pat have taken them to the wildlife park and will keep them for the rest of the weekend.' Mia raised her hand when Kiki sought to protest and her words died on her lips. 'Matty and Charlie will stay with them for the rest of the weekend. The kids need some downtime too, Kiki. You need to pull yourself together before you see them again. Matty is worried sick about you. Charlie is confused but hopefully too young to understand what's going on.'

Mia took a mouthful of hot tea and relished the burn as she pressed on. 'Matty tells me that Neil has a nickname for you.' Kiki flinched and Mia shook her head as her worst fears were realised. 'Your husband calls you Stupid. In front of the children. And you let him.' She paused between each statement, feeling awful at witnessing her sister's pain but determined to have everything out in the open.

Kiki didn't speak. She just kept her eyes lowered to the mug of tea in front of her and Mia wanted to shake her. How had she allowed herself to become so beaten down, so cowed by life? Even in the depths of her grief over Jamie's death there had been an indomitable part of Mia's spirit that had driven her forwards.

Kiki seemed to have no spark, no sense of purpose left, and it made Mia furious to behold it. She couldn't honestly say whether her anger was aimed at her sister or Neil. Both probably, and her parents too for being such useless role models when they were growing up.

Kiki had always been the softest of them, the sweetest of hearts and therefore so easily damaged. Their mother took full advantage of it when they were older, pleading with Kiki to help her ease the pain of whatever non-existent ailment she was claiming. Just a little nip, just a small shot to help her sleep, and Kiki couldn't refuse. She couldn't or wouldn't see the manipulative gleam in Vivian's eye when she got her way and Kiki snuck her a drink.

Mia had tried to persuade her father to remove the alcohol from the house but he refused to acknowledge the problem, hiding from the truth in his study. *Bloody coward.* An unexpected wave of anger swamped her. If George had only stood up to Vivian, things might have been different.

Kiki had been prime fodder for the likes of Neil. A few years older, originally a protégé of their father's, he had paid small flattering attentions to Kiki. A CD he thought she would enjoy, a ragged posy of flowers. All he could afford so he claimed and Kiki had swallowed every sweet thing that he said, desperate for affection and validation. Neil had seemed harmless enough at first and Mia had not discouraged his attentions towards her sister, as it was just a relief to see her smile and blossom a little.

Kiki was the prettiest of the three of them—it did no harm to Mia's ego to acknowledge it. But Kiki had never been able to see it for herself. Her modesty and shyness had drawn Neil, who lapped it up every time Kiki looked at him with such devotion. Her desperation fed his ego and before anyone knew what was happening, the couple were away to the registry office and married.

Jamie had courted Mia whilst they were still at school and Mia had been too caught up in her own happiness to recognise that all was not well in her sister's marriage until it was too late. Kiki was pregnant and Neil was furious at the extra expense on his modest salary. He had made it clear that he blamed Kiki for the problem.

After the baby had been born, Kiki had revelled in motherhood, finally able to connect with a being who would love her unconditionally and who she could love equally in return without fear of reprisal.

Neil, however, did not take well to the loss of Kiki's attention and began to sulk and pick at her, in an effort to get it back. Still in love with him and inured to years of being the one at fault, Kiki took it all to heart and soon believed that everything that was wrong in her marriage was down to her. *She didn't work, so why didn't she have time to get everything in the house straight? How difficult was it to make sure that there was a meal waiting for Neil when he got home? Why hadn't she noticed that his suit needed dry-cleaning when he had an important meeting?*

The more he undermined her, the more useless Kiki felt, and the last shreds of her confidence deserted her. Whilst Mia could understand and rationalise how things had ended up so bad, it was time to put a stop to it now that the children were starting to be affected by Neil's behaviour. She would not allow history to continue repeating itself and she was damned if she would let Kiki be the victim any longer.

'So I assume Neil has issued an edict on the food for tonight. Do you have everything we need or do

I need to make a shopping list?' Mia kept her voice brisk. There was too much to get sorted out so she would not press Kiki too hard for the minute.

Kiki didn't speak, just continued to stare into her tea and Mia scrubbed at her hair to give her hands something to do other than reach across the table and shake her sister until she rattled. 'Kiki!' Her sister flinched so hard she spilled her tea across her hand and Mia grabbed a cloth to mop it up. 'What's wrong with you, darling? You're like a zombie. I need you to focus for me, just for a little while. Can you do that? Can you help me so that I can help you?'

Mia held her sister's face and forced her to meet her gaze. The naked pain she saw there was heartbreaking but she pressed on. 'I need you with me, Kiki Dee. Okay?'

Her sister raised her hands to cover Mia's and she nodded slightly. 'Okay. Sorry, I'm okay, I'm okay.' Perhaps if she said it enough times she might even begin to believe it. 'I've got everything we need for the meal tonight. It's all in Dad's fridge already. I have a key so I was going to go over there this morning and prepare everything.'

Mia held her sigh of relief in as Kiki started to sound a little more with it and they reviewed the menu for the dinner party. Nothing too difficult or controversial, thank goodness. After a few protestations from Kiki, Mia persuaded her to go back to bed and sleep for a few hours whilst she would go to their parents' house and get everything ready.

She would also make time to call into the hospital and see their mother in the hope she would be a little more present. She accompanied her sister upstairs to make sure she had an outfit selected for that evening and laid out the clothes on Matty's bed. She wanted to give Kiki every chance to rest and gather herself together as it would be a difficult evening with her husband watching for any opportunity to pick fault.

Chapter Twenty

Mia had already decided she would stay and serve the meal. It wouldn't be much fun, but Kiki could focus on being a guest and not panic about the hosting. If anything went wrong then Neil could blame Mia, if he damn-well dared.

She pulled the hire car into the driveway and sat for a moment, staring at the familiar red-brick structure. The woodwork and garage had been painted since she was last there and they were now a bright white. The garden was immaculate but lacking in any kind of personality. Neatly weeded flower beds nestled on either side of a dark and light striped lawn. It looked like Centre Court at Wimbledon and Mia was filled with longing for the wild, untamed sprawl of the gardens of Butterfly Cove.

Her hands ached and she looked down to see her knuckles had turned white from gripping the steering wheel so hard. Forcing her fingers to uncurl, she grabbed her bag and burst from the car in a sudden fit of motion. Sitting and dwelling would only give the ghosts of her past the chance to rise and haunt her. *Keep moving. Keep active.* That was the motto; that was the mantra that would get her through.

She wiped her feet on the external mat as she turned the key in the well-oiled lock. She wiped them again on the inside mat before toeing them off and placing them neatly against the skirting board. The ingrained habit gnawed at her belly and the devil on her shoulder wanted her to stomp through the flower beds and traipse dirt along the length of the beige hallway. The devil on her shoulder was a childish little shit sometimes and she would not give in to his suggestions.

The walls were the same off-white as before, bare except for a few impersonal generic prints that were available at any department store. Nothing that reflected the personality of the inhabitants, or perhaps the blankness was a perfect reflection. No family photos rioted across the walls as they did in Bill and Pat's home, no stray coats or scarves lurked, escapees of the under-stairs cupboard. *A place for everything and everything in its place.* The strictures of her childhood came back full force.

With a little nod to the devil, Mia flung her coat over the bannister and dropped her bag untidily at the foot of the stairs. A minor rebellion, but one she could not resist. She drew in a breath and absorbed the scents of her past—furniture polish, a faint trace of her mother's perfume and the slight musty trace of the books lining the walls of her father's study. The door to the study stood ajar and Mia paused on the threshold. Her hand rested on the door as she contemplated pushing it wider and entering the inner sanctum that had always been off limits.

A noise behind her startled a shriek and Mia spun towards the front door, embarrassment flushing her face as a couple of envelopes hit the mat. Raising a shaky hand to her thudding heart, Mia shook off her nerves and pressed on down the hall towards the kitchen. *Keep moving. Keep active.*

She hadn't expected it to be quite this difficult, but the disappointing memories were nothing she couldn't handle after the horrors she'd faced in her adult years. She busied herself with preparations for that evening and resolutely ignored the whispers of the past as they swirled around the kitchen, trying to find a way into her head.

She took a break to visit her mother and wondered why she bothered as it was pretty much a replay of the previous day, only the nurse was different. Did her dad understand how far gone Vivian was? Her vague behaviour had to be from more than just shock from the accident.

Sitting next to the bed, she wondered what she was hoping to get from the encounter. She stared at her mother, traced the red lines on her face; observed her once beautiful nails now bitten to the quick. *An explanation? An apology? An acknowledgement of past failures maybe?* Whatever she was looking for, it hadn't been forthcoming as Vivian had proved as self-obsessed as ever. Mia checked her watch and wondered how much longer she needed to sit there and listen to a replay of Vivian—the early years.

She called Kiki from the hospital car park, to check in on her and make sure that she was okay getting ready for the party and was reassured by the steadiness of her sister's voice. A few hours' sleep had worked wonders and a soak in the bath had added its powers of restoration also. Satisfied that she was not needed for the moment, Mia returned to her parents' house to finalise the preparations for dinner.

A large, black saloon car squatted in the driveway and Mia felt her stomach lurch. Her dad had come home early. With a sigh and a silent, if likely futile, prayer for patience Mia parked her shiny red hire car behind his and approached the front door. She reached for the key in her pocket before changing her mind and knocking briskly. His familiar silhouette appeared in the distorted glass pane of the door a moment before it swung open and her father contemplated her in astonishment. 'What are you doing here, Eunomia?'

Mia took a moment to study him. He had aged in the past few years; the once ramrod straight spine was softening into a noticeable stoop and his always neatly trimmed hair was pure silver now. The woodsy scent of his aftershave was the same, as was the uniform—crisply pleated dark trousers, striped, collared shirt and a plain cardigan with drooping pockets where he habitually stored his daily paraphernalia of handkerchief, glasses case and notebook.

'I came because Kiki needed me so I'll be the one catering for this evening. I can't believe you let Neil talk you into hosting the party, especially after we talked about it.' She knew it wasn't entirely his fault, but seeing both her mother and sister in such a piteous state had Mia spitting mad. She shouldered past him and marched towards the back of the house.

George trailed after her, seemingly bewildered by her presence and attitude and he stood just inside the kitchen door, watching as she rinsed her hands under the tap and rolled up her sleeves. She headed over to the fridge and drew out the beef, which had been marinating for the past couple of hours. Mia paused as she glanced over at him before sliding the meat back onto the shelf and closing the fridge door. She crossed her arms and leaned back against the cold, white metal and contemplated George. 'What is it?'

'Nothing. I'm just surprised to see you here. Neil told me Dikê was happy to help. What was I supposed to do?' He at least had the decency to look embarrassed.

'Neil is a bully and Kiki wouldn't say no to anything he said—you know that.' She watched the slight flinch around her dad's eyes. Yes, he knew, or at least suspected how things lay between his daughter and son-in-law. Thoughts of the ugliness reminded her what her mother had said the previous day.

'I've been to see Mother. I think we need to look at how you're going to care for her when they release her. I couldn't make head or tail of half the things she said. She even told me at one point that you pushed her down the stairs.'

He deflated before her eyes, as though her words had stolen all the breath from his body. George stood there gasping like some bony fish hauled out on the deck. His reaction stunned her; she'd expected a flat denial, proof her mother's broken mind had conjured it up.

Mia unfolded her arms and took a purposeful step forward. George seemed to shrink back under her approach and she pressed forward again. 'Did you push Vivian down the stairs and break her leg, Dad?'

'Wh...what are you saying?' Shock drained the colour from his face and Mia reached out to catch him, fearing he would collapse. She pulled out a chair and George dropped like a stone onto the seat. His hands dangled between his spread knees as he hung his head forward, refusing to look at Mia. She crouched down beside him, hemming him in with one arm against the table and the other braced against the chair back.

'I'm saying I saw Mother yesterday, and she told me you pushed her. So, let me ask you again, did you do it?'

George raised his face and the haunted look in his eyes made her want to vomit. She hadn't given any real credence to her mother's accusation, but the guilt on his face was unmistakable. She pushed to her feet and turned away, heading for the hall to grab her coat and bag. Her father sobbed loudly, the sound like a rusty hinge giving way under strain and she spun back to face him. His face was buried in his hands and his whole frame shook as he barked and gasped.

'You should speak to the police, Dad. It would be better if the call came from you, rather than me.' Mia's throat closed and she strained to get the next words out. 'Why did you stay with her? After all these years, both of you so unhappy? I don't understand it. Why didn't you get some help before things got so bad?'

George raised his tear-stained face sharply and then shook his head as if in denial. 'You don't understand…'

'You pushed her. She's in hospital. What's to understand?'

'Not this time,' he whispered. Mia walked back into the kitchen and pulled out a chair to sit before him. She watched quietly as George gathered himself together somewhat, wiping his face on the handkerchief from his pocket. He toyed with the piece of material, folding and refolding the white square.

'I didn't have anything to do with it this time. She was drunk and she stumbled on the stairs. I think her slipper came off and she tripped. I was in the study when I heard this terrible thudding noise and there she was at the bottom. There was blood and it looked just like before, but then I realised that she had cut her hand on the glass she was holding as she fell...' The words hung there like rotten fruit on the bough. *This time...like before...*

'When did you have anything to do with her falling?' Mia kept her voice soft and even, pushing her rising horror deep down. She needed to get to the bottom of the story even though she was afraid that it would destroy them all in the process.

'You were six, I think. It was the day after your party. You had a new dress, yellow as the sun, and ribbons in your hair. I remember it streaming behind you as you spun around in the garden until you were dizzy. You always had such beautiful hair, Eunomia. Why did you cut it?' George reached out his hand as though to stroke her head and Mia jerked back in her seat.

He sighed and dropped his hand into his lap. He began to smooth and fold the handkerchief again. 'I came home from work the next day and you were in here, making sandwiches for your sisters. Eirênê was crying, and Dikê was holding her in her lap. There was rubbish everywhere, all the leftovers from your party, and there you were, still in your uniform from school. When I asked where your mother was you told me she had a headache and was lying down. I knew what you meant: she was drunk again and I was

221

so angry. She'd promised me she would try harder, that she would stop drinking for the baby.'

'Baby? Nee was hardly a baby then. If I was six, she must have been two,' Mia interjected.

Her father shook his head. 'Not Eirênê. Vivian was pregnant again; we wanted a boy. I wanted a boy is probably closer to the truth of it. When I went upstairs, she wouldn't put the bottle down. She'd run a bath of scalding hot water and downed most of a bottle of gin. I think she was trying to get rid of it. We fought, and she slapped me, so I pushed her away and she fell...she fell. My poor boy was lost.' George's voice trailed off as the sobs hit him again and Mia wrapped her arms tightly around herself, afraid she would splinter and fall apart. How had they not known about this? How could their parents have kept such a terrible secret for all these years?

Mia tried to remember the party her father had mentioned, but the memories wouldn't come. The trouble was, having spent so long actively avoiding the past, the few good memories were lost to her. She was sure there had been some better days, days when her parents had cared about them, but they were hidden behind the same walls as all the bad times. Mia was sure her father had never cried for any of the girls the way he was mourning this boy child who had never lived.

Could that be the reason he had turned away from them all? Withdrawn into his world of books and research and left three little girls to struggle alone?

The noise of his desperate sobs was starting to grate on Mia's nerves. How dare he feel so much for a child he had never met when he had all but thrown away the three that he'd had? She moved away from the table, frightened by the sudden wash of anger in her veins.

She needed to be away from George in that moment; if she lashed out, she would never forgive herself. Mia grabbed her bag and dug around for her phone, which seemed determined to stay hidden from her in the cavernous depths. In frustration, she tipped the bag upside down and dumped the contents on the hall carpet, her phone nestling cheekily on the top of the pile of tissues, receipts, notebook, make-up and other detritus which most women accumulated over time.

Taking a seat at the bottom of the stairs, she scrolled through until she found Kiki's number. Mia had to grab her wrist with her other hand to hold the phone still enough against her ear that she could hear when her sister answered. 'Is Neil there?' Mia croaked and then cleared her throat and tried again. 'Kiki Dee, is Neil there? Dad's not well so we need to call the party off. I'm hoping that Neil knows who else is on the guest list. Can you ask him to do a bit of a ring around?'

Mia could hear her sister talking to her husband, although her hand was clearly muffling the speaker. Mia winced as she heard the tone of Neil's voice change, rising sharply and angrily before he was suddenly there ranting in her ear. 'What's the problem, Mia? George was fine when I saw him an hour ago at work. This dinner is important. What the bloody hell have you done? I knew you'd sabotage everything. You just can't let it go, can you? I bloody told Kiki not to drag you up here—you always interfere and cause problems. Marching in here, taking my kids like it's anything to do with you. No wonder your sister's so fucking useless with you taking over all the time.'

On and on and on he raved, and Mia could imagine him in her mind's eye. Face red, mean little eyes squinting in his fury, spittle gathering at the corners of his mouth. She held the handset away from her ear until the words were no longer clear and waited for him to run out of steam.

The diatribe ran its course eventually and when there was silence, Mia put the phone back against her mouth and spoke very quietly. 'Fuck you, Neil.' She clicked the phone off and shoved it back into her bag. Kneeling on the floor, she gathered the rest of her stuff and threw it all in after the phone, leaving only her car keys. The sobs from the kitchen had quietened during the call and Mia turned to look at her father still sitting at the table.

He looked broken, a shell of the man who had always loomed so large in her life. Mia opened her mouth and then closed it abruptly. She had no words for him. Gathering her coat, she tugged it on before tucking her feet into her shoes by the front door. She paused once more at the door to look back. George remained frozen in place. Much as she longed to walk away and pretend the past half an hour had never happened, she couldn't do it. Too much the fixer, the solver of problems, the soother of hurts.

'Damn it.' Mia dropped her stuff by the door and hurried back into the kitchen. She crouched down beside George and placed a hand on his shoulder. 'It'll be all right, Dad. We'll sort this out somehow.' She had no idea how though.

Chapter Twenty-One

Daniel leaned against the side of the car and watched anxiously as the few passengers straggled out of the station and towards the car park. There was no sign of Mia and he began to wonder whether he'd got the time wrong when she finally came into view, towing her small case behind her. She looked pale and hollow-eyed—too much like the sad woman he had first met.

He steeled himself not to run towards her and gather her up. He deliberately maintained a casual stance and forced a smile to his face. It scared him a little how much he had missed her and he didn't want to overwhelm her when she had clearly had a tough time of it.

An answering smile was his reward, although it wavered a little at the edges. Daniel waited until Mia was almost at the car before he opened his arms and, with a soft sigh, she nestled against his chest. He enfolded her tightly and pressed his lips to the top of her head. They stood like that for a while and Daniel was content to wait and just enjoy the feeling of holding the woman that he loved in his arms.

When Mia finally stirred, Daniel loosened his arms to let her create a small space between them. He watched her swallow hard and knew it wasn't the time to press for information, so he just shook his head lightly and steered Mia around to the passenger seat in the car. He stowed her bag on the back seat and curled his long legs into the driver's seat.

He reached across and fastened Mia's seat belt for her. He patted her thigh before starting the car and flicking the radio on low, creating enough background noise that Mia wouldn't feel any pressure to talk. He drove them home at a leisurely pace, rubbing his hand across her leg occasionally as he changed gear or they paused in the traffic. He kept an eye on her surreptitiously and felt his own tension melt as Mia's body language gradually relaxed on the short drive home. He had made some plans since receiving the brief text detailing her return train details and was glad now that he'd done so.

He left Mia to exit the car whilst he gathered her bag. She trotted quietly behind him into the kitchen. Daniel turned to unbutton her coat and pulled off the thin cardigan she was wearing beneath it. He gathered up the huge Aran sweater that was her favourite and tugged it over her head, kissing her nose as she popped out from the enveloping cream wool. He winked at her when she quirked an eyebrow at him and then knelt to relieve her of her shoes before helping her into a thick pair of socks.

Daniel grabbed her hand and pressed a kiss into the palm before he rose and gently propelled Mia towards her wellington boots, which were perched handily next to the back door. He toed off his own shoes and replaced them with matching boots before shouldering the rucksack and blanket, which were also by the back door. Gathering Mia by the hand, Daniel led her back outside and across the yard and the garden towards the steps to the beach.

The sky was blue and the few clouds that scudded across it were more white than grey, so Daniel didn't think they would have to worry about rain for a bit. The wind was brisk and the grey sea was topped with foam as the waves danced and tossed across the dark sand. He kept to the upper reaches of the beach, heading for the perfect spot he had discovered a couple of days previously. There was a stretch of small dunes a few hundred yards down from the house, which would provide just enough shelter.

Daniel shook out the blanket and sat on the edge to remove his boots. He tapped Mia on the leg and she dutifully lifted each foot in turn so that he could remove her boots before she stepped onto the blanket beside him.

Daniel scooted to the middle of the blanket and spread his knees wide, patting the soft checked material in front of him. Mia settled down between his legs with a soft sigh, her eyes trained on the roiling sea. He opened the rucksack and pulled out another blanket and a flask of tea, which he poured into a large mug and handed to Mia. He wrapped the spare blanket around his shoulders and scooted forward until Mia's back was firmly against his chest. He raised his arms to drape them lightly over her shoulders so that she was enclosed in both his embrace and the warmth of the blanket.

She sighed again and settled back against him, sipping the hot tea, and Daniel knew he'd had the right idea. He turned his head and brushed his lips against her temple. Mia lifted her head to meet his mouth in the softest press.

'Thank you,' she whispered softly against his lips.

'Take your time,' he replied softly. 'There is no rush, no need to make any decisions just yet. Tell me as much or as little as you want about it and only when you are ready. I'm just glad to have you home, with me.'

'Yes,' she murmured, 'home with you,' before turning back to watch the seagulls wheeling and diving into the foaming waves.

He listened with growing horror as she told him about the episode with her dad, the argument with Neil and the fragile state of her sister's marriage. 'Oh, love. You should have told me. I would have helped you.'

She rested her head on his shoulder. 'I know, but I didn't want to get you involved. Not because I don't trust you or anything, I just needed to hold on to the thought of you waiting here for me.' He tightened his arms and she snuggled into his side, where she belonged. He was never letting her out of his sight again.

'I got Dad to talk to the GP. I'm not sure he'll do anything about the grief counselling he was offered, but at least he's admitted Vivian is beyond his care. We've found her a place in a care home close enough for him to visit. One of the things they specialise in is the management of alcohol-induced dementia.'

'And what will you do about Kiki?'

What would she do about Kiki? That was the toughest question of all. By the time she had dropped Matty at school and Charlie back with her sister, it had been well into the morning. Mia hadn't answered any of Kiki's questions about their dad, in the same way that Kiki had refused to answer any of Mia's about Neil and the consequences of the night before.

Pale and red-eyed, Kiki had flinched away when Mia hugged her. She'd sat stiffly at the table and Mia could tell that there were bruises that Kiki was hiding under her jumper. She'd begged Kiki to leave Neil, promised her and the children a place to stay at Butterfly Cove. There was plenty of room and she could afford to support them all until Kiki could get her feet under her. They'd had a terrible fight and Mia had left in tears, frustrated that her sister could still feel any loyalty to Neil after all he'd done over the years.

She'd sent Kiki a text on the way home to apologise and extend again the offer of somewhere to stay. There was no point in saying any more, she just needed to leave that door open and hope that Kiki would walk through it someday soon. She would talk to Pat and Bill—ask them to check in on Kiki when Neil would be at work. She'd give it a couple of days then call her.

She hadn't told any of them what had happened with her father. It was still too raw and Mia wasn't sure what she would do with the information. She couldn't tell Kiki, and Nee was still out of contact. Did they need to know? It wasn't a decision that she was ready to make. She was just glad to be home.

Mia settled closer against Daniel and let the vista before her settle her whirling thoughts. She was so grateful for him in that moment, more so than at any other time in the few short weeks since they had met. Maybe it was too soon to think it, but his actions today had proven he had come into her life for a reason and she would do whatever she could to nurture the shoots of their love.

Mia held the tea mug up and Daniel took it, draining the contents before he refilled it from the flask and tucked it back between her hands. She turned to look at him over her shoulder and he smiled and kissed the tip of her nose. Mia lifted her chin and he took her invitation and pressed another kiss to her lips. Nothing heavy, just sweet and heart-warming, and she sighed in contentment.

Daniel was right; it wasn't the time for big decisions. She would just hunker down and focus on the positive things in her life and work on getting the house up to scratch. She would keep communicating with Kiki, but only in the most positive way, and just hope that her sister would come to her before it was too late.

Easter was a few weeks away and Mia had promised a room to Pat and Bill for the long weekend. She wanted to keep them in her life and the only way to do that was to actively demonstrate that she wanted and needed them around. She would invite Madeline and Richard around as well and she was sure that the two older couples would get on like a house on fire.

Needing to talk of happier things, she told Daniel about her time with her in-laws, mentioning their impending visit. He didn't say much but she felt a tension in his body so she twisted around on the blanket to face him properly. There was a crease between his brows and Mia reached out to smooth it with her thumb. 'They really want to meet you, Daniel. They won't be making comparisons between you and Jamie, if that is what you're worried about. They were genuinely relieved to hear I'm starting to move forward with my life and I would like them to remain a part of my future. Our future.'

Mia felt her face heat as she dropped her gaze to the checked blanket beneath them. She traced the pattern with her finger and pressed on, although her voice was more tentative. 'That's if you want there to be an "us". I certainly want there to be, and I want all the most important people in my life to be friends if possible.'

Daniel remained silent and Mia chewed her lip, keeping her eyes downcast, her fingers tracing the same part of the blanket pattern repeatedly. *Say something, please say something,* she repeated over and over in her head as the silence stretched on.

'Look at me, Mia.'

Although his voice was soft, she shook her head, afraid to see what he was thinking. It was ridiculous really—now that she'd said it, there was no going back. *What if he doesn't want the same thing as me? Oh, God! What if he does?* The future with him was a beautiful thing, theoretically. Whilst it was tucked safely in her heart and in her dreams, it was a thing of wonder and possibility.

Bringing it out into the real world was the problem. The reality would never match the dream. It would be rough and bumpy, ugly in places. As long as she kept it a dream it would be hearts and flowers and rainbows and unicorns and...and she was losing the plot. Dreams were empty; dreams didn't keep you warm at night, didn't pay the bills—didn't do anything.

She'd spent too long in her head since Jamie died, hiding from the world, and now that she was finally living again there was no way she could turn tail and hide. The future was sitting patiently just a few inches away from her. She just needed to gather her courage and seize it.

Mia raised her head, glancing up through her lashes until she met Daniel's eyes. They were sparkling with amusement, and his lip twitched as though he was struggling to keep a serious expression on his face. 'Mia Sutherland, did you just ask me to marry you?'

'What? No! Um, possibly? No! No! Maybe? Bloody hell, did I? Will you? Should we? No!' By the end of her stuttering response, Daniel was literally roaring with laughter. He pressed his hand to his side, gasping for air and Mia scowled fiercely at him. His laughter continued until she launched herself at him, knocking him flat on the blanket.

She leant over him, blocking out the sun so that his face beneath her was cast in shadow. The mirth fled from his green eyes and they darkened perceptibly as his face grew serious, intent. She felt his body stiffen beneath hers where she straddled his hips and she rocked forward into him. Daniel lifted his head from the blanket, intent on capturing her mouth, but Mia maintained the distance between them and held his gaze.

She rocked again and watched the green deepen further and she knew she was pushing him towards the edge of his restraint. Good. She wanted him off-balance; she wanted him as messed up and emotional and ragged as she felt in that moment. This thing between them, this connection, *this love,* was consuming her and she was terrified and exultant in equal measures. She needed to know that Daniel was feeling the same way too.

She pressed her hips down again and Daniel reared up, his abdominal muscles pulling tight as he sat up and captured Mia in his arms. He snatched at her mouth, capturing her bottom lip between his, and he sucked hard before releasing her only long enough to drag her jumper, shirt and vest up in one go and rip them over her head. He bowed Mia back over his arm and sucked hard on her breast through her light cotton bra. Her nipples stiffened instantly. The contrast between his hot tongue and the cool sea air enhanced the erotic pull of his mouth and shot straight to the centre of her body.

Daniel used the edge of his teeth on her sensitive flesh and Mia cried out, grabbing at a handful of his hair. She didn't know whether she wanted to pull his mouth away or press him closer as the sensitivity built to an almost unbearable point. She couldn't control her hips as she rocked repeatedly against him and Daniel pulled away from her breast abruptly with a tortured groan. 'Christ, Mia, you need to stop that or I am going to go off in my jeans like some unpractised kid.'

She couldn't stop her laughter at the edge of desperation in his voice, which made her body shake and Daniel groan, setting off another chain reaction of giggles. He clamped his hands on her hips, lifting her up to break the contact between them. The pressure of his grip urged her to stand. Mia let him take control, shivering from a combination of the cold wind and the desire burning through her.

He stripped her jeans and underwear with urgent fingers, leaving her clad in only her thick socks and bra. Daniel tore open the front of his own jeans and dragged them down his hips before pulling Mia back down to straddle him. They both gasped as their bodies met, and it was only then that Daniel seemed to notice the goose pimples racing up her arms.

'Bloody hell, woman, you are freezing. This is madness,' he muttered as Mia reached between them, taking him in her hand to guide him where she needed him the most.

'Don't care, I don't care,' Mia said as she rolled her hips and worked him deeper inside. Daniel fumbled beside them until he shook her jumper free from the rest of the tangle of clothes and tugged it back over her head. The scratch of the wool against her nipples was rough and welcome. Bracing his hands on her hips, Daniel held her steady as Mia shoved her arms into the too-long sleeves.

The thick wool was enough to shield her from the worst of the wind and Mia leant forward, her hands braced on Daniel's chest as she drove down against him, desperate for friction. His hold tightened as he pushed up to meet her downward motion, and it was good, so good, but not quite what she needed.

'Lean back, Mia,' he said roughly and she altered her position as instructed, bracing her hands behind her on his thighs. The change gave him better access and Daniel licked his thumb before reaching between her legs to tease the tight bud of nerves at her apex.

Her eyes rolled back as the sudden burst of stimulation pushed her to the edge and every muscle in her body clenched.

'That's my girl, that's my beautiful girl.' Words of praise spilled from his lips as they drove together, chasing that perfect moment, desperate to find the peak of their pleasure together. He pressed his thumb harder between her thighs and the shock was enough to push her over the top. Mia cried out to the rolling clouds above her as she came. An echoing cry from Daniel and a flood of heat as he filled her brought tears to her eyes and she collapsed forward, boneless, her head buried in the crook of his shoulder.

Home. She was home at last.

Chapter Twenty-Two

Daniel sat at the kitchen table, his laptop before him as he transferred the latest round of pictures from his camera to his cloud storage. He had continued to document the progress on the house, including a rewarding session with the furniture restorers showing the revival of the beautiful table now gracing the dining room.

Mr Robinson and his son Jordy had been full of knowledge about the area and were clearly masters of their craft. Daniel had already discussed a couple of feature projects with them for the conversion of the barn into art studios.

They'd taken a tour of the old workshops next to the barn and Daniel was already well into the planning of the spin-off project to convert them into a gallery. Mia had ducked her head briefly through the door before withdrawing on a laugh and leaving him to it.

Jordy was proving to be a good sounding board for his ideas and Daniel had it in mind to ask him to consider taking on something of a project management role for the conversion works. He certainly had the local contacts and Daniel was determined that he would use local labour wherever possible. He wanted to be part of the community here, and if the studios and gallery were to be a success then it would do no harm to foster local support early. He hoped that by providing opportunities for the locals during the off season, word of mouth recommendations would then bring the tourists flocking.

He was getting well ahead of himself again but it didn't do any harm to lay the groundwork as early as possible. He had every intention of making himself a permanent fixture in the area.

He turned his attention back to the close detailed shots of the wind-out mechanism for the dining room table. It had been fascinating to watch Mr Robinson bring the piece back to life, and he marked a couple of shots to frame up as gifts to the man for his patience and willingness to share his knowledge with a nosy amateur.

Daniel dragged a couple of other images into the folder he was building for the album he wanted to present to Mia. Madeline had let slip that it was Mia's birthday in May, so he had decided he would present it then as one of his gifts to her.

His phone vibrated on the table and Daniel smiled to see Aaron's name flash up on the screen. He was waiting on some updated blueprints for the barn and now the weather had picked up, Daniel was hoping that work would be able to get underway after the rapidly approaching Easter holidays.

He was trying to be cool about meeting Jamie's parents, but his gut carried a knot of fear that they would find him lacking somehow. He dragged his finger across the screen on his phone to connect to Aaron and flicked the speaker on.

'Aaron, great to hear from you. How are those drawings coming along?' Daniel continued to click and drag images into the folder on his laptop as he spoke.

'Umm, yeah, they are progressing well. Luke should have the final set with you in the next twenty-four hours. He's also champing at the bit to get back down to you guys to help with the harem suite. Tell Mia not to do it all without him.' Daniel laughed. Luke had become obsessed with the little side project sending Mia endless messages and suggestions.

Aaron cleared his throat. 'But that is not why I am calling, mate. Have you seen *The Standard* today?' *The Evening Standard* was a daily evening paper that delivered national and international news, as well as being London-focused. It was prerequisite reading for much of the capital's population, providing—amongst other things—reviews and details of social, arts and media events in and around town. Daniel hadn't had cause to look at it since he had arrived at Butterfly Cove. *Was it only two months ago? It seemed a lifetime.*

'Can't say that I have. It's not really relevant to my life these days.' Daniel was surprised at how true that statement was. He was completely removed from his old life and concerns.

'Can you get on the internet? I really think you need to have a look.' The strain in his friend's voice put him on alert, and he minimised his folder to flick open the browser window.

'I'm on. What am I looking at?' He typed in the search box and the familiar homepage rolled open.

'Under the events tab, you can't miss it. You have no idea about it, do you? I thought at first you must know, but then we only talked a couple of days ago and I was sure you would have mentioned it. How the fuck did he get hold of them?' Aaron sounded angry now.

Growing more concerned and confused by the second, Daniel selected the events tab and scrolled through the headlines. An icy feeling crawled up his spine as he read the sidebar in growing disbelief.

Mystery of Fitz's disappearance solved—new exhibition announced.

'What the hell is this?' he muttered, scanning through the story. His agent, *his ex-agent*, Nigel, was pictured outside the gallery that had hosted all of Daniel's previous exhibitions. The owner, Maggie had taken a chance on him, and he had stayed loyal to her throughout his career. The story talked about Fitz being on retreat, looking for a new direction and a load of other bullshit Nigel had invented. There were a couple of teaser shots included with the story and Daniel blanched when he saw them.

They were all images he had taken since arriving at Butterfly Cove. The top one was from inside the barn, the first time he had been in there. A murky shot of the sea taken through the filthy, cobweb covered window. The second image was a close-up of the vine-and-butterfly-patterned tiles around the dining room fireplace.

It was the third shot that was the killer, though. It was one he had taken of Mia standing at the top of the steps leading down to the beach. She stood in silhouette looking out to sea, her hand raised to shield her eyes. A storm had been brewing. The sky purpled with the threat of rain and the sea a mass of white horses. It was a private image—one she hadn't been aware of him taking. No-one was ever meant to see it—other than himself, and Mia when he gave her the album.

'I'm going to kill him. How the hell did he get his hands on these?' Even as he said it, Daniel knew. He'd uploaded everything to the cloud, just as he'd always done. Nigel had shared access to it. They'd used it to discuss and review plans for previous exhibitions, shuffling images around and weeding out the final approvals. It had never occurred to Daniel that Nigel would access it without his knowledge or permission.

Flipping open the folder, he dragged everything from the shared area and moved them all back to his hard drive as quickly as he could. He could hear Aaron in the background, asking him if everything was okay but he didn't answer until everything was cleared down and back in his sole possession. There was no way of knowing whether Nigel had copies of everything but Daniel would have to assume the worst.

He finally turned back to the phone and Aaron's increasingly worried voice. 'Sorry, I didn't mean to ignore you. He had access to the cloud and I never dreamed he'd do anything like this. I need to come up to town, and get this sorted out.' The very thought of returning to London turned his stomach to acid, but there was no time to waste. The show opened on Thursday, and it was already Monday afternoon.

'Get what sorted out?'

Daniel spun in his chair, his hand automatically closing his laptop as he turned to face Mia who had entered the kitchen behind him. He pasted a smile on his face, which he hoped looked less false and stiff than it felt. 'Oh nothing, I just need to pop up to London for a few days, see the guys about the designs for the barn. It's proving a bit complicated with us toing and froing over the phone. If we can sit down together then we can get things finalised...'

His voice trailed off as he heard a sharp cough from the loudspeaker of his phone. He snatched it up and flipped the speaker off as he raised it to his ear.

'I'll text you when I've sorted my train times out, all right? Yeah, yeah I know. See you later.' Daniel hung up and swallowed, trying to clear the sour taste on his tongue from so many lies. He didn't know why he hadn't just told Mia the truth about the exhibition but now that he had started on the path of untruths, he had no idea how to backtrack without making things worse. It had been an instinctive move to protect her, to protect himself really.

He couldn't bear it if she found out and somehow thought he'd planned this all along. He just needed to get to London and get his hands on bloody Nigel. Get a retraction printed and make sure all the copies were deleted. If he could just make it all go away, then he could get back to Mia and explain it to her afterwards. Somehow.

***

Daniel Fitzwilliams was a terrible liar. If that was his idea of a poker face, he'd get fleeced every time he sat at a card table. She might have taken his visit to Aaron at face value except for two things. His mouth had twisted over the mention of London, and the guys were supposed to be joining them in a few days for the long Easter weekend. She knew he found the prospect of meeting Bill and Pat daunting, and thought he'd feel more comfortable with a bit of support at his back. She and Madeline had planned a huge feast for the Sunday, and an enormous turkey occupied pride of place in the freezer.

Whatever this sudden trip was about, it didn't have anything to do with the plans for the barn, she was almost certain of it. It hurt her to think he was hiding something from her, but she brushed it aside and gave him her best smile. Relationships were damn hard— she'd forgotten just how much. Since their morning on the beach, it had seemed silly to make him sleep in the room next door. She just wished he didn't take up quite so much space everywhere.

He was a snuggler, she'd discovered, with a natural body temperature to rival any Ready Brek kid. Two and half years of sleeping alone had turned her into a starfish, sprawling across the mattress in a wide array of arms and legs. He invaded her space at every turn, leaving stray socks beside the bed and his watch and phone tumbled carelessly between the carefully placed set of bowls on her dressing table. Silly, niggly things that counted for nothing when he took her in his arms, but it would take time to adjust to the reality of him.

Maybe he was struggling with her need to have everything just so. His clothes still hung in the wardrobe in the other room because she hadn't quite got around to making room for him in hers. Perhaps she should take the opportunity while he was away to clear a few things out so he had some proper places for his own things when he got back.

'When do you need to go?'

'First thing in the morning. I'll get the early train, if you don't mind dropping me off?' He kept his eyes fixed on the half-closed laptop in front of him. Her stomach twisted. Something was definitely wrong.

'But you'll be back in time for the weekend?' He gave her a blank look over his shoulder. 'It's Easter. Pat and Bill are coming down, remember?' She kept the reminder gentle. What if his trip to London was an attempt to avoid meeting them? Why else would he be in such a panic?

'Oh, damn. That's this weekend?' He scrubbed his hands through his hair, leaving a chunk at the front sticking straight up. The bleak look in his eyes was more than she could bear. Closing the space between them she petted the strands back into place, then cupped his head to hold him to her in a tight hug.

'I'll be on the first train Friday morning, I promise. If I could put this off I would. I'm sorry.' He muttered the words into her shoulder.

She stroked his hair again. What was she to do? If things were going to work out between them then she needed to trust him. Whatever his reason for the trip, he didn't sound happy about it. Fighting against her need to take control, she kept her mouth shut. If he wanted her help, he would ask for it. There was no cause to feel rejected. *Keep telling yourself that, Mia.*

Chapter Twenty-Three

Daniel stayed in his seat as the train pulled into the terminus in London. Everyone else seemed desperate to be first off so he hung back and left them to push and shove and barge their way off the train. He was in no hurry; the closer he'd got to London the worse the sick feeling in his gut became until he was swallowing convulsively to keep the bile down. He hated that feeling, that sudden gush of saliva just before his stomach muscles contracted and his body did a fine impression of something trying to turn itself inside out. He'd had too many mornings in the recent past when he had felt like that. The heat and crush on the commuter train was doing nothing to ease his anxiety.

He wasn't ready to face this life again. He wanted desperately to stay in his little cocoon with Mia and the house, looking to the future, always to the future, not back. In his heart, Daniel knew that he needed to resolve things in London once and for all. It had been cowardly of him to cut and run the way he had.

Thankfully, Aaron and Luke had both stood by him, even though he had been a less than stellar friend in the last few months of his life in London. They'd both done their best to keep his head on straight, to talk to him about the parties and the booze and his occasional foray into illicit substances, but Daniel had been too stupid and, if he was brutally honest with himself, too egotistical, to care.

It still stung to acknowledge how hard he'd fallen for his own hype, believing the bullshit about his own genius fed to him by sycophants and hangers-on. They'd only been interested in his money and basking in the reflected glory that his fifteen minutes in the spotlight had earned.

A cleaner entered the empty carriage, clearing the empty cups, newspapers and food wrappers discarded everywhere into a bin bag. She gave Daniel a quizzical glance and it was enough of a push to persuade his reluctant feet to move. He would head to Aaron's first and dump his bag before heading over to the gallery. He'd toyed with the idea of returning to his own flat, but he couldn't face it. He would try and speak to his landlord while he was here, terminate his lease and arrange for his things to be packed up and shipped home.

Mulling it over on the journey, he'd decided his best course of action would be to speak to Maggie, the gallery owner, directly. She had been the first person to show his work and had always dealt fairly with him. He wondered what Nigel had told Maggie about his absence from planning the exhibition, as Daniel had always been insistent on approving everything.

The betrayal was still a fresh wound in his heart. Stupid really, as he'd known what a ruthless bastard Nigel was before he'd agreed to be represented by him. Daniel had never taken to the man, or the way he operated. Anyone who was anyone was on Nigel's books, however, and Daniel had been persuaded he needed his representation to take the next big step towards success. Nigel boosted the price tags, got the special commissions, which Daniel might have found unbearably boring, but the money had been too good to refuse.

He pushed his way through the crowds milling around the station, so different to the homely, welcoming platform at Orcombe with its hanging baskets of flowers and old-fashioned waiting room. Here it was harsh lights, coffee shops and crowds. Commuters grumbled as they chopped and weaved through the tourists and day trippers who dawdled along, tube maps in hand as they pointed out the exit signs to each other.

Daniel knew his way around, but he took his time, wondering anew at the need for accessory shops. Who got off the train with an urgent need to buy a tie or a scarf? Who honestly thought a pair of novelty socks would be the perfect gift for their host? The little shops were bursting with people so clearly there was a call for it.

The escalator down to the underground was steep and slow; Daniel made sure to obey the rules and stood on the right, to let those in a rush run down the moving stairway. He turned to watch the rows of posters that lined the walls, advertising the latest theatre shows, comedy tours and *shit!* There was the same image he'd taken of Mia on poster after poster, advertising the opening of the exhibition in just a couple of days' time. Even worse, the posters were interspersed with a mood shot of Daniel himself looking every bit the tortured artist.

Daniel ducked his head away from the taunting images and pulled the collar of his coat up. The last thing he needed was anyone recognising him. He stepped into the busy flow and joined the rushing commuters, running down the remaining steps of the escalator and escaping into the tunnels beyond.

The gallery looked the same as always: stark black painted wooden frames around huge picture windows, a black wooden door with the name of the gallery owner picked out tastefully in gold script. The windows would usually display selected works of the featured artist but today they were blanked out with white screens plastered in posters for the forthcoming exhibition.

Daniel scrubbed his hand through his beard and leaned on the doorbell. He kept the button depressed and could hear the insistent buzz notifying the owner of his presence. The gallery was closed to visitors until opening night and he didn't want to risk being ignored as an eager punter.

He hoped that Maggie would be around, rather than one of her assistants, and he was rewarded by the clacking of heels on the tiled floor and the sound of her crisp, sharp voice approaching the door. 'I hear you, I hear you. Take your finger off the bloody buzzer.' The door yanked open, the fierce scowl on Maggie's face instantly erased by a huge smile when she saw him. 'Oh, Fitz, darling boy!'

Daniel was enveloped in a discreet cloud of Chanel perfume as Maggie flung her arms around him. She looked just the same as always, cream silk blouse tucked into a black pencil skirt, stockings—'*tights are for schoolgirls and bank robbers' masks, darling*'—and black patent court shoes. Her blonde hair was fixed in a simple, elegant chignon and pearls at her throat and ears completed the look.

'Come in, come in! It's so wonderful to see you at last. Nigel has been bloody cagey about your whereabouts and I was starting to worry. He's got some very strange notions for the displays, not our usual thing at all. Between him and that obnoxious girlfriend of yours they have been driving me to absolute distraction!' Maggie hooked her arm firmly through Daniel's and towed him into the gallery.

The walls were plastered with images he had taken at Butterfly Cove. Interior shots of the house, as well as around the garden and down on the beach. There was no finesse to the display, no careful grouping of images; they were just *everywhere*. 'What the hell, Maggie?' Daniel turned in a slow circle as he tried to take it all in.

'I know, darling, I know, but you're here now and we can fix it. I told them both, less is more. Subtle is the name of the game, but they wanted everything putting out.'

'Less is definitely the way forward, Mags. A lot less.' Daniel strode towards the wall in front of him and started to remove the prints as quickly as he could. His hands shook with fury and he pulled them down faster and faster, stacking them on the floor with no care, desperate to get them off the walls as quickly as possible.

'Fitz, wait darling, you are going to chip the frames. What's the matter?' Maggie's voice was high with her distress as she pulled on Daniel's arm, trying to stop him and make him turn to look at her.

Daniel shook her off and tore at the wall again, throwing a quirky shot of the green man statue down with such force that the glass in the frame shattered. The noise made Maggie scream and she jumped back to avoid the splinters of glass. Her scream was enough to shock Daniel into stillness and he turned to face Maggie, still clutching one of the photographs.

'There is no Fitz anymore. There is no exhibition. I quit town—quit all the bullshit—and I've found a new life. These are private, personal pictures. Mementos that were only to be shared with one person. I will not sell my future to strangers for a few quid and a bit of critical acclaim!'

Daniel placed the picture more carefully on the pile of others on the floor and stepped towards Maggie who was staring at him in absolute horror. 'No exhibition? That can't be right. I've spent a small fortune on advertising. Nigel said it was the only way he could justify keeping your work here, that so many other galleries were clamouring to show your new collection. I had to demonstrate to him I was serious about retaining you as a client.' Maggie hiccupped as her words trailed off and Daniel wrapped his arms around her petite frame, worried that she would keel over, she was so ghostly pale.

'Maggie, Mags, you can't have believed that I would desert you after all we've been through?' Even as he said the words, Daniel was struck by the fact that he had indeed left Maggie without a second thought. She was someone who had stood by him from the very beginning and certainly deserved better than this. He squeezed her tighter and rubbed his hand up and down her soft, silk-clad back.

'I'll cover the costs. Nigel had no right to put you in such a position. I'll post an announcement tomorrow, explain there has been a misunderstanding; it'll be all right.'

Maggie pulled back from Daniel and glared up at him, her eyes were red-rimmed and her perfect, subtle make-up was smudged across one cheek. She was furious. 'It won't be all right; the bloody phone has been ringing off the hook. Your vanishing act had everyone intrigued. I've had dozens of people willing to reserve a piece, based only on your reputation. The fact that a couple of gossip columns have been speculating on your whereabouts and your girlfriend has stirred the pot with her enigmatic statements. You can't cancel now; it'll be a bloody disaster! My reputation will be ruined!'

'Girlfriend? What girlfriend?' As angry and confused as he was, in his heart he knew that Maggie was right about the exhibition.

'That skinny piece you were carrying on with, Giselle, is it? I've had it on good authority that her name is Louise and she changed it to appear more sophisticated. Silly little girl.' Maggie paced backwards and forwards, heels clicking on the tiled floor of the gallery, her arms folded tightly across her body.

Daniel watched her pace and tried to get a rein on his thoughts. How the hell was Giselle mixed up in this? Daniel assumed he'd seen the last of her and yet somehow she was involved in the exhibition. Maggie had said something earlier about his obnoxious girlfriend being around, but Daniel hadn't caught on to it, too busy trying to get his pictures down from the walls. 'Giselle has been here? Nigel has involved her in the preparation for the exhibition?' He shook his head, trying to piece everything together.

'Yes, I told you she's been making a nuisance of herself. Trying to tell me how to run things, interfering with the catering. Bossing my staff around until I was ready to throw her out on her ear.'

'She's not my girlfriend, Mags. We split when I left town. I assumed she'd moved on when she texted me a picture of her in bed with someone else. She's nothing to me, nothing at all.' Daniel turned to the pictures still hanging on the wall of the gallery, seeking out a picture of the woman who had become everything to him in such a short space of time. He stepped away from Maggie and towards the image that had caught his eye. It was a half-profile shot. Mia had her hand covering most of her face so all you could see was her left eye, cheek and temple and a smattering of dark, spiky hair.

He'd taken the picture just a couple of weeks previously. The weather had turned filthy in one of those sudden spring storms when the skies opened and it felt like it might rain for ever. The temperature had plummeted and Daniel and Mia had decided to take a day off and huddle in front of the fire in the sitting room. They'd enjoyed a wonderful lazy day, watching films, listening to music, reading and just being quietly content in each other's company.

Daniel had ventured off with his camera for a while. The green-grey light of the storm outside had created some fantastic shadows in the untouched rooms in the attic and he'd lost an hour or so capturing some great shots of the sky through the upper windows and the dusty corners of the rooms on the third floor.

Daniel had uploaded the pictures and was sorting through them, sprawled out on the big comfortable sofa, his feet tucked cosily in Mia's lap. She had been watching a film that made her laugh and cringe at the same time. Daniel had been captivated by the play of emotions across her face.

It was one of the things that he loved about Mia, how she gave herself over to whatever she was watching or reading or listening to. He was constantly fascinated by her ability to laugh so joyously over a ridiculous film or weep uncontrollably when the story in a book swept her away. Daniel was more practical, more grounded, and he envied her ability to connect so easily with a story, or a line of lyrics. The only time he felt like that was when he held his camera.

He'd taken a few shots of Mia, including one of his favourites when she had been stroking his feet where they rested in her lap. Her soft hands contrasted against the thick woollen socks he'd been wearing, the denim of her jeans providing a framing backdrop. It was a simple shot, but one of those secret moments of absent affection that spoke to him. So much sweeter and somehow more intimate than a candid shot of a couple embracing. It spoke of a quiet domesticity that everyone yearned for. Daniel tracked his eyes across the wall and there it was.

Maggie stepped up beside him and leaned her head against his arm as she studied the images in front of them. 'What's her name?' she asked quietly.

'Mia.'

'Does she know what's happened?' Maggie kept her voice soft, casual even, and Daniel looked sideways at her. She was too perceptive by half; it was one of the reasons she was so good at what she did. Maggie could see through people and pictures to the heart of the matter. Every time.

'The pictures are for her. I've been putting together an album for her, a memento of the work that we've been doing to restore her house. She has plans to open it as a guest house in the summer. I wanted it to be a surprise.'

'That's a no, then.' Maggie smiled to take the sting out of her words but Daniel still felt their bite. Why hadn't he told Mia? Why had he felt compelled to lie to her about the exhibition? He looked around the room, at the mess he'd made on the floor, and it struck him that this was the perfect metaphor for his previous life in London. If you looked in one direction then there was his work, adorning the walls. If you looked in the other: mess and chaos, ugliness.

Daniel realised that his lies had been born of fear. Fear that he would be dragged back into the life he'd run so hard from, fear that Mia would be tainted by the seedier side of that life he had been living. Fame had been intoxicating and Daniel was terrified that if he let the exhibition go ahead that he would be sucked back into that world again.

He turned to Maggie, unable to stop the sudden shaking in his body, and she drew him into her arms. She was so much smaller than him that it seemed ridiculous to seek strength from her, but Maggie had a spine of steel. She held him tight for a few moments before releasing the embrace and stepping back to meet Daniel's eye.

'Why don't you call her, darling? I can see from the pictures how much she means to you. Why don't you let her help you? It's what family does, after all.' Maggie patted his cheek sympathetically and then walked away to start gathering up the pictures that were strewn across the floor.

Daniel watched her for a few moments as she picked her way through the broken glass, rescuing the framed shots that were still in one piece and stacking them carefully away from the mess. Maggie was right—as usual, he thought ruefully—and reached for the mobile phone in his pocket.

Chapter Twenty-Four

Mia was making supper for Madeline and Richard when the phone rang. She'd been worried about Daniel's sudden departure and when Madeline had called earlier for a chat, Mia had asked them over for a visit. Within five minutes of getting through the door, Mads had stripped away Mia's brave face. Through floods of tears, Mia had poured out every painful moment of her visit home. Richard pottered around, making tea and tidying up, giving his wife room to work her magic and bring their beloved girl the support and comfort that she needed.

Once the worst of the tale was out, Mia had started to breathe more easily and some of the burden of guilt she felt had lifted. They agreed her mother going into a home where she could get the right treatment would be a positive step. Madeline and Richard had also supported her decision not to tell Kiki about their brother that never was. They'd also been angry, but sympathetic about the intolerable situation her sister faced at home.

An impassioned discussion had followed—Madeline all for storming up there and stealing Kiki and the children away. Richard more controlled, although no less furious, had argued that Kiki had to make the choice to leave herself or they ran the risk of her resenting Mia for interfering.

Madeline had grudgingly conceded the point and then moved on to more pleasant topics, including the impending visit of Pat and Bill who she was excited to finally meet. Daniel's rush visit to London was glossed over with little more than a raising of eyebrows between the older couple when they thought she wasn't looking.

Talk had moved on to things to do over Easter, when the phone interrupted them. Mia rested her spoon on a cloth on the counter, then wiped her hands on a tea towel before picking it up. 'Mia?' The pain in Daniel's voice vibrated down the line and Mia braced her hand against the wall as she turned away from the room, her posture guarded.

'Daniel? What's happened, darling? Are you all right?' Mia knew he wasn't, but it was one of those involuntary questions everyone seemed to ask in moments like this. Madeline came up behind her, placing a comforting hand on Mia's shoulder. She turned her arm upwards so she could touch Madeline's hand, acknowledging her support with silent thanks, her attention fully focused on the man at the other end of the phone line.

'Oh Mia, it's such a fucking mess. I don't know what to do about it.' Daniel's voice cracked and Mia felt her stomach clench in fear.

'Are you hurt?' Mia prayed that he would say no. If he was uninjured then everything else could be fixed.

'No, no. Nothing like that. I'm okay, it's just... God, Mia, I need you.' He sounded desperate and Mia knew that she just needed to get to him, wherever he was, so that she could help him.

'I'm coming. I'm coming right now. Is Aaron there? No? Well, you call him as soon as we've finished speaking and then tell him to call me and let me know where I need to meet you. I'm not sure when the next train is...' Mia broke off as she heard a rattle and she looked over to see Richard jangling his car keys. Madeline moved away to turn off the oven and tidy around the kitchen.

Mia tucked the phone under her chin as she bent over to pull on her shoes. 'We're driving up so it'll be a few hours at least. The traffic won't be too bad this time of day. Madeline and Richard are with me. Just call Aaron and then sit tight and I'll be with you before you know it. I love you.'

Mia hung up the phone and turned to face Madeline and Richard. Madeline cupped Mia's pale face in her hands and kissed her forehead. 'Whatever it is can be fixed. Run upstairs and throw some things in a bag as we might be a few days. We'll take the car and do the same at ours and then you can drive and meet us there, okay?' Mia nodded weakly and then again with more determination. *They would sort out whatever the problem was. Together.*

They'd been on the road for about half an hour when Mia's mobile phone rang. She'd been holding it in her hand, like a talisman, willing it to ring from the moment they had all piled into Richard's Mercedes. The joys of a good pension and no kids to steal all his money meant they'd been able to treat themselves to a few high-end luxuries, the sporty sedan being one of them. They'd kept their old estate car as a run around, but the long drive to London warranted a more comfortable ride.

Mia pressed the speaker button on the phone, expecting to hear Aaron's sensible, deep voice. 'Halloo! Mia, lovely girl, is that you? I'm getting myself in a dither about the weekend so Bill said I should stop fiddling about and just call you for a chat.' Pat's sweet voice filled the car and Mia bit her lip to make sure she didn't snap in frustration.

'Pat, I'm sorry but we're having a bit of a crisis. I might have to put things off this weekend.' She started to explain things when Madeline turned around from the passenger seat and hollered towards the phone.

'We're riding to the rescue of our Daniel; he's got himself into a bit of a pickle, Pat. You and Bill should come down to town and meet us. You can come back to Orcombe with us once we sort everything out. All hands to the pump!'

262

'I'm not sure that's a good idea. We don't want to overwhelm him,' Mia tried to interject but Madeline kept on talking over her. Mia glanced up, catching Richard's eye in the rear-view mirror. He gave her a shrug and a wink, knowing his wife was not one to be thwarted once she seized upon a plan.

With a resigned sigh, Mia passed her mobile over to Madeline and within minutes she and Pat were in total agreement that the other couple should get on the next train into London and join the rescue party. Madeline and Pat swapped numbers and with a promise to call once they were on their way, Pat hung up to keep the line free.

Mia took her phone back, rested her head against the back seat and closed her eyes. She hoped that Daniel would understand and appreciate them arriving mob-handed, she thought ruefully. Her hand squeezed around the handset, willing it to ring again with news from London. It was hard to make any kind of a plan when she didn't know what they were facing, but at least she would have a support team behind her.

Aaron called when they were about an hour from the city. The traffic had thinned out as night had fallen and they were just pulling away from the service station where they'd stopped to grab a snack and to allow Richard to refuel the car. He wanted to make sure he had a full tank in case there were any errands he needed to run once they reached their destination.

Aaron's brief explanation about a problem with an exhibition left Mia mystified. 'I didn't know he was planning an exhibition; he never said anything.' Mia turned to face her own reflection in the darkened car window and scowled at herself. It wasn't the time to start feeling insecure. Daniel must have had a reason to keep the exhibition from her and she would let him explain it to her when she saw him.

Aaron must have sensed something in her tone because he softened his voice as he replied. 'Mia, Daniel didn't know anything about the bloody exhibition either. It's a complete mind-fuck for him and he's in a real state. I'm over at the gallery now. I was going to suggest you meet us at my place but I think it would be best if you came straight here. There is a decent bed and breakfast place near my flat so I'll call them and see if I can book a room for Madeline and Richard.'

'Better make it two rooms, Aaron. I've got more reinforcements coming. The grey army is on the march!' Mia laughed and Aaron gave a chuckle when she explained about Pat and Bill being on their way as well. Once she got the address and some general directions to the gallery, Mia rang off and let Aaron get back to helping Daniel. She still didn't understand about the exhibition but hopefully things would become clearer soon.

'Hang on, Daniel. I'm nearly there,' she whispered into the dark night.

After an unexpected diversion along one of London's many one-way systems, they arrived at the front door of the gallery just after nine-thirty in the evening. Mia was stiff from being in the back of the car, but her discomfort was all forgotten as the familiar tall silhouette of Daniel filled the doorway of the gallery.

She threw off her seat belt and flew from the back of the car, straight into his arms. Daniel buried his face into her neck and she stretched on tiptoe to pull him down closer into her arms, where he belonged. She smiled at Aaron over Daniel's shoulder as he squeezed past them to greet Madeline and Richard, and her smile broadened to watch them engulf him in hugs and pats and kisses. Aaron was one of theirs now, whether he realised it or not.

Mia turned her attention back to Daniel and rocked him slightly, the position awkward as he was that much taller than her, but she didn't care about anything other than giving him the comfort that he needed. He eventually drew back and gave Mia a watery smile as he pressed their foreheads together. 'Thank you, thank you so much for coming, love. I don't know what the hell I'm going to do about this. I didn't know, I swear it. I didn't know. The pictures are yours; they were all for you. It was supposed to be a surprise. They're not public; they're yours.' He was babbling almost, trying to explain but not making a lot of sense.

Mia pressed her finger to his lips and smiled gently. 'Let's get inside and then we can talk about it properly. Is there any chance of a cup of tea?' Mia addressed this to the smartly dressed woman in the doorway of the gallery. The woman looked chic and perfectly put-together even this late into the evening. Mia felt like a country bumpkin in her holey jumper and scruffy jeans. The woman gave her the warmest smile and Mia saw that there was a genuine person behind the perfect demeanour.

'I'm Maggie; welcome to Gallery Sinclair. The kettle's on and I have some beer and wine in the fridge. I've sent one of my assistants on a mercy run to the local takeaway so we'll have some food soon as well. Come in, please, all of you.' Maggie stepped back and ushered everyone inside.

Mia paused on the threshold, captivated by the images scattered around the walls. They were her home: the beach, the gardens. Butterfly Cove filled her eyes everywhere she looked. All these photos that she'd hadn't been aware of him taking. After the first couple of weeks, his camera became an extension of him—the way so many people were attached to their phones or tablets these days—and Mia hadn't paid that much attention to it.

It was fascinating to see her familiar world in a completely different light, through the eyes of someone else. She wandered silently through the gallery, her attention dazzled by what she saw. Daniel stayed with her, a death grip on her hand but he stayed quiet and Mia knew he was dreading her reaction. She wasn't entirely sure how she felt about her private spaces being on public display so she kept her thoughts to herself until she could be more certain about how she wanted to react.

Pictures of her were spread throughout the other images and her initial reaction was to shy away from them, so she focused more on the pictures of the house and the surrounding gardens. She could hear Madeline and Richard in the background, looking at the pictures behind her, talking quietly to Maggie, but they kept their voices low. She walked a bit further away, almost to the end of the wall to give her and Daniel a bit more privacy, stopping in front of a fantastic seascape. She recognised the spot; it wasn't far from where they'd made love that first time.

Daniel hovered, a brooding weight at her shoulder, and she reached back to capture his arms and pull them around her middle. She leaned back into him and felt his weight settle a bit more firmly against her. 'They're very good, Daniel. I'm no expert, but you have such an eye for the details I miss. I thought I knew everything about the house and its grounds, but I am seeing so many things afresh. It's a lot to take in.'

His warm breath ghosted against her cheek on a deep sigh. 'This wasn't how I wanted you to see them, Mia. I was working on an album for you, for your birthday.' Daniel explained about his cloud storage and how his agent had stolen the images without permission. He told her about his history with Maggie and the gallery, his loyalty to her shining in every word. No wonder he was in a muddle.

The doorbell rang, disturbing their reverie, and everyone turned towards the young man who entered the gallery, laden down with brown paper sacks from the local Chinese takeaway. Mia drew a reluctant Daniel back towards the main group and she watched admiringly as Maggie marshalled her young assistants and Aaron into action. Plates, cutlery, napkins and drinks were soon distributed and everyone settled on a big white sheet that Maggie threw across the tiled floor.

It was possibly the most bizarre picnic that any of them had ever been to but there was a sense of camaraderie amongst this group of relative strangers. Everyone pitched in and the general chatter quietened as plates filled and then gradually emptied. Mia nudged Daniel into eating something and she pressed a cold bottle of beer into his reluctant hand. 'One won't do you any harm, Daniel. We're not exactly the party-hard crowd now, are we?' He stiffened visibly at what she had meant to be a joke and Mia gave herself a mental slap for being so insensitive.

She cupped her hand around his head and drew his face down close to her, uncaring of the audience sprawled in a circle before them. 'Look at me.' Her voice was firm and she made sure to hold his gaze, keeping her hand in place to hold his head still. 'You are mine now, and I will take care of you. I am not going to let anything bad happen to you, Daniel. Your past is just that.' She leaned closer and pressed her lips to his. He returned the pressure briefly and then they drew apart as another knock at the door heralded the arrival of Pat and Bill.

Daniel looked a bit wild around the eyes when he realised who the new arrivals were, but Mia didn't give him time to work up into a full-blown panic. She jumped to her feet and pulled him up with her. Before he could blink, he was enfolded in Pat's arms and Bill was right next to her, his hand resting on Daniel's shoulder, smiling broadly at him. Madeline and Richard joined them and Daniel was powerless to resist the sweet, powerful warmth of their joint affections.

Mia slipped away from the group and headed over to where Maggie and her two young assistants were standing. It was time to face the problem head-on and work out what to do for the best.

Chapter Twenty-Five

Daniel found himself in front of some of his pictures, the untouched beer going warm in his hand. Bill and Richard flanked him, discussing the images in front of them. Richard was explaining about the progress made at Butterfly Cove to Bill and Daniel chipped in with the odd remark. It was a slightly surreal experience and yet he felt more grounded and more in control as every minute passed in their company.

He'd been adrift since the loss of his own parents and it wasn't until that moment that he realised just how much he was gaining through his relationship with Mia. It wasn't just her, although she was the lodestone that charged his heart now. Somehow he had also gained a family. A hotchpotch of people who were unrelated by blood but who all wanted the best for each other and would drop everything to help one another.

Daniel looked around the room and exchanged a resigned grin with Aaron who was similarly hemmed in by Madeline and Pat. The ladies had their arms looped through his and were talking a mile a minute across him, but they were keeping him close. Aaron and by extension Luke were also a part of this new family they were building and Daniel was glad to see his friend relax under the attentions of the two older women. He'd had such a difficult time, losing his mother so young and then dealing with his stepmother's bitterness. Aaron was in desperate need of some mothering and it looked like Madeline and Pat were going to provide it.

Whether he liked it or not.

Switching his attention to the third group in the room he grinned at the sight of Mia and Maggie, heads close together as they plotted away. The two gallery assistants were tidying up the remnants of the meal, ferrying everything to the small kitchen area in the rear of the gallery, opposite Maggie's office. Maggie was very animated in her conversation and Mia was nodding along in agreement. Christ only knew what they were cooking up between them.

Daniel thought he'd better go and find out, but before he could excuse himself, they stopped talking and Mia clapped her hands sharply together to draw everyone's attention. Her hair stuck up in all different directions as usual. Her face, bare of make-up, was pale apart from the dark smudges under her brown eyes. She'd never looked more beautiful to him.

She fiddled with a hole in the sleeve of her jumper as she spoke, the only betrayal of any reluctance she might be feeling. 'I've had a chat with Maggie who has explained the situation. There isn't any way to get out of the opening night now, so we are going to make the best of it. I know this isn't what you wanted, Daniel, but Maggie has convinced me it's the right thing to do. If we cancel now, there will be so much attention on us and we won't be able to control it.'

Mia held out her hand to him, drawing him to her side, his lodestone, always. Daniel raised her hand to his lips and pressed a heartfelt kiss to the centre of her palm. Why he'd worried for a moment about her reaction to the situation was beyond him. She was a practical, sensible person at heart, and he'd been stupid to let his own fears blind him to that for even a moment.

'You're sure about this? You really don't mind that strangers might buy some of these pictures and own a piece of our life?' Daniel struggled with the idea still. He'd never meant for these images to belong to anyone other than himself and Mia and this was the first time he had not wanted to share his work with anyone else.

'Just think about it as great advertising, Daniel. We can tell people the story of Butterfly Cove, share our plans, and who knows, we might get a few of them interested in a break by the sea.' Mia grinned cheekily and Daniel just shook his head, knowing he was defeated.

He shrugged at Aaron who had a gleam in his eye. You know she's right.' His friend rubbed his hands together. 'There are bound to be lots of your artistic mates along. We can tell them about the studios too. We'll be booked solid before you know it. I'll give Luke a call and he can bring copies of his designs over.

We can set up a display in one corner.' Never happier than when he was contemplating a financial deal, he drew out a notepad and started jotting down numbers at a dizzying rate.

Maggie cleared her throat and stepped forward. All eyes turned to her. 'The biggest problem we have is there is no design here, no story to tell people. I was confused by Nigel's demand to put everything up on display but now I get it. He wanted to sell everything, make as much money as he could and hope Daniel wouldn't find out. We can't open on Thursday like this, but I'm not sure where to start. We normally plan for weeks...' Maggie trailed off as she contemplated the walls around her.

Daniel knew she was right but he didn't know where to start either. His exhibitions had typically been themed around a single topic, and whilst the images had often been of a personal nature, the subjects had not been his own life. Madeline asked about some of the previous exhibitions and Maggie explained about the theming structure.

The conversation whirled around him. He couldn't separate himself from the images enough to get any kind of perspective and a wave of nausea swept through him. The Chinese takeaway was a lead weight in his stomach and he felt beads of sweat pop out on his forehead.

Suddenly, Mia was there by his side, ushering him into the bathroom at the back of the gallery. She pressed him down onto the closed lid of the toilet and ran the corner of a towel under the cold tap. Daniel let

273

her soothe him, as she had the very first day they'd met. He sucked in oxygen, trying to maintain some control over his unruly stomach. *What a wimp.*

Everyone had rallied around him and here he was hiding in the bathroom, trying not to puke on the love of his life. He kept his eyes closed as she wiped his face with the cool towel and tried to focus on what needed to be done to try and bring some order to the chaos on the walls outside.

Mia took the towel away and ran it under the water again before encouraging Daniel to put his head down so she could apply the damp material to the back of his neck. 'Stop thinking so hard, Daniel, just for a few minutes.' She combed her fingers through his dark hair.

The motion was hypnotic and he let himself drift away on a little wave of bliss as the sickness in his stomach subsided and rational thought seemed possible again. He lifted his head slightly and Mia laughed as he found his face buried in her breasts. She started to step back, but quick as a shot he snaked his arm around her waist and kept her pressed up against him.

He took another deep breath and drew strength from the familiar scent of her soap, a lingering trace of sugar, and that essence that was purely her own. She smelt like home and Daniel felt his body stir unexpectedly. He turned his face to nuzzle her breast through her shirt and smiled in satisfaction as she gasped and arched into him.

A hesitant knock on the bathroom door had Daniel cursing and Mia breaking away, cheeks flaming like a teenager caught in the back seat of her boyfriend's car. She pulled the bathroom door open in a rush and Daniel angled his body slightly away from the open door to hide the evidence of his arousal. It was Claire, Maggie's assistant, and she stammered out an apology for interrupting. Mia waved the apology off, glanced down and hurriedly folded her arms across the damp patch on the front of her T-shirt.

'I didn't want to interrupt but I had an idea about the exhibition. I don't want to presume, of course; I just thought it might be of help.' The young woman was practically stuttering with nerves.

Mia smiled in encouragement. 'We are in dire straits, Claire, and you've already been amazing with your support tonight. Any ideas you have will be gratefully received.'

Claire blushed and explained her idea in rushed tones. 'I was looking at the pictures and thinking about how lovely Butterfly Cove must be. And then it struck me. Every image is about metamorphosis. You're taking the ugly chrysalis of a ruin and transforming it into a beautiful butterfly. Just like the name says.' She ducked her head shyly. 'And I can see a change in your perspective too, Fitz. Sorry, *Daniel*. A growth and transformation in the way you frame your images. I've always been a huge fan of your work, see, that's why I came to work for Maggie.' She cut herself off with a wave of her hand. 'This isn't the time for a fan-girl moment.'

Mia nodded enthusiastically. She clearly liked what she was hearing, but Daniel was struggling to get his head around the young woman's perceptive analysis. It felt too personal, too raw for public consumption. If she could see it, so would everyone else.

'I've already asked the others and they really like the idea—' Claire cut off when Daniel stood up abruptly, and she took a nervous step back from the doorway.

Mia turned to face him, the bright smile on her face turning to a scowl when she saw his own hesitation. Planting her hands on her hips, she crowded him back against the bathroom wall. It should have been comical—her diminutive presence shouldn't have been intimidating when he was so much taller and broader—but Daniel felt himself shrink slightly under her fierce gaze.

'You ungrateful sod! Everyone is trying to do everything that they can to help you and this is how you react? Do you have a better idea? Do you?' Her sharp tone demanded a response. Feeling like a heel, he couldn't do anything other than shake his head.

'Then get the fuck over your artistic temperament and say thank you!' Mia whirled away from him, brushing past poor Claire who was still lingering just outside the bathroom door. Daniel winced. Mia marched back into the main gallery, in full flow now. Several less-than-flattering comparisons flowed behind her to slap him in the face as her diatribe continued unabated.

Daniel bent to pick up the towel that had fallen to the floor when he'd stood. He folded it neatly, hoping Claire would take the hint and leave him in peace.

He took his time with the task but could still feel her shy presence just outside the door. With a sigh, he lifted his eyes to meet his own reflection in the bathroom mirror and spoke, both to himself and to Claire. 'I'm sorry. I do appreciate your efforts today, tonight, whatever.' He glanced at his watch and frowned; it was getting late. 'I don't think you can understand how hard it is for an artist to hand over control of their work in the way you are asking me to.' He turned away from the mirror and he saw a flash of pain in the young woman's eyes.

Christ, man! Will you listen to yourself? The kids who worked for Maggie were all art students, hoping to gain experience and here he was acting like some superstar and dismissing the girl as not being able to understand what it meant to be an artist. Daniel turned and placed his hand on her shoulder. 'Claire, I'm sorry. I'm acting like a colossal dickhead, and I had no right to be so dismissive of you. I'm tired and stressed and stupid. This is what London does to me. I can't wait to get out of here and back home.'

He paused and grimaced. Mia had moved on from his personality faults to a monologue about dirty socks and bed-hogging. 'Assuming I still have a home to return to. Which doesn't sound too promising at the moment.'

Claire giggled, and he squeezed her shoulder gently. 'Seriously, I appreciate your idea and Mia is right, I have no clue what else to do about the exhibition so let's give it a whirl.' He steered the now beaming girl towards the main room and paused as everyone turned to face him. They were all smiles, seemingly enjoying his discomfort, and Daniel felt himself shrink inside a little.

He wanted to run, but knew he had to face this challenge. They'd come all this way to help him and he owed it to them all not to let them down. He swallowed hard, his hand still gripping Claire's shoulder, holding her slightly in front of him like a shield. 'I think Claire has come up with a great idea. The theme for the exhibition will be Metamorphosis. I'd like to group the images into three discrete sets—Past, Present and Future. I'd appreciate your help again tomorrow—that is, if you want to stick around. I've been such an utter idiot.'

They crowded around him even before he'd finished speaking, the women patting and stroking his arms, the men with shoulder claps and handshakes. He looked over their heads to where Mia stood, hanging back from the crowd. He shrugged at her, and gave her his best hangdog look. His heart surged with joy when she threw her hands up in the air with a laugh. It seemed he wasn't homeless just yet.

Chapter Twenty-Six

Mia pushed her damp fringe away from her forehead before starting to unpack the next box of wine glasses onto the table in the corner of the gallery. Claire was with her, helping to set up the refreshments whilst Madeline and Pat folded canapé serviettes into pretty shapes, chattering a mile a minute. Daniel was in the office with Richard, reviewing the images they'd selected for 'Future'. Maggie and Bill were busy arranging the 'Present' photographs on either side of the back wall, bracketing the centre corridor.

Aaron had returned, having taken the day off work, and Luke had joined him. The brothers had set up a display in one corner showcasing the house. Pictures of the finished bedrooms and dining room were pinned to a display board, interspersed with photos of meals and cakes Mia had made. Luke's concept designs for the art studios were fixed to a board next to it, together with internal and external shots of the barn. The blueprints were laid out on a table in front, together with a sign-up sheet the ever-enterprising Aaron had drawn up for a mailing list.

They had decided to leave the gallery on Tuesday night almost as soon as Daniel had apologised, the general opinion being that a few hours' sleep and some fresh heads would do a better job than pushing through into the wee small hours. The older couples had disappeared off to the B&B Aaron had secured for them and Mia and Daniel had hopped on the tube with Aaron for the trip to his flat.

Lying in the dark together, Mia had analysed her sudden blow-up at Daniel. Curling close to his side, she had admitted most of her frustrations had been brought on by fear and worry. He'd scared her with his call for help and once she realised that he wasn't hurt or ill then she'd had to release the tension somehow. He'd accepted her apology, offered his own, and they'd come together in a tender act of renewal.

They had both slipped into a dreamless sleep and Daniel had woken that morning full of determination and positive energy. Mia was relieved at the turnaround and hoped it would carry him through into tomorrow's launch party.

The hammering of a fist on the door of the gallery made everyone jump. Mia clutched a hand to her heart with a startled laugh, while Claire hurried to see who was there. Leaving the quiet, capable girl to deal with their visitor, Mia carried on unpacking the glasses. Voices rose behind her, and she abandoned her task, curious to see what the problem was.

The problem was a rail-thin blonde woman, every inch the model in a jet-black trouser suit and spiked heels high enough to give anyone else a bout of vertigo. Mia rubbed her hands on her scruffy T-shirt, trying not to compare their appearance. The blonde shouldered her way past Claire and stalked into the gallery.

A presentable, if slightly too sleek-looking, man followed behind and they both scowled around the room as they made their way further into the gallery. Flicking her iron-flat hair over one shoulder, the blonde made a beeline for Mia. She paused in front of her, a little too close for Mia's liking, the pinched expression on her face tightening when Mia folded her arms, refusing to be intimidated.

She glared over her shoulder towards the table and then back down her nose. Mia stood her ground, forcing herself to relax and smile at the woman. She had more than an inkling of who the couple were and she would need a calm head to deal with them. 'This is a private event. Is there something I can help you with?' She kept her tone light and breezy, swallowing a grin when the woman's glare intensified.

'I don't know who you think you are. This is *my* event. You'd better only be here for the setting up. I gave the caterers very specific requirements regarding the staffing this evening.' She swept a disdainful glance over Mia. 'You really won't do at all.' The sneering tone made Mia's job all the easier, as did her proprietary tone. This must be Giselle, Daniel's

281

ex-girlfriend, and the weasel lurking behind her could only be Nigel, the double-crossing bastard.

'I think you must be confused.' It was tempting to snap, but Mia forced herself to remain polite as she delivered the killer blow. 'This event is for the opening of an exhibition for my fiancé, Daniel Fitzwilliams. You must have your dates mixed up.' Mia stepped around the woman and gestured towards the door. 'Now if you will excuse us, we have a lot of work to do.'

Giselle flushed an ugly shade of puce, her mouth gaping open and closed like a fish, and Mia felt a touch of venom sharpen the smile plastered across her face. She held Giselle more than partially responsible for the mess Daniel had been in when he landed on her doorstep. She gestured impatiently towards the door, nodding to Claire who dutifully swung it open.

The blonde spun towards her companion, who was shifting uncomfortably under the dual glares of Madeline and Pat. 'Nigel!' she shrieked. 'What the hell is going on? Who are these people?' She swivelled on her spiked heel towards Maggie who was standing with her hands on her hips, enjoying the show.

'What did you do, you interfering old cow?' Spittle formed at the corner of Giselle's lips as she stepped towards Maggie, her fingers curled, sharp nails like claws ready to strike out.

Mia blocked her path. 'Enough!' She grabbed the taller woman by the wrist, marching them both towards the door. She might be smaller than the other woman, but you didn't grow up with two sisters without knowing how to hold your own. Keeping her grip on Giselle's arm, she forced her to keep moving until they'd cleared the door and taken half a dozen steps down the pavement. She let her go and leaned back against the window of the shop next door to the gallery.

'It's over, Giselle. You lost. Fitz is gone and he's not coming back. Why don't you do yourself a favour and just walk away?'

The blonde rubbed her wrist, feigning hurt, although Mia had been careful not to dig her nails in, much as she might have wanted to. 'Who are you?' she hissed.

Tired of being polite, Mia dropped her casual pose. 'I told you already. I'm Daniel's fiancé.' Okay, so they hadn't settled on marriage, but this woman needed to get the message. 'There's nothing here for you. After the exhibition, Daniel is coming home with me. We love each other; we've made a home together. He's happy.'

A glint of moisture shone for a moment in Giselle's eyes and Mia almost felt sorry for her. With a downward sweep of her mascara-thick lashes, the hint of vulnerability vanished and Giselle pursed her lips in a sneer. 'I might have known he'd end up with someone like you. You look like a housewife, for God's sake.'

If that was her idea of an insult, Mia would take it any day of the week. The other woman would be fine. People like her always survived. It wouldn't take her long to shrug this off and find some other man to latch on to. 'Goodbye, Giselle.'

The blonde hesitated, then stalked off with a dismissive flick of her hair. Mia took a deep breath.

One down, one to go. Nigel was still in the gallery, but she would leave Daniel to deal with him.

She found Madeline lurking on the gallery doorstep, a broad grin on her face. 'That's my girl.' She slid her arm around Mia's waist and gave her a squeeze. She leaned her head against her friend's shoulder for a moment, then let her steer her back inside towards the table where they picked up the task of unpacking glasses.

Daniel glared at Nigel then pointed towards the back. The agent ran a hand over his gelled-back hair in a nervous gesture before following his furious client. A brief, awkward silence filled the room before Bill turned to Richard and said mildly, 'Did I tell you about the time that Pat put a brick through my car window?'

Mia snorted loudly and she felt Madeline shake beside her as she tried to suppress her own laughter.

Pat turned to Bill and replied in an equally mild voice, 'Well it served you right for taking that trollop, Veronica Bailey for a test drive. I told you then and it still holds now, William Sutherland. I won't stand for any shenanigans.'

A ripple of laughter spread through the room as Bill grabbed his wife and dipped her over his arm for a kiss worthy of an old-style film star. Pat clutched at his shoulders and gave as good as she got. The ladies clapped and laughed whilst Aaron and Luke quickly turned away and made a big deal of pinning and repining a few of the photos on their boards.

Glasses set up, Mia moved to help Richard position the 'Future' pictures on the right-hand wall. The three distinct groupings described the journey both she and Daniel had started since his arrival at Butterfly Cove, ending in their aspirations for the future. Maybe it would be a bit sentimental for the cynical London art crowd, but she didn't care. These were personal images and they needed to be displayed in an emotional, emotive way.

The door to the office opened and Mia watched Nigel step out into the gallery, with Daniel on his heels. She barely glanced at the greasy agent, her concern all for the man behind him. He looked okay. A little sad perhaps, but not too upset. She caught his eye and raised her eyebrows. He nodded to indicate that everything was fine, so she turned her attention to Nigel.

A ruddy flush glowed on his cheeks and his previously slicked-back hair looked rumpled. His hands were jammed tightly in his suit jacket pockets, ruining the line, and there was a faint tick in the muscle of his jaw. He didn't speak as he ran the gauntlet of disapproval through the gallery and Claire hurried forward to open the door to the gallery.

Nigel stepped out onto the pavement and turned back towards the group who had drifted closer to the door, forming a barricade of support behind Daniel. He seemed to have caught a glimpse of his reflection in the gallery window by the way he quickly tidied his hair and straightened the front of his jacket. With a few brushes of his hands, he transformed his outer appearance from defeated to impervious. He brushed an imaginary speck of dust from his collar and shot the cuffs of his shirt. 'Can't blame a fellow for trying now, can you?' he said in a faux-jocular manner.

'Yes,' said Daniel quietly. 'Yes, I can.'

Nigel blinked once before regaining his composure quickly. He raised two fingers to his temple in a sarcastic salute before turning away and marching down the road as though he owned it. He and Giselle deserved each other.

Mia wrinkled her nose in disgust as she stepped forward to place her hand on the small of Daniel's back. He curled an arm around her shoulders, drawing her to his side to press a kiss to the top of her head. The others melted away back to their self-appointed tasks.

Mia turned into him, raising her hand to scrub through the soft dark beard on Daniel's chin. His green eyes sparkled as he pressed a kiss to the tip of her nose. 'So, fiancé, is it?' he said with a smirk on his face.

'Hey now! Don't get any ideas. Boyfriend just sounds stupid at our age.' She folded her arms, but couldn't keep the laughter out of her voice. 'I haven't asked!'

'You will, though,' he said with absolutely certainty.

He was right; she would.

But that was for another day.

Turn the page for an exclusive sneak peek at the next book in the enchanting Butterfly Cove series, *Wedding Bells at Butterfly Cove*!

Chapter One

'Mummy.' The whispered voice next to her ear woke Kiki. She swam up through the layers of drowsiness, noting the darkness in the room, and wondered what time it was. 'Mummy.' A little shake of her shoulder added this time.

'Matty? Is everything all right, darling?' She matched his whisper, but it wasn't enough to avoid disturbing Neil.

He rolled over with a grumble. 'Whatever it is, take it somewhere else. I've got to be up in a couple of hours.'

Kiki slipped from beneath the quilt and used her toes to locate her slippers. After tucking her feet in the thin mules, she ushered her son towards the sliver of light shining from the landing. She pulled the bedroom door closed behind her, then crouched down to look at her beloved boy. Sweaty strands of dark-brown hair clung to his forehead and his cheeks shone with a feverish glow. He nibbled his bottom lip. 'I didn't mean to wake Daddy.'

The gleam of worry in his eyes stabbed her in the heart. Neil was perfectly capable of making everyone's life a misery at the slightest provocation. She forced a smile as she smoothed the damp hair from his brow. 'Don't worry about that, he'll be fast asleep again by now. Did you have a bad dream?'

Matty shook his head. 'I don't feel very—' He cut himself off with a hand over his mouth and his whole body convulsed in a shuddering heave, sending a stream of vomit through his splayed fingers and down the front of them both. Tears of shock and upset glinted in his eyes and she scooped him up in her arms, swallowing down the echoing hitch in her own stomach.

She carried him quickly into the bathroom and just managed to settle him on his knees in front of the toilet before another gush of bitter-smelling liquid spewed forth. 'Poor poppet. Poor darling,' she murmured, rubbing circles on his back as he shivered and shook. The front of her nightdress clung damply to her body, but she pushed the unpleasant sensation to the back of her mind to focus on Matty. He gasped like a little fish out of water, swallowing and panting. She knew the pattern well. This was just a brief respite in the process.

'Uh-oh,' he muttered and lurched forward again. This would be the last of it now. Kiki stroked his hair until he subsided into breathy sobs, sinking down until his head rested on the cold rim of the toilet.

'Better out than in, that's what they say.' She rose from her cramped position by his side to rinse her hands under the tap. Grabbing a dark-green flannel from the edge of the sink, she soaked it in cold water then bent down to turn Matty towards her. 'Look up, darling.'

He lifted his pale little face and she held his chin in a light grip as she wiped the tears, sweat and other less pleasant things from his skin. A quick rinse of the cloth and she folded it into a square. 'Hold this against your head a minute, can you?' He nodded weakly and clutched the flannel with a shaky hand.

Confident he would be okay for a couple of minutes, she left him to go and check his bedroom and fetch some clean pyjamas. His bedding and carpet were mercifully clean and she sent up a silent prayer of thanks that at least she wasn't faced with changing the sheets at...she glanced at the LEGO Batman clock on the dressing table and winced...three a.m. Pausing at the airing cupboard on the landing, she dug out a T-shirt and a pair of leggings for herself and returned to the bathroom. A quick change and a teeth-clean and they were both soon tucked into Matty's single bed.

'How's your tummy now, still sore?' She feathered her fingers through his silky-soft hair. The deep-brown strands matched her own, but his soulful blue eyes were all his father's. She'd fallen for a bigger version of those baby-blues before she'd known the truth—a twinkling look and a sweet smile could mask a monster. Neil had smiled, flirted and flattered his way into her life and she had lapped up the attention like a parched flower, blooming into a blushing, eighteen-year-old bride.

His earnest focus on her, his need to know her every movement, had seemed exciting. He needed her with him, couldn't stop thinking about her, worried someone else might snatch the prize of her from under his nose. Oh, the lies he'd told her had been music to her innocent ears. Like Helen of Troy and Paris, theirs was a love that would burn through space and time. Like Heathcliff and Cathy, like Jane and Rochester, nothing could keep them apart. Only she'd glossed over the ugly, hard truths of those childhood love stories in her burning need to feel special to someone.

And how exciting for a naïve girl to capture the heart of an older, wiser man. Neil had been in his first year as a postgraduate student when they met, and at twenty-two he'd seemed a fount of knowledge and experience from the moment they bumped into each other in the Ancient Greece section of the university library. Taking a classical studies course had been Kiki's transparent attempt to please her father, and when Neil found out she was the daughter of one of his intellectual heroes, he'd been hooked. He painted a fascinating picture of a man nothing like the withdrawn, preoccupied one who ruled her home with more neglect than care.

A soft snore drew her attention and she eased her arm out from under Matty's head to settle him more comfortably on his pillow. Content he was asleep, she slipped out of his bed to clean up the mess left behind on the landing carpet. Once that was done, she might as well tackle the ironing pile. She cast a quick glance at her closed bedroom door as she passed it. There was no way she wanted to risk waking Neil again, and she could always have a catch-up nap once the kids were sorted in the morning.

'Mummy?' Déjà vu. Only this time the voice was Charlie's sweet, piping tone, still carrying a babyish lisp. And the hard, wooden table beneath her cheek was no substitute for her pillow.

Forcing open her grit-filled eyes, Kiki tried to ignore the sick, groggy pain in her head and sat up. 'What's the time, darling?' A rhetorical question to a three-year-old, but her brain was still too full of cotton wool to think straight.

'It's gone eight o'clock and I'm going to be late, thanks to you,' Neil snapped as he stormed into the room.

She blinked, noting his suit and tie, rather than the casual-jacket-and-jeans look he favoured when lecturing. 'Oh, your meeting. I'm sorry, I must have dozed off.' Jumping up, she hurried over to switch the kettle on and stuff a couple of slices of bread into the toaster. 'Give me a minute, just one minute, and I'll bring your breakfast to your study.'

Neil glared at her, not an ounce of warmth in his blue eyes. 'I already told you, I don't have time. Which part of late don't you understand?' He dodged back to avoid their daughter's attempts to clutch his legs for a hug. 'No, Charlotte! You'll crease Daddy's suit.' He left the kitchen, muttering to himself.

Kiki leaned back against the board, wondering how she'd managed to screw up the day before it had even started. Charlie, lower lip quivering, her dark hair sleep-tangled and knotted, painted a picture of abject heartbreak. Kiki swooped on her, gathering her little girl into her arms for a tight hug. 'Daddy doesn't mean to be cross, Charlie. He's just got a busy day and Mummy didn't help by falling asleep.' Even as the words left her mouth, she wondered why she was making excuses for him. Neil was an adult and perfectly capable of getting himself up and ready for work on time, but the default blame in the Jackson household for any problem fell squarely on her shoulders.

She could just imagine what her big sister would have to say if she could hear her. Mia had never warmed to Neil. Kiki suppressed a bitter laugh. There she went again, painting the situation in a rosier light than it deserved. Mia couldn't stand him. Had even tried to persuade Kiki to leave and bring the children with her to Mia's new home in Butterfly Cove. As if she could just pack up and start again! She hefted Charlie onto her other hip, 'Come on, poppet, let's go and see how your brother is feeling this morning.'

Matty appeared untroubled by his early morning misadventures, so she dropped him off at school, then a bubbly Charlie at crèche for her morning session. Strictly speaking, the rules required her to keep him off for forty-eight hours, but he usually bounced back after an episode and Kiki preferred not to make a fuss about it. His bouts of sickness had started a few months previously, frequent enough for her to have taken her son to the doctor. After a range of tests, they'd not been able to find anything wrong with him, and Kiki was keeping a food diary to see if there might be an allergic connection. She hadn't found an organic link to his problem, and she was beginning to suspect the doctor's other suggestion—stress—might be the real cause.

The resilience the children showed filled her with pride, and not a little guilt. They shouldn't have to tiptoe around their father the way they had been recently. She would have to try and talk to him, ask him to be a little more patient around them. Her stomach churned at the thought, but if she broached the subject when he was in a good mood, maybe she'd get through the conversation without it turning into a shouting match. Not that she did any shouting of her own. Perhaps if she made his favourite meal for dinner...she turned left at the next set of lights towards the supermarket.

Brushing the flour off her hands onto her apron, Kiki ran to the hall to fish her mobile out of her bag where it hung over the end of the bannister. The damn thing had found its way to the very depths and she almost dropped it in her hurry to answer before the caller rang off. 'Hello?'

'Jesus, Kiki. Can't you even answer your phone without a drama?'

'Sorry, darling. I was in the kitchen and I'd left my bag in the hall...'

Neil sighed. 'I don't need to hear your latest line in stupid excuses. Just go into my study, will you? There's the name of a hotel and a phone number on my jotter and I need it.'

'Hotel?' She crossed the hall and pushed open the study door. The room reminded her so much of her dad's, and it, too, was off limits unless she was cleaning. The high-backed leather chair behind the desk had cost a fortune, but Neil needed to be comfortable when he was working in the evenings. She nudged the chair to one side and scanned the familiar scribble on the cream-coloured jotter. 'What's it called?'

'If. I. Knew. What. It. Was. Called. I. Wouldn't. Be. Wasting. My. Time. Talking. To. You.' She winced at the deliberate pause he put between each word. 'It's on the left-hand side somewhere.'

Using her finger, she traced the scribbled notes. 'Oh, here. Lilly's Island Hotel? Number starts with a plus-thirty?'

'That's the one. Hurry up, I need to get back to the meeting.'

She reeled off the number, then paused. 'Antiparos? Isn't that near Despotiko?' The island was one of the most famous archaeological treasures outside of Delos. Neil's research focused on the cult of Apollo and he had been trying to get on a dig at the sanctuary for the past few years. 'Did you get your approval?'

'I won't get anything if you don't stop chattering, but yes, looks like I'll be there for the summer.' He hung up without saying another word.

Kiki sank into the deep leather chair. How many times had they talked about a summer trip to the islands when they'd first got married? Curled up in Neil's bed in his tiny flat, they'd spun dreams of days spent uncovering hidden treasures buried deep in the rocks and nights sipping ouzo and eating local delicacies. Then she'd fallen pregnant with Matty and those dreams were put on hold while they struggled to make ends meet. She'd dropped out, knowing there was no way she could finish her degree with a new baby and Neil needing all the help he could get with his research.

Life had got in the way, as it so often did, but maybe this would be a chance for them to spend some quality time together. A tiny bubble of hope stirred in her heart. Away from the stresses and strains, perhaps they could find a way to make things right between them. The kids could run and play in the sunshine, and she could help Neil catalogue his findings. She bit her lip, unable to stop a smile. If they could just get back to the way things used to be...

She reached for the wireless mouse on Neil's desk and shook it gently to wake up his computer. A word document filled the screen, so she scanned the lower toolbar looking for the browser icon, but accidentally clicked on the email one. The screen changed, displaying an open message and she gave it half a glance, before looking back at the bottom bar.

Darling...

Her finger froze on the mouse as the word registered. Who would be calling Neil darling? Ignoring the little voice in her head that warned he would be furious at her for snooping, Kiki rolled the mouse to the top of the message and began to read. Incredulity became denial, became horror, as she followed the email exchange back over several weeks. She wanted to shut her eyes, refuse to see the truth laid out in black and white, but her finger kept clicking on the previous arrow. Every click was punctuated by the same word, the admonishment Neil threw in her face on a regular basis—stupid, *click*, stupid, *click*, stupid.

He was right.

ACKNOWLEDGEMENTS

I have lots of people to thank for bringing Mia and Daniel's story to life.

First and foremost, my husband who has supported me every step along the path of my author journey. Thanks, bun x

My writing buddies from the Chat Chalet and beyond for all their encouragement, enthusiasm and support as I put pen to paper (or fingers to the keyboard) for the first time. Roxy, Tracy, Kayleigh, Scott, 'Nathan and Amie – thank you for helping me believe I could do this.

The lovely team at HQ who have been so warm and welcoming from the very first email. Charlotte, Rayha, Hannah and everyone else who is part of this very special team – you keep making me cry very happy tears.

To the other HQ authors, both old hands and newbies like myself, thank you for making me feel so very welcome. It's a privilege to part of the HQ family with you.

And of course, to you, the reader. Thank you for taking a chance and picking up this book. I hope you enjoy your first (and hopefully not last!) visit to *Butterfly Cove*.

ONE PLACE. MANY STORIES

Bold, innovative and
empowering publishing.

FOLLOW US ON:

@HQStories